Mystery in the Village

REBECCA SHAW

An Orion paperback

First published in Great Britain in 2015
by Orion
This paperback edition published in 2016
by Orion Books,
an imprint of The Orion Publishing Group Ltd,
Carmelite House, 50 Victoria Embankment
London EC4Y ODZ

An Hachette UK company

1 3 5 7 9 10 8 6 4 2

A CIP catalogue record for this book
is available from the British Library.

ISBN 978 1 4091 4727 5

Printed and bound in Great Britain by Clays Ltd, St Ives plc

The Orion Publishing Group's policy is to use papers that
are natural, renewable and recyclable products and
made from wood grown in sustainable forests. The logging
and manufacturing processes are expected to conform to
the environmental regulations of the country of origin.

www.orionbooks.co.uk

Caroline slid into her parking spot in the hospital car park, braked, and hesitated for a moment before getting out. Eyes closed, heart thudding she sat waiting for common sense to take over. It didn't. After five minutes of deep thought she was no nearer to an answer.

A sharp tapping on her side window brought her back to earth.

'Caroline? All right?' It was a nurse from the department.

She made to open her door. 'I'm fine, thanks.'

'You don't look it. In fact you look ghastly, as though you've come face-to-face with a terrible truth.'

Surprised by the nurse's acute perception Caroline shook her head. 'No, not at all. Now what terrible truth could someone like me have to face, I ask you? I'll catch you up. Won't be a minute.'

She watched as the nurse dashed away. Had she arrived at some terrible truth? Of course not. She still loved Peter. Really loved him. Of course she did.

Rebecca Shaw was a former school teacher and the bestselling author of many novels. She lived with her husband in a beautiful Dorset village where she found plenty of inspiration for her stories about rural life. Rebecca sadly passed away in 2015.

INHABITANTS OF TURNHAM MALPAS

Ford Barclay	Retired businessman
Mercedes Barclay	His wife
Willie Biggs	Retired verger
Sylvia Biggs	His wife
James (Jimbo) Charter-Plackett	Owner of the village store
Harriet Charter-Plackett	His wife
Fran	Their daughter
Katherine Charter-Plackett	Jimbo's mother
Alan Crimble	Barman at the Royal Oak
Linda Crimble	His wife
Lewis	Their son
Maggie Dobbs	School caretaker
H. Craddock Fitch	Owner of Turnham House
Kate Fitch	Formerly village school headteacher
Dottie Foskett	Cleaner
Zack Hooper	Verger
Marie Hooper	His wife
Gilbert Johns	Church choirmaster
Louise Johns	His wife
Greta Jones	A village gossip
Vince Jones	Her husband
Barry Jones	Her son and estate carpenter
Pat Jones	Barry's wife
Dean & Michelle	Barry and Pat's children
Revd Peter Harris MA (Oxon)	Rector of the parish
Dr Caroline Harris	His wife
Alex & Beth	Their son and daughter

Tom Nicholls	Assistant in the store
Evie Nicholls	His wife
Greenwood Stubbs	Head gardener at Turnham House
Chris Templeton	Johnny's brother
Deborah Templeton	His wife
Sir Johnny Templeton	Head of the Templeton estate
Lady Alice Templeton	His wife
Charles and Ralph	Their sons
Dicky & Georgie Tutt	Licensees at the Royal Oak
Bel Tutt	Assistant in the village store

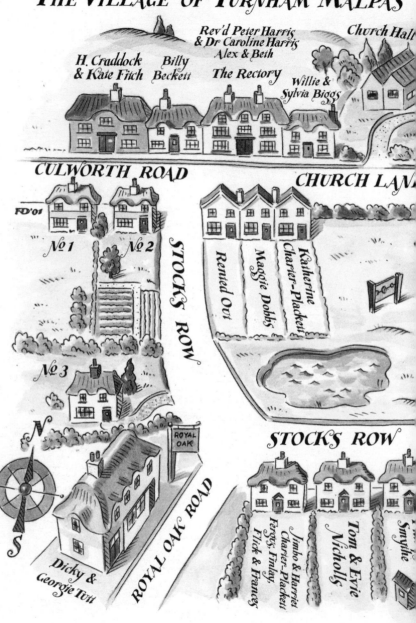

Chapter 1

Chris Templeton stood quietly in the doorway of Turnham House looking out over the estate. In the distance he could see the thatched roofs of Home Farm, the regimented tall trees that framed every yard of the one-mile drive to the house, and the Old Barn, renovated and providing a steady income for the estate coffers. He could just catch the sound of cows leaving the milking parlour on their way to the fields and inside the house he heard his brother coming down the main staircase, obviously escorted by his two little boys, Charles and Ralph, because he could hear them endlessly chattering to their father as they negotiated the stairs. An end to the morning peace, then.

The day had begun. His day. Deborah's day. A day for the entire village too, it seemed. He'd wanted a quiet ceremony, just himself, Peter the rector, and his beloved Deborah: she who knew his next thought before it had even crystallised in his own brain. She who loved him with a depth he had never encountered before, she who loved the very few good things about him, she who had brought about the transformation of Christopher Templeton.

He turned to say good morning to his nephews. 'Hi, you two! Had your breakfast?'

They both nodded. 'If you're not too busy, Uncle Chris is going down to the lake – would you like to come too?'

The two nodded and rushed to take hold of his hands, one on each side, eager to be off.

Johnny nodded at his brother and said, 'I'm going to Home Farm. OK?'

'We might join you there, but don't wait about for us just in case we don't.'

'Twelve noon prompt.' Johnny smiled.

'I know, I know. I'm not likely to forget, am I? My wedding day . . .'

'Alice and I are delighted, really delighted, Chris. She's a lovely, kind, thoughtful woman, a real treasure. You're lucky she's said yes.'

'I know that.' Chris grinned. 'It's thanks to her I've changed my ways.'

'How has she done that, then? We all of us tried but with no success.'

'She sees through my massive ego to the real person waiting to get out.' Chris, with two little boys clamouring to get to the lake with him, added, 'Must go! I shan't be late. Say, bye-bye, Daddy!'

Johnny watched them meandering down the path towards the lake, thinking how grateful he was that at last Chris had improved almost out of all recognition. Deborah was certainly the best thing that had ever happened to him. Then Johnny heard his mother's imperious voice demanding to know if anyone knew where Chris was? He turned to go back inside.

'Don't panic, Mother, he hasn't run away, he's taking the boys to the lake.'

'Oh, what a relief. I can't wait for half past twelve.'

'The ceremony is at twelve.'

'I know that, Johnny dear, but twelve thirty means he's well and truly married . . . that's if he turns up. He will, won't he?'

'I do believe he will. He's besotted with her.'

'My dear Johnny, he's been besotted before – so many times I've lost count!'

'Believe me, this time it's different! Very different!'

It felt like the right moment for giving his mother a kiss. He didn't need to bend his head for she was as tall as he was and she almost jumped with the surprise of his gesture. 'Oh! Johnny! Well, it is a special day, isn't it? Very special. I'll kiss you, shall I?'

Her rare kiss landed on his left cheek, and then he got a second one on his right cheek. Special day, special kisses. He knew she hated the cold of an English winter but Johnny knew she would not have missed Chris's wedding, no matter what the weather. Chris was her special boy; he and Nicholas had known that all their lives. In earlier years it had been the cause of jealousy and argument between the three boys, but now ... well, now it didn't seem to matter any more. Both he and Nicholas had accepted the inevitable – Chris would always come first with their mother.

Johnny kissed his mother, saying, 'Home Farm here I come, only for an hour, so don't worry, I shan't be late for the wedding.'

'You love living here, don't you? Really love it.'

Johnny had to agree. 'This is where I belong, heart and soul. Didn't know it till I got here, but it's true. This must have been what I was waiting for all my life. I will never go back to Brazil to live, not ever. I have to look after this land for my boys. And you've still got Nicholas in Brazil, haven't you? And his children.'

His mother turned away so he couldn't see her face and said, surprisingly pathetically for her, 'Will Chris ... do you think ... will he stay here or come back home to me? Has he said?'

Johnny placed a comforting hand on her shoulder. 'He's not said. I think he might stay here. Rio doesn't seem the right setting for Deborah, not quite her kind of thing, is it?'

'No. I suppose not, though she might get to like all the fun.'

'Mother! Will you check Deborah has everything she needs?'

'Of course, dear, of course.' Despite her promise, she didn't. There was no way she would indicate by the slightest of gestures that Deborah was acceptable to her. Chris had always been as free as air; woman after woman after woman, he just beckoned to them with his little finger and they were his for as long as he wanted them. Sometimes a week, sometimes a month – bright, vivid, entertaining girls they'd always been – and now he was marrying and she'd never thought he would. If there'd been bets on him marrying someone like Deborah she would have bet 100 to 1 he wouldn't marry. The woman wasn't his sort. I mean, where did she go when she disappeared for a few days every month? She never said, not even to Chris. But disappear she did and though he was plainly hurt by this, Chris never questioned where she'd been.

She, Perdita Templeton, had asked Deborah outright once where she went but all Deborah said was, 'I am not *chained* to Chris.' But she was, because she always came back to him, and now she would be her daughter-in-law.

Perdita went back inside the house; the wind was getting up and her hair would be ruined, that is, if it wasn't already by that ridiculous hairdresser who'd come to the house at some ungodly hour this morning because she'd made a mistake and booked two weddings on the same day! Shop owners in Rio knew no one messed Perdita Templeton about, that what she wanted she got, but that wasn't true here. In Rio she came first and everyone else second – and Deborah would come twenty-second or possibly even *thirty*-second if there was a queue.

Give Deborah her due, she had classically beautiful features, a thrilling speaking voice and a figure to die for, but she was dull – well, Perdita found her so. Dull as ditchwater, with no spirit whatsoever, and as a fashion icon ... huh! All her clothes were so restrained, so simple!

At that exact moment Deborah appeared at her elbow, looking divine. She glowed just as a bride should on her wedding day. 'Perdita! There you are! Nicholas is on the phone, the one in Johnny's office.'

In Perdita's opinion Johnny's office was delicious. Ancient wood-panelled walls, antique desk, Victorian furnishings she was told, and curtains that had hung at that very window for well over a hundred years. It was so splendid even a modern up-to-date woman like herself could feel its ambience creeping through her veins. But Nicholas! 'Here I am, darling,' she sang. 'Nicholas, darling, how is everything back there?' Perdita plumped herself down in Johnny's chair and waited to be entertained. Nicholas was always such fun to talk to. He gave her fascinating details about the consternation circulating around Rio on the question of Chris's marriage. Let them speculate!! All those disappointed mothers wishing it was their daughter he was marrying! When she put down the receiver she knew she was glad Chris was marrying an Englishwoman even though she didn't like her – a fact she endeavoured to keep entirely to herself. Perdita checked her watch. Two hours to go. She looked out of Johnny's office window, contemplating the forthcoming wedding service. If her husband had still been alive it would have been him who inherited and she would have been Lady Templeton. That really would have been wonderful. Lady Templeton. Lady! That would have scored points for her in the opinion of everyone in Rio. Not that she needed any help in that direction. She knew her place and so did everyone who came in contact with her. At the top! Oh! Yes. Her place was at the very top. So unfair, really, that it was her daughter-in-law, Alice, who was Lady Templeton …

Alice Templeton was in her and Johnny's bedroom laying out her clothes for the wedding. Deep in her heart she was glad that Chris was getting married to Deborah. She and Deborah got on wonderfully well with each other, even though Deborah was a businesswoman through and through and she, Alice, was a musician. They couldn't have been more different in outlook, but they gelled wonderfully well. The people in the village had taken to Deborah too, and in such a small community that was incredibly important; much more important than her mother-in-law realised. Alice smiled. As far as Perdita was concerned, all these dratted village people being guests at the wedding was insane. Waving and cheering outside the church, may be, but not guests to whom she had to appear gracious. Gracious! That was a laugh! Johnny and she accepted everyone as friends and not as her mother-in-law did, as something beneath her notice.

★

As the bride and groom emerged from the church the bells rang loudly and joyously. Jimbo Charter-Plackett, now proficient at the job of bell ringing, swung on the rope with relief, glad that it wasn't his darling Fran who was leaving the church on the arm of Christopher Templeton. There had been a time not long ago when he could have murdered the groom without blinking an eyelid. Greeting him at the reception afterwards he gripped Chris's hand with enthusiasm and genuinely congratulated him on his choice of wife. 'You both look so very happy. And I wish you the very best in the years to come.'

Harriet, Jimbo's wife, waiting her turn to shake the happy couple's hands, found it very difficult to be genuinely pleased. 'Lovely day for a wedding,' she said. 'You look fantastic, Deborah, really fantastic!' That was true anyway. It was the simple flowing style of the dress with its high, close-fitting V-neck, the long tight sleeves coming to a point on the back of each hand, and the train with its two feet of material lying spread out on the ground behind her. So elegant, yet plain, almost virginal in style.

This new Chris looked triumphant. His eyes shone with love – everyone who saw them close up thought that. And for once it appeared to be true love. As far as Chris was concerned it *was* true love; he'd never felt so proud of anything he had done in all his life so far that made him feel so filled to the brim with love. Just looking at Deborah filled his heart with a glow never experienced before and he knew, from the top of his head to the soles of his shining brand new shoes, that this was love for an eternity. Feeling as he did now he knew nothing could go wrong with his life ever again. She was his anchor, his soulmate ... his everlasting friend. Nothing and no one could spoil things now. Chris smiled at his bride and she smiled back at him, and for one splendid moment they felt as one: just the two of them, filled to the brim with love for each other.

One person who had refused their wedding invitation was

Frances Charter-Plackett. The distance of time since Chris had hurt her so devastatingly had lessened the pain, but it was still there right inside her and couldn't be ignored. If she attended the wedding, every single person present would remember what had happened between her and Chris. Long memories were a feature of life in the three villages, so long sometimes that two centuries could pass and the resentment and pain still existed in the memories of the families whose ancestors' lives had been blighted all those years before.

And she wasn't having them all remembering her pain and tut-tutting, scandalised that she'd turned up. Was that a tear they could see on her cheek? they'd be asking. She couldn't give them the satisfaction and therefore stayed away, grateful for the understanding that Alex Harris offered her by suggesting a day's excursion to London with a theatre visit to round it off and then a long drive back to Turnham Malpas so the celebrations would be well and truly over by the time he'd delivered her back to her home.

Late up on the Sunday morning, Fran found her mother in the kitchen about to start preparing Sunday lunch.

'Darling! I heard you come back last night. Good time?'

Fran dragged her dressing gown belt and tied it slowly to give herself time to think of what to say. 'Yes. But ...'

'But what?' Harriet turned to look at her and recognised that what had been meant to be a lovely escape from her memories had not come up to scratch. 'Well?'

'I've told him it's no good. Alex Harris and I are no longer an item,' Fran said, and exploded into floods of tears.

By the time she'd told the whole story to her, Harriet was devastated. 'He must be heartbroken.'

'He is, but second best is no good, is it? And that's what he is. Second best. Although reason tells me I'm being a fool because he's charming, considerate, charismatic, and very attractive to

7

look at, like his dad. He's fun, kind, thoughtful ... but where's the magic? It's there very, very briefly and then it's gone. It's no good, Mum, I can't marry him. So ... a possible lifetime of regret has been rejected after a great deal of thought. He's driving back tonight for a tutorial tomorrow and I just hope he's OK. Driving back after such a long day, you know. And yes, I know I must be the biggest fool ever for turning him down ...'

'Has he actually asked you to marry him, then?'

'He has. Yes, last night. That was when I knew I must be honest and tell the truth. No good letting him hope, is there? That wouldn't be fair.'

Fran spooned a luscious pile of froth from the top of her mug of coffee, paused for a moment remembering an incident in a restaurant when Alex had done the very same thing and got a blob of froth on the end of his nose. How they'd laughed, the two of them together in unison, so young, so happy and now ... all that laughter had ended in the space of a few words.

Time she grew up, did what she knew she must: get a place at university and put to good use all that hard work she'd done at school to get top grades. It had to be goodbye to the old Frances, living at home to avoid dynamic decision-making and hello to the new Frances, kicking her life into action. Instantly she imagined the touch of Alex's hand on the back of her neck as he kissed her and she knew she'd long for his gentleness, his sweet, sensitive touch, his kindness and ... No, he wasn't the only man in the world! There must be men like him, but with the magic she longed for, somewhere ... Oh, better single than full of regret.

'After lunch I ... By the way, is Grandmama coming?'

Harriet nodded.

'Don't say a word, Mum, she'll only go on and on.'

'My lips are sealed.'

'I can hear in your voice you think I'm a total idiot for turning him down.'

'The decision is yours, Fran, not mine. It's your life, after all. There's time, too. You're only twenty-two and what's twenty-two nowadays? I heard two women talking in the posh dress shop in Culworth the other day and one who'd given up hope of her two daughters ever getting married was now facing hosting two weddings within five months and her daughters were thirty-four and thirty-nine. So, if it's meant to be etc., etc. If you're not one hundred per cent sure then it's best to say no.'

'Thanks, Mum, for being on my side. I'm certain I'm right in saying no. I love working in the store with Dad, and—'

Harriet patted her shoulder. 'I know, I know. But right now I need the table for starting lunch. Off you go and do what you have to do, darling. There's no one else but yourself who can make the decision about your life.'

And Fran wasn't the only one to turn down their invitation to the wedding. Out of the kindness of his heart, Johnny had invited Ben Braithwaite along with his sister Becky and Becky had decided no. It only needed Ben to be in one of his peculiar moods and the wedding service and the reception could be ruined, so she'd decided not to go just in case. His upsets at the moment were caused by the fact that old Greenwood Stubbs had not yet invited Ben to join him in the glasshouses, and that was what Ben wanted more then anything in the whole world. He constantly mentioned it to Becky who dreaded him asking her yet again why Greenwood wouldn't have him to help. He even knew the names of those who did work in there and they had become his enemies.

So by the time the wedding day arrived Becky was glad she had refused. What surprised her the day after the event was when the doorbell rang after lunch and there was Sir Johnny with a bouquet of flowers, a box with wedding cake in it, and a request for a word with her.

'Have you time for a quick word, Becky?'

With Ben safely engrossed in front of the TV watching a

cowboy film she stepped outside and closed the front door behind her. 'It's about Ben, isn't it? Causing trouble? Are you wanting him not to work for you any more?'

'No, no, no. Firstly, the wedding. We all had a wonderful time and I just wish you'd been able to come. This is a flower arrangement from the reception for you, seeing as you couldn't come, and Deborah insisted I brought a big piece of the wedding cake. She thought that perhaps you would enjoy a taste, to say nothing of Ben.'

'It's so kind of you! Thank you very much indeed. The flowers smell lovely, and as for the cake, the two of us will certainly enjoy it. It's a very big piece – are you sure you can spare it?'

'Whatever Deborah decides is fine by me.'

Becky grinned. 'She's an absolutely lovely person, isn't she? As for Ben, he's upset, you see, because he longs to work with Greenwood Stubbs in the glasshouses. I'm sorry, but the truth is he desperately wants to work with the peaches and grapes and such, and Ben, being as he is, he can't understand why, when he wants to, he can't. He'll get over it. Eventually.'

'Is that all it is?'

'Yes. Definitely. Believe me, he loves working on your estate; he tells everyone he meets that he's your gardener, he's so proud of it. I'm so sorry. He's causing a lot of trouble is he? If so . . .'

'No, no. Somehow we'll accommodate him. I'm determined to make a success of Ben coming to work for us because he tries so hard. Always on time, always wildly enthusiastic, and that's the kind of person I like working for me. I shall solve it. Somehow. Greenwood belongs to the old school, you see, and finds it difficult to . . . to handle Ben. According to him Ben should be hidden away in an institution the way people used to be, not out in the world earning a living.'

'I'm grateful you make allowances for him, and that's not a word I like to use in the same breath as Ben, but I am, grateful you've so kindly given him a job.'

'It's not a kindness; it's a business decision. He gives good value for money, he works diligently and thoroughly, and there's absolutely no reason for complaint. Leave it with me, I'm dealing with it.'

Johnny turned away, intending to leave, then changed his mind. 'Sorry you couldn't come to the wedding; we all had a fabulous time, no nasty shocks, no unfortunate incidents, it all went like clockwork and the bride looked perfect. Which she is. I took photos. Want to look?'

'Yes, please I'd love to.'

So they stood out in the cold wind admiring the photos on Johnny's iPhone.

'The bride looks beautiful, absolutely fabulous. Chris is a lucky man.'

'He is.' Johnny paused for a moment and then added, 'And he knows it. He's changed almost out of all recognition.' He smiled, switched off his phone, and while opening his car door he said, 'Leave the Ben situation with me. Right?'

'Thank you, I will. And thanks for the cake, and the flowers and thinking so well of Ben.'

Johnny placed a finger on his lips saying 'Shush! Not a word to him indoors!' He waved and drove away.

Honestly, thought Becky, who would believe he was the Lord of the Manor, wealthy beyond belief and yet so pleasant and so easy to talk to and above all so considerate to her and her brother. 'Look, Ben! Want a piece?'

So Ben and Becky sat together watching TV, drinking tea and eating thick slices of the delicious wedding cake, with the scent of the flowery table centrepiece wafting round the room and feeling rich in all the best things in life; like friendship and kindliness and caring and sharing.

Chapter 2

The following morning Johnny left a message for Greenwood Stubbs on his answerphone and an hour later Greenwood was saying in his Northern accent, 'Good morning, Sir Johnny. You want a word with me? Nothing wrong is there?'

'What on earth could be wrong, Greenwood, just want a word about the glasshouses. Will you be there in the next hour or so?'

'I can be.'

'Excellent. See you there then.' Johnny smiled to himself; Greenwood always kept that slight edge of independence. He wouldn't say, 'Yes, of course.' Or, 'Certainly, sir.' Or, 'What time?' or 'Would half an hour be all right?' Johnny laughed as he put down the receiver. There it was again, his Northern independence, letting the boss know that he didn't own Greenwood Stubbs body and soul.

Sure enough he was smoking his pipe seated on a bench placed outside the main glasshouse. Waiting. Smoking. Enjoying the pale winter sun.

Greenwood endeavoured to stand up but Johnny signalled him not to even try, saying, 'Please don't.'

Johnny sat down beside him, opening the conversation by saying, 'Cold, today.'

'It is.' Greenwood continued smoking his pipe leaving his employer to lead their discussion.

'I want to talk to you about Ben Braithwaite. He's getting very upset because you haven't mentioned to him about working in the glasshouses and yet you seemed to get on well when you let him spend time with you there, way back.' Johnny left a long silence.

Finally Greenwood answered. 'In my day people like 'im were shut up in big houses and you didn't see 'em. Safe, you know. Fed. Kept clean. Cared for. Nothing to worry about. Now ...' He shrugged his shoulders. 'Now they're all over the place.'

'Why shouldn't they be?'

'Some of 'em fail to be looked after, fall through a hole and get lost right in the midst of the social services.'

'Come on, Greenwood, that's not the real reason is it? Mmm?'

Greenwood shuffled about to make himself more comfortable. 'Can I be honest with you?'

'That's exactly what I want. Honesty from a man who is honest through and through, because that's you all over.'

'I don't really know what to say to him.' Greenwood blew his nose, twice, coughed and added, 'And he looked confused a lot of the time. Does he understand things?'

'Yes, he does, but one thing at a time is best.'

'Well, I will need someone in another few months, probably just before Christmas.'

'Then we'll give him a chance now. Just sweeping up and cleaning the windows and, let's face it, there are plenty of those now, aren't there? I'll come the first time or two. It may not work out at all. On the other hand, it might. So we'll have an experiment. And I'll help where I can. Not all day every day at first for Ben, give him a trial period, see how he shapes up.'

Greenwood agreed. 'So long as you come the first time or two. I shall know if he has wine running in his veins straight away. It has to be in his heart, working in a greenhouse. There's something instinctive about grapes and vines and peaches and things. I'm willing to give him a trial. But if he's not right I won't have him anywhere near my glasshouses because the vines will die, believe me they will. Of their own accord they'll fade away. They know, do them vines, they really do.'

Johnny smiled inside himself. This about vines dying was Greenwood's escape route, saying the vines would die of their own accord! All a load of nonsense but he'd go along with it. 'I'll go get him now. This very minute. I have a couple of hours to spare.' Before Greenwood could object Johnny had sprung up from the seat and was heading for the kitchen garden.

Ben glowed with excitement at the prospect. 'He does? The Green Man wants me?'

Johnny nodded. 'He says you can have a *try*, just for an hour or so, and he'll watch and see how you get on with the vines. He says vines know if a man is right for looking after them, so you have to be very careful indeed and do exactly what he says or else . . .'

'Or else?' Ben puzzled over this statement. 'Or else?'

'Or else they'll . . . they'll die.'

'Die?' Ben looked horrified. 'Not with me. No, not with me. I shan't make them die, they'll love me.'

'They need their windows cleaning.' Johnny said solemnly.

'I clean the windows for Becky, Ben's good at that.'

'Off we go then.'

So Ben spent two hours cleaning windows and did a marvellous job of them. Greenwood couldn't find fault at all. 'I'll take you on. Two hours each morning, cleaning the rest of the windows. There's plenty to keep you going. We've got a lot of windows in the glasshouses, and I like them to be shining.'

Ben noticed a length of dead stem on the nearest vine, snapped it neatly off and placed it in a bin. Then he went back to the living part of the stem and stroked it. 'You keep going; you're doing very well. Just keep going.'

Greenwood, very surprised by this turn of events, realised Ben might perhaps be a man after his own heart.

Ben raced home that evening to tell Becky. 'Two hours every morning cleaning the windows!'

Becky, preoccupied with preparing their evening meal, didn't respond immediately.

Furious, Ben shouted, 'Listen, listen! Never mind chopping stuff. Listen! The Green Man's put me in charge of the vines. Do you hear me?'

Unable to believe it she asked him outright: 'That's wonderful. But did he say so, "*in charge of the vines*"? Those words?'

Ben hesitated. Half of him knew Greenwood hadn't used those words, half of him couldn't quite remember, but not wishing to disappoint Becky he declared firmly, 'Yes, that's right.' He *had* been put in charge. He'd been in there and pulled that dead bit off, hadn't he? He wouldn't have been allowed to do that without being in charge, would he? Green Man hadn't been cross. He'd looked pleased. 'All day in the glasshouses. I shall like that.'

Becky couldn't believe where Ben had got the idea from. 'Are you sure?'

Ben nodded. 'Oh yes. I pulled a dead stalk off and Green Man looked pleased. I found the bin and put it in. Must keep a vine clean and tidy.'

Becky just knew he'd got completely the wrong idea. Ben simply wasn't clever enough to be in charge with all that money at stake at harvest time. But how to tell him he was wrong? He'd explode.

'Ben, come and get your supper. It's your favourite. Cauliflower cheese. With the cheese really browned. Sit down.'

Ben sat down to eat. He didn't say a word until he'd finished. Every last scrap was eaten and he asked to eat the leftovers in the casserole dish she'd used to grill the topping.

Whilst they ate their pudding, Becky related a story Roger had told her about the school where he taught and made Ben laugh, then another story she'd heard in the Store when she bought the cauliflower. For once, he'd understood the stories weren't about her but other people and, deciding he must be in a good frame of mind, she told him the truth about the glasshouses. 'You see, Ben, I think you will be cleaning the windows and that sort of thing, not be *in charge* as you thought. You'll have to *learn* first, *then* be in charge.'

As she fearfully expected, Ben exploded.

She was glad she'd explained it to him at home because the ruckus he caused would have persuaded even a kindly disposed witness to think he was mad. He screamed and shouted and hit her harder than he'd ever hit her before and they were both shattered by his outburst, Ben sobbing because he'd hit her far too hard and brothers didn't, shouldn't do that, and she regretting how much the truth had hurt him, this brother of hers for whom she would have given anything in the whole wide world if she could stop him being hurt. But he was hurt, right to the core. She wished Johnny had never given him a job and that she had him at home all day where he could be safe from being hurt. The bruise on her arm was the worst he had ever given her, but at least it was winter her sweater's long sleeves covered his damage to her so no one would ask her how it had happened.

But now she not only had Ben to protect but herself too. There was something very adult, very grown-up about his attack on her, that she hadn't experienced before and she was worried. It wasn't the petulant outburst of a child like it used to be, and next morning he appeared to remember nothing about the previous night; it was as though it had never happened. He was up and off to the big house in time for his eight o'clock start with not a care in the world, apparently happy at the prospect of being in charge. 'I'm clever Ben Braithwaite, I am,' he reminded her as he shut the front door with a bang.

With the cloths he'd borrowed from Becky, Ben went immediately to the glasshouse, still convinced he was in charge. Becky's cloths were the best, much better than the Green Man's cloths. He worked away, oblivious to the fact that the man in charge of the kitchen garden was wondering why Ben hadn't turned up for work. 'No,' he told Johnny 'he hasn't turned up. Not like him, that, regular as clockwork he is.'

Johnny suspected what Ben had done and went to check, totally unaware of the storm that was about to descend on him. Confident that he knew how to handle Ben, Johnny found him cleaning windows.

'Ah! There you are. We were worried you weren't well.'

Ben paused for a moment to say, 'I'm in charge in here and the windows need doing. The vines said they did and so ...'

Aware he had a very difficult situation to deal with Johnny chose his words carefully, but mistakenly he came out with the truth immediately. Better be up front, no gentle footling about, straight out with it, he thought. 'I think perhaps Greenwood didn't mean straight away, I think perhaps he meant little by little. Take it steady, there's a lot to learn. I think perhaps he meant you to start slowly ... It's Greenwood who is always in charge, anyway. Of everything. The flower garden, the vegetable garden, the woods, the drive, the glasshouses, the—' At this moment Ben crashed his fist into Johnny's jaw with all his strength and felled him. For a split second Johnny was unconscious.

As he began to come round he found Ben was stroking his head and saying 'Sorry' time and time again. A contrite apology, which Johnny accepted, but he remained at a loss as to what he should do next. To begin with he sat up, tenderly soothing his jaw with delicate fingers. Then with Ben's help he attempted to get to his feet. It had been an almighty blow and Johnny simply did not know what to say or do. Be angry? But he could get thumped again. Be polite? But in truth, Ben should not be hitting his employer – or anyone else for that matter. An employer who was hoping to make his life more useful and set him on a path that would lead to something bigger. As his head cleared and his temper cooled Johnny did think that perhaps he was aiming too high on Ben's behalf, that digging in the vegetable garden was the best he would ever achieve. Sack him, here and now? Ring Becky and tell her what had taken place?

He did ring that evening. 'Johnny Templeton here, Becky. Have you a moment?'

Becky listened with horror to what he had to say. 'I am so sorry. So very sorry. He loves the idea of working in the glasshouses, it's his one aim in life to get in there to work. I explained to him last night that I really didn't think Greenwood Stubbs meant him to be in charge but he wouldn't listen – and obviously he isn't clever enough anyway – but of course he's so desperate to work with the grapes and such he believes he *is* clever enough. Please don't take him to court, it could be the end of him if you do, him being how he is . . .'

There was a strange anxiety in Becky's voice that made him ask 'Becky, tell me – it'll go no further than you and I.' He paused for a moment and then asked outright, 'Does Ben hit *you*?'

The prolonged silence at the other end of the phone convinced Johnny he was right, but Becky said, 'No, he doesn't. Ben gets cross but . . . no . . . he doesn't hit me.'

Johnny was not convinced she was speaking the truth. But he made it sound as if he believed her. 'Good, I'm glad he doesn't, because that wouldn't be right. I'm not going to sack him, which is what I should do, but one more incident and that's it; I've got my other employees to think about. Thank you for talking to me, I thought you ought to be warned. I know it will be all over the village by tomorrow – can't avoid it, my jaw is both purple and swollen! He has some strength and not half. Goodnight, Becky, don't worry about it, will you? I'm tough!'

Don't worry about it? Becky wept, unable to hold back the tears. She pulled up her sleeve to stroke the bruising that had come up after Ben's attack on her. It was dark purple and, fortunately for her, a long-sleeved sweater covered it up beautifully, but you can't cover your face so yes, he was right, everyone would know.

This latest news, as it always did, finally arrived in the Store just before five o'clock on the day it happened. A man was in there buying cigarettes, a man who'd had an appointment with Sir Johnny that very afternoon.

'Some blow and not half. His face is badly swollen, purple coloured it is, and very painful. So bad he can't speak properly. Said he'd walked into a door, some door I must say, if that's the truth. So if someone comes in here and his fist is swollen and purple that's him what did it. Take care not to cross him!' The man laughed, picked up his change and left, grinning at the man behind him in the queue at the till. That man said to Jimbo, 'I've been up there today quoting for putting double glazing in two of their old windows. Every word is true because Sir Johnny apologised when he came to talk to me about the quote. The chap who did it must be mad. Wonder he didn't break his jaw.'

Someone choosing a birthday card overheard the conversation and asked, 'Who hit him, then?'

'He wouldn't say.'

'Wouldn't say? He's covering for someone. I wonder who it is. Not his brother Chris, he's on his honeymoon. I'll ask my sister's husband; he works up there. He'll know, I bet.'

'Just about everyone round here works for 'im,' said Maggie Dobbs. 'Lovely man and he pays well too. Them two little boys of his are lovely. Image of him they are. I can't wait for 'em to begin at the school.'

'They won't be going there, not to the village school, not with their money. Huh!' The man who scoffed at such a ridiculous idea came from Little Derehams.

'They are! I've seen the list.'

'Well, only time will tell, but when, *when* the time comes they won't be going there. Believe me. Men like 'im do that to make gullible people like you think they are wonderful down to earth people despite all their money, and not the rich bombastic so-and-so's they really are.' He stormed chirpily out of the Store, convinced he was right.

'Well,' said Maggie, 'let's hope *he* doesn't come in here too often, the nasty beggar. I've seen it with my own eyes, both of 'em registered. I'm not a fool. Believe me, they'll both be there like Templetons have been for years. Sir Ralph went there, and if it was good enough for him it's good enough for them two lovely boys.' She glared at every customer standing behind her in the queue waiting to pay, daring anyone to contradict her, paid for her groceries and departed head held high.

Fran, on the till that afternoon, knew that Maggie would be right. Johnny was like that about traditions and so on, she'd learned that from his brother Chris when she was going out with him. Not that Chris agreed with Johnny, far from it. During a brief lack of customers coming to the till Fran thought about Chris and his heart-breaking attitude to women and was glad it wasn't her who had gone down the aisle on his arm. God! She'd had a narrow escape there. Now she had decided to get a place at university next year she would be leaving all this behind and beginning her new life, and she couldn't wait. She liked Alex so much, but he didn't excite her and after being with Chris liking simply wasn't enough That extra sparkle Chris had, even though he'd been savagely unkind to her, was what she was looking for. On the day of Chris and Deborah's wedding she'd thought about the bride and knew that an older woman with strength and charisma was really what Chris needed to keep him, and that was what he got with Deborah Charlesworth. A younger woman would have found he'd slipped away from her after two or three years – and to Fran total commitment was essential.

Perhaps when she was thirty and still unmarried she would regret her decision to refuse Alex but she didn't, not yet, and knew there were other things she had to do before settling down to married life and, in particular, babies, because she knew that she would want a large family. Not just one or two children but at least four. She saw the pleasure and the hard work that a large family had brought to Louise and Gilbert Johns and to her own parents and she wanted that for herself. So though she loved working in the Store with her dad, she knew she needed three years of freedom to allow her to mature. Stuff weddings.

At that moment her grandmother walked in.

'And a good afternoon to you, Grandmama! How are you today?'

'All the better for seeing you, dear. Busy?'

'Yes.'

'Good! Just what your father likes. The sound of the doorbell jingling is music to his ears. Is he in?'

'He is.'

Grandmama headed for Jimbo's office. She had to tell him. There was no doubt about that. She sat down on a chair and made herself comfortable, saying, 'For heaven's sake, Jimbo, stop tapping on that blessed machine and listen to me.'

Picking up on the anxious tone of her voice, Jimbo stopped and swung round to listen to what she had to say.

'I'm just back from the hospital.' She paused. 'Turns out I need an operation. They've got the results of the tests they've been doing and it's what they suspected: a tumour on my right adrenal gland. There's no need to worry. Very rare, but perfectly routine, they say. In about three weeks or perhaps four. they say.'

Jimbo heard a slight wobble in her voice and knew she was trying hard to be brave, and not quite getting there.

'Mother! I'm so sorry. Where?'

'Like I said, in my right adrenal—'

'No! I mean which hospital?'

'Culworth Hospital, of course.'

'Private?'

Grandmama hesitated for a moment and then said, 'No.'

'Look here, I can well afford to pay for you to go private, so please let me.'

'Well, *I* can't, so I'm going NHS, full stop. I'm not letting you pay.'

'You are, Mother, You are. I can well afford it.'

'Absolutely not. I'm very determined that I'm going NHS and you are not paying for me. And that's that. Please, Jimbo, I have more than enough to do scraping up the courage to face it all without having to fight you too. Just be a good boy and do as I say.'

'But Mother—'

'But Mother nothing. I worry they might find its spread and ... anyway, that's my news, what's yours?'

Jimbo's news was the astonishing way in which the website he'd created for selling meat had taken off right from the first day. Vince Jones had almost immediately needed full-time help and had found an unemployed butcher to do just that, and they were both working all hours. He was thrilled at the success of it but faced with telling his mother after her devastating news ...

Cautiously he said, 'My news is wonderful, but I don't think ...'

'Good! Well, then go on, tell me.'

'The meat website has brought us such success you wouldn't believe. I've never had a new venture get off the ground so well. But enough of that, you're far more important. I'm so sorry. And Harriet, too, she'll be upset. Now—'

'Listen to me. They've found out what's wrong and they are going to do something about it and I should be glad they caught it so soon. So no more of the gloom and doom. We have to be positive.'

'Let me say this. I am so sorry, Mother, about it, and please, please go privately. I can easily pay for it so let me pay. It'll be so much more *comfortable*.'

'Jimbo! I'm struggling to be brave, so please don't make me have other hurdles to deal with, I've enough on my plate as it is.' She bowed her head, fighting back her tears.

Jimbo saw what he'd done and leapt to his feet. Neither of them had been demonstrative in the past but he saw he needed to be now. Putting his arms around her shoulders he said, 'You're the one who has it to go through, so it will be exactly as you want it. But if you change your mind let me know.'

His mother nodded her gratitude, 'I won't tell the others until I get a date. OK?'

'As you wish. I'm so sorry, Mother. I really am.' Jimbo kissed her cheek and then sat down at his computer again. 'You've never had an operation before, have you?'

'Never. Apart from having you in hospital, I've never lain in a hospital bed. Ever. So it'll all be a very new experience. All this gossip about the NHS failing their patients – I shall have first-hand experience of it, won't I? Let's hope I can give a good report of Culworth Hospital. I could always write an article for the newspaper and send it to them. Time someone said something good about it.' Then she burst into tears, no longer able to draw on her defence mechanism.

Jimbo had never seen his mother weeping before and felt at the same time embarrassed and deeply sympathetic. 'Mother! Mother! I'll get you a cup of tea. Stay right where you are.'

Greta Jones was the first person he saw. 'Greta! Cup of tea, please, right away.'

'I'll do that when I've sorted these parcels out with Tom, won't take me a tick.'

'Hang the blasted parcels! A cup of tea *immediately*.'

Greta, shocked to the core that she was being asked by Jimbo, of all people, to put his business second to a cup of tea, stood as though paralysed.

Jimbo snatched the armful of parcels she was carrying and said through gritted teeth, 'Cup of tea, not a mug, a *cup* of tea, immediately, please. Milk. One sugar. In my office, pronto.' The parcels were then unceremoniously perched on top of the cupboard in the passage outside his office. 'Now!'

When Greta carried the cup of tea into his office she still didn't know why it was so urgent and said cheerfully, 'Cup of tea, for you, is it, Mrs Charter-Plackett?'

'It is. Thank you, Greta. Most kind.'

Greta noticed her hand trembled as she took hold of the saucer. 'Take care.' Jimbo sat as though carved in stone so Greta decided on a tactful exit. 'Good afternoon to you both.' As she picked up her abandoned parcels Greta guessed there had been some bad news involving Jimbo's mother, the old battleaxe that she was. She'd caused more trouble ... but put that all aside – it would seem to be something serious involving good old Grandmama. Still, they'd all know in time.

Chapter 3

That night in the pub Greta decided to tactfully mention that all-important cup of tea. 'We all use them mugs that Harriet bought in a sale, we never, never use cups, so there's a little collection of cups and saucers at the back of the cupboard behind the mugs. Now, why, I thought to myself, does he want a cup and saucer? Which I have to wash first since it's so long since they were used. Then he grabs all the parcels I was carrying to Tom to post, drops them on to that cupboard he always keeps locked and demanded – and I mean, *demanded* – a cup and saucer. *Immediately*! That was the word he used. I've never before heard Jimbo put something, *anything*, before his business. Always he would have said send the parcels off and then get a cup of tea. And surprise, surprise it was for his mother and ... her hand trembled when she took it from me and she was grateful. Go on then, tell me, whenever has she been grateful to anyone for anything at all?'

Maggie said, 'Never!'

Pat said, 'Well, I never. Something must be wrong.'

Sylvia and Willie both said, 'Not as long as we've known her.'

Dottie agreed and the conversation fell apart.

Sylvia saved them from a long silence. 'Course she wasn't invited to the wedding. All the Charter-Placketts were, but not Grandmama. I'm surprised Jimbo and Harriet accepted when she wasn't invited.'

'Johnny Templeton, and Chris for that matter, are good customers at the Store,' Willie said. 'I was in there once when Chris was collecting an order and you should have seen what he bought!

25

All kinds of stuff that weren't Jimbo's usual stock. Posh wine and funny stuff like we'd never order in a whole lifetime. Believe me. Jimbo told him the total and Chris just handed over the cash like it was normal. Fistful of notes he had in his hand. Over a hundred pounds the bill was, and it was just bits and pieces he said.' Willie took another sip of his homebrew and waited for his news to filter through the group.

'For bits and pieces?' Greta was appalled.

'Over a hundred pounds? For bits and pieces? That's more than my weekly bill comes to,' said Sylvia. 'We all know they're well off but that is disgusting! And there's people starving all over the world.'

Dottie, better off than she'd been for years with her cleaning jobs and helping Pat at the Old Barn and, of course, Maurice now they were married. 'Disgusting, that. Still, they do a lot of entertaining, don't they? They've always got people coming over from Brazil. Even so . . .'

'Johnny's much more discreet where money's concerned – he doesn't flash handfuls of it about. Usually pays with his debit card, and Alice too, so nobody's any the wiser,' said Vince. 'I wonder why Grandmama Charter-Plackett wasn't invited? Rather rude, wasn't it? Leaving her out.'

'Nobody knows why, but she was very upset about Fran and her . . . well, we don't talk about it, but we all know for a fact it was an early miscarriage, and we all know it was Chris's baby. Fran was invited but declined and I don't blame her, poor kid. But he is the kind of man who would sweep you off your feet – in fact, he'd sweep anyone off their feet, he would. Gorgeous man.' Dottie fell into a reverie after this little piece of conversation. Maurice, now her husband, patted her hand. He smiled, she smiled and everyone looked away, not wishing to spoil their moment.

Then, very unexpectedly, Peter came in with Caroline and passed the time of day with them all and then drifted over towards the bar where Dicky was serving. 'Good evening, Dicky. How did the Scouts do in the canoe racing? I saw them practicing and thought they had a good chance of winning.'

Dicky beamed with delight. 'You were right. We won hands down. No doubt about it. It was almost embarrassing, they won so easily. It was the Craddock Fitch grandchildren who did it. Those girls are brilliant. Never rowed before they came to live here and now they are stars. Absolute stars! Now, doctor, what's your choice?'

'Gin and tonic, please, Dicky. Make it a double, I've had a hard day.'

'Right, double it is.'

When Dicky had served them their drinks they went to sit at the only unoccupied table and that was the one nearest to the inglenook fireplace. It was slightly apart from all the others due to the shape of the saloon bar and gave the occupants the most privacy of any other table. Why he had a dreadful feeling that he was about to hear something he didn't wish to Peter couldn't say, but he did, and he sat down at that secluded table wishing he was anywhere but here. Caroline began to speak, even before she'd taken a single sip of her gin and tonic. 'I'm going to tell you something, Peter, but it's strictly between ourselves.' She took a sip of her gin.

Peter waited.

'Remember Morgan Jefferson? That doctor specialising in research, looking for new drugs, that kind of thing?'

Peter remembered him all too well but decided to keep his response light. It was years ago now, after all ... 'Yes, I do. Big, well-built chap with a brilliant sense of humour. I remember once he told me—'

'Peter! Forget his sense of humour, *just listen, please.*'

Suddenly Peter sensed it really wasn't anything at all to do with Morgan's sense of humour, but something much more important. There was such urgency in her voice, such determination.

'Now, are you going to listen?'

'Yes. Shall I like what you have to tell me?'

'Well, of course you will, you being who you are. Morgan worked in the States for years and then came back here – he's been living up north – and now he has the most fantastic opportunity to take up another research post in America.'

'Good for him. At his age.'

'Exactly. He told me all about it.'

'I don't remember you getting a phone call last night.'

'I didn't. He wrote to me. I opened the letter after I got to work. The salary is phenomenal.'

'Good for him.'

'And he needs an assistant.'

'There'll be plenty of people only too glad to pack their bags and join him.'

Caroline smiled her agreement.

Peter asked her, 'For how long?'

'A year. And I thought, with both Beth and Alex away from home now . . .'

'Yes?'

'You don't sound very interested?'

'I'm listening. Caroline, are you thinking of Alex or Beth? But neither of them are studying a medical subject; they wouldn't be suitable and they can't just take a year off.'

'Not them, of course not. I'm not daft. No, I meant *me*.'

'*You*?' Not being a selfish person he bit back the words that flooded into his mind and instead said, 'How can you? You already have a job.'

Caroline flicked her hand with disdain as though her current job was not an issue. 'I can give in my notice, easy as that. I've been doing it far too long. Far, far too long. Time I had a change. Can't you see how brilliant it would be? America for a year. I met you just when I was ready to do something tremendously world shattering, but I didn't, did I? I fell in love with you.'

28

'And I fell in love with you – and I still am. In love with you.'

'Then we married because we couldn't help ourselves. And then the children came along so I couldn't.'

'Of course you couldn't, and didn't want to at that time.'

'So, this is my moment all these years later and I've just got to do it, take life by the scruff, as you might say. I've got to do it, Peter. Haven't I? I can't turn it down, can I?'

'He's offered you it, you mean?'

'Yes, he has. As you know, we've kept up an infrequent correspondence all these years and he says who else would he offer it to but me? Beth and Alex will still be up at Cambridge ... I mean, what better moment is there but now for me to go? I said yes straight away. I couldn't believe it. And Morgan's delighted.'

'I can imagine. Yes. He would. Being the kind of man he is. There isn't a better moment. Congratulations, darling. Congratulations.'

Caroline came down from her cloud saying, 'You don't sound very happy about it. "Being the kind of man he is." In that tone of voice. Aren't you happy for me?'

'Of course I am.' Peter stood up. 'I'm sorry. I've developed the most tremendous headache; I'm going home to take one of those new headache tablets of yours, OK? See you when you get back. I may be in bed.'

'Darling! I'll come with you. I didn't know you felt so bad.' She began to gather her coat and handbag together, fully intending to escort him home. It was so unusual for Peter to have a headache; he *never* had headaches. But being so full of her own news she didn't recognise the significance of it. 'Wait for me.'

'No, don't come. There're plenty of people who'd love to talk to you so stay here, they'll all be delighted. No, no, don't come, I shan't be good company anyway.' He raised his hand to the crowd, calling out 'Goodnight, everyone!' and left before she could protest.

And this was he who valued absolute truth every day of his life, and he'd lied to the woman he loved more than anything in the world. But of all people, Morgan Jefferson. He couldn't take the risk of the two of them being together for a whole year! Yet on the other hand, he had sinned all those years ago, and he'd not even left home, let alone gone away for a year. Now he'd sinned again by lying. How about that for faithfulness? In all honesty he couldn't complain. Because of the love she bore him, Caroline had given him the amazing, unbelievable opportunity to bring up his own children; at the very least he owed her this year away in America. He'd have to let her go. He owed her so much. But ... Morgan Jefferson!

Back home, he didn't go to bed. He sat at his desk in his study, terrible pain surging through his head. How on earth would he survive? And he didn't mean the shopping. The cooking. The ironing. The housekeeping.

He meant sheer survival. Without her ... for twelve gruelling, jealous months. He remembered Morgan's looks, his dark hair and complexion that was almost Italian looking, but that was his Welsh parents who'd brought that about. Very tall, lean and energetic. He'd never married, though he'd had lots of women friends, one of whom had been Caroline. Peter had met him twice when he and Caroline were seeing each other, and though, since their marriage, they'd never met, he guessed his appeal to women of every sort would not have diminished. Wherever he went, whatever the occasion, Morgan was always the centre of a laughing crowd of people. As he poured out his second glass of the whisky Jimbo had given him for his birthday, Peter swore. This was so unlike him that he knew he'd never survive twelve days without her, never mind twelve months. When he'd had a difficult day he always knew that coming home to her well-grounded common sense would put everything into perspective. And he *did* have difficult days, dealing with death, especially that of a child, and it happened, not often but it did happen, and it always left him shattered. He recalled when Louise and Gilbert

Johns lost their newborn son, Roderick, it had been so difficult to be strong and reasonable each time he saw them, when in truth he felt like weeping as they were doing. But Caroline, as always, had carried him through.

Peter stood up intending to go to bed but he heard Caroline's key in the door. He glanced at his watch and saw she'd only stayed fifteen more minutes after he left. He stood in the hall and watched as she locked the door for the night and switched off the outside light.

'Oh! Peter! You made me jump, I thought you would be in bed.'

Caroline looked directly at his face.

Peter looked back at her, realising the pain he felt was clearly visible.

'Oh darling! Please! I've got to go,' she pleaded. 'It's a wonderful chance to be *me*, not your wife or the parish skivvy, or the mother of twins – well, not really, but you know what I mean. *Such* an opportunity. Please let me go?' She reached up to kiss his lips, but they were cold and unresponsive, and though she recognised the pain he was suffering she brushed it aside. He'd manage without her; she knew he would. He'd have to.

'You see, Peter, things are different now. I'm older, so is he, and we shan't see each other in the same light at all, and you can always come over to the States for a holiday. You have six weeks so you could come two or three times to see me. Couldn't you?'

'Yes, I could. Of course. And you could come over here to see me, too.'

'Well, I had thought I might take the opportunity to use up my holiday weeks seeing all the places in America I've never seen. I shall miss you, of course, but I truly need this chance.'

'Wonderful opportunity, of course it is. Why ever not? Just me being envious. You'll be able to do talks when you get back home – the WI will be booking you for one as soon as they know.'

'Don't tell them until it's definite I'm going. Right. Thank you so much for being so understanding, darling.' She reached up to kiss him again, but kissed his cheek this time so as to avoid those cold, unresponsive lips.

Chapter 4

The following morning Dottie noticed the chilling atmosphere as soon as she opened the front door and called out, 'It's only me. My word, it's a cold morning. I shall have to get my warm gloves out, no doubt about it.'

After this comment she would normally have said something about Maurice, him being a very large factor in her life nowadays, but this morning she left the words unsaid.

Caroline agreed with her about the weather but the reverend merely nodded acknowledgement of her arrival. Oh dear, she thought. Something's wrong. So instead of going into the kitchen and starting clearing the breakfast table she hid in the hall cupboard, sorting out her cloths and things, hoping by the time she emerged equipped for cleaning upstairs the atmosphere might have lightened a little. It hadn't, so she fled upstairs to strip the bed in the master bedroom and get out the clean sheets from the airing cupboard.

While she worked she half listened for their conversation to see if she could pick up anything. But she couldn't. Then Caroline left the house and she heard the reverend close his study door. So that was that. She and Maurice had had a misunderstanding last night but it was sorted in a trice, because they were like that; they each said what they thought was right, said it, no holds barred, and the whole problem could be cleared in a second. They'd agreed on that before they married because Dottie had decided there'd be none of that business of keeping quiet in the hope the matter would resolve itself because she believed problems didn't resolve themselves without someone saying *something*.

She glanced at the bedroom clock and decided it was time she made coffee for the reverend, else he'd be off out without it which would only make matters worse for him.

She started off down the stairs and straight into the kitchen to put the kettle on. Tray. Coffee pot. Coffee grinder. Sugar. Milk. There, that looked nice. Seeing the last flowers blooming in the back garden she found a small vase and placed a few tiny flowers in it. There, they'd cheer him up. Whoops! She'd forgotten the water.

Dottie tapped on his door and walked in. 'Your coffee, Reverend. Thought I'd catch you before you left. Lovely morning, very chilly though.'

He made a tremendous effort to reply to her. 'It is indeed. Quite warm too.'

Warm? She saw immediately that the bright, compassionate light they all loved and that was especially his, had gone, and she knew he was troubled beyond endurance. Daringly she patted his shoulder, saying as she did so, 'Sorry you're not so well today, cheer up. There's a lot of it about. They'll all be waiting for you in Little Derehams this morning for their special do now the village hall's been decorated and is open for business again. I'll leave you some lunch ready before I go.' Dottie rushed away, not wanting to wait for him to reply.

Grateful as he was for her sympathy, Peter was appalled that she'd recognised his anxiety. He really would have to pull himself together; it simply would not do for everyone to know. He was being ridiculous, behaving this way. He knew Caroline would never, ever brush aside the love she held for him. Nor the love he held for her. But this damned Morgan ...

The phone rang. It was someone from Little Derehams,

worried he was late. 'We're waiting for you, Peter, for the hall, you know, the decorations and the new chairs and tables. Just so glad to catch you.'

'Sorry. I'll be there, just a few minutes. Hold the fort. Got delayed with a phone call. Sorry.' Now he'd lied again. Then he genuinely did get held up by a phone call and finally arrived ten minutes after he should have done. But he braced himself, said what needed to be said, cheered them all enormously, presented Lady Bissett with her gift for organising everything so wonderfully well, shades of the tremendous amount of money she'd raised all that time ago when he and Caroline and the children were working in Africa in a church that desperately needed it. Now Little Derehams' village hall almost compared favourably with the Turnham Malpas one that had been revitalised by a generous refurbishment funded by Johnny Templeton only six months ago. It was only Penny Fawcett village hall that required a first-rate clean sweep and then all three of the village halls would have had a spanking new refurbishment. But by comparison with the other two villages Penny Fawcett always lagged behind, the effort too much to even contemplate, the villagers too listless to make a start on anything at all, no matter how vital. Their hall had been the shabbiest of the three for years, so much so that no one wanted to hire the hall for any event, no matter how humble. Consequently, they never even began fund raising.

Johnny Templeton had said he would at least double the amount of money Little Derehams raised, so they had set about the task with impressive energy and he had offered the same to Penny Fawcett. But in truth, Johnny knew they would never raise enough money to improve anything at all.

Almost everyone, even those with a meagre dose of sensitivity in their make-up, noticed the lack of glow in Peter's face that morning. He always shone with love and compassion for everyone, saint or sinner, but not today when it was such a triumphant day for Little Derehams. They'd slaved for two years to get the money to match Johnny's promise and this should have been a brilliant celebration for them all. Peter said all the right things but somehow he lacked joy.

Jimbo, who had organised the refreshments as always, recognised that the flame had gone out of his eyes, but said nothing. Harriet, in response to a mobile call from Jimbo arrived with a tray of freshly decorated muffins to bolster the rapidly disappearing buffet and recognised what Jimbo saw lacking in Peter's face and knew that the piece of gossip circulating Turnham Malpas for the last few hours was apparently true. Poor Peter! A whole year without Caroline's love and common-sense support that was the jewel in his crown! Surely she wouldn't go? The name being spoken of rang a bell with Harriet, Morgan something or other, and she clearly remembered Caroline's delight when she mentioned his name once and felt that there would be more trouble with that Morgan and one year in America with him than anyone could imagine. She raised her eyebrows at Jimbo and he intuitively recognised what she meant and his heart sank.

Peter went back to the Rectory after the celebrations in Little Derehams to find a note on his desk from Caroline.

Peter! Hope you have nothing much planned for the coming weekend as Morgan rang to say he is up in London overnight on Saturday and has invited me to go up so we can have an in-depth discussion on Sunday morning about what this research will be all about. I may not like the idea when I hear it in detail, so it could all be off. Love C.

Caroline had come home at lunchtime so she could tell him face to face what was happening, completely forgetting that Peter would be in Little Derehams. Her mistake served to illustrate how out of touch with her everyday life she had become since that initial letter from Morgan. She could have phoned him, of course. Indeed, why not? But saying it to him face-to-face seemed important to her. She was still going even if Peter didn't like the idea, so why was she being so particular about the face-to-face situation? Because she already felt guilty about something that had not even happened since ... Not since the week she met Peter for the first time and knew that any other man in her life had been blown clean out of the water as far as she was concerned. It was Peter, Peter, Peter, for ever. And now look what she was doing. Intending, eagerly she had to admit, to spend a whole year with Morgan. Why?

She avoided answering her own question until she was driving back to Culworth Hospital and came to that difficult crossroads which the council had been going to make easier to cross for something like fifteen years but couldn't agree how amongst themselves, let alone find the money to actually do it. She paused and gingerly edged further out until she could see a little better. Nothing coming! She pressed on the accelerator and went for it.

The blood drained from her face when she realised she'd missed an oncoming car from her right by a foot. The car screeched to a stop and so did she. Caroline waved an apology to the driver, swallowed hard, and drove on. Altering the line of sight at the crossroads immediately became her next passionate campaign. It would mean the council buying up a short stretch of land from the owner, felling three trees and ... then she recollected that she wouldn't be here to lead any kind of campaign at all. She'd be in the States with Morgan and her heart leapt at the prospect. Whatever the project was actually about she'd make it important to her, because somehow she had to get away. Right away. Away from gossip, away from stagnation, away from doing the same job at the same hospital for what seemed an eternity of a lifetime. Alex would have to sort his own love life out, Beth would have to stand on her own two feet instead of relying on her mother and her brother and especially her dad for emotional support. Time she did. At her age. Twenty-one. Was it really twenty-one years since she had held Beth in her arms with such overwhelming gratitude? Twenty-one years since she'd found out about Peter's infidelity? Twenty-one years since she'd hugged Alex to her with a depth of feeling that she thought would break her heart apart. And despite her shock at Peter's infidelity she had loved him all the intervening years. But had she? Had she truly loved him all these long years or simply fed off that first huge, overwhelming flood of passion that had occurred when they'd first met?

Caroline slid into her parking spot in the hospital car park, braked, and hesitated for a moment before getting out. Eyes closed, heart thudding she sat waiting for common sense to take over. It didn't. After five minutes of deep thought she was no nearer to an answer.

A sharp tapping on her side window brought her back to earth.

'Caroline? All right?' It was a nurse from the department.

She made to open her door. 'I'm fine, thanks.'

'You don't look it. In fact you look ghastly, as though you've come face-to-face with a terrible truth.'

Surprised by the nurse's acute perception Caroline shook her head. 'No, not at all. Now what terrible truth could someone like me have to face, I ask you? I'll catch you up. Won't be a minute.' She watched as the nurse dashed away. Had she arrived at some terrible truth? Of course not. She still loved Peter. Really loved him. Of course she did.

But the idea lay at the back of her mind all morning. She was lucky compared to some of the patients who consulted her. So many of them *did* have difficult lives; lack of money, lack of company, lack of mobility, lack of love, their hospital appointment often being the most exciting happening of the week, if not the month.

Something one of them said made her wonder if Peter had only stayed with her because of the children and the debt he owed her for deciding to bring his children up as her own. No, she was wrong there! He really did love her, as indeed she loved him. But then the dreaded question raised its ugly head again and she paused between patients to straighten out her thinking. If she loved him, why was she so set on leaving him for a whole year?

Chapter 5

Grandmama Charter-Plackett always considered herself a cut above most of the people in the village. Which she was, let's face it, but on this particular day she felt dreadful. Tomorrow she would be at the mercy of Culworth Hospital having her adrenal gland, well, the tumour on it, cut away. She'd faced life full on for most of her days on this earth but today she was feeling old and couldn't challenge life at all. Harriet, taking up her position as daughter-in-law-in-chief, had invited her to lunch to help pass the time.

Grandmama didn't know that Harriet had also invited Perdita Templeton to help liven the day, so when she arrived at Jimbo's house there, in all her glory, was Perdita tossing back her pre-lunch sherry. This got Katherine Charter-Plackett angry before she'd even taken a bite of what she knew from past experience would be a classy lunch.

Perdita had never intended staying in Turnham Malpas more than a few days; two days to recover from the flight from Brazil, one day for Chris's wedding, another day to repack her things and then the following day off home. But there was something about the old house, this Turnham House, which captivated her. She'd twice booked her plane seat, twice cancelled it and was still here three weeks longer than she'd ever intended. Now lunch, with this superior person, well, this woman who *thought* she was superior – but then, she had no idea of how important Perdita Templeton was back home.

'Katherine, my dear! How lovely to see you. Isn't it a lovely day for this time of year?'

They'd met at the wedding and at coffee mornings and at two services in the church and, as far as Katherine was concerned, Perdita was a tart. Not that Katherine ever used that word in public but inside her head that was how she classified Perdita. Katherine could always recognise them, right from the first moment she met one.

'Perdita! How lovely, I'd no idea you were invited. So considerate of Harriet – she is the loveliest daughter-in-law anyone could hope for. Your daughters-in-law – are they lovely too? Of course I know Deborah, lovely girl, an absolute treasure, and Alice, very talented, and your third one back home is she lovely too?'

'Nicholas has always had good taste. His wife is very distinguished and their children are a delight.'

Katherine seated herself in an armchair nearby not beside Perdita on the sofa and prepared herself for a challenging afternoon. At least it would take her mind off the blessed operation tomorrow. But there was no chance of that. Perdita's first words were, 'I suppose you'll be glad to get the operation over tomorrow. You're going privately, I expect, so that will make a big difference, a different class of people there to going on the National Health.'

'Actually, I *am* on the National Health. I intend living until I'm one hundred years old at least, so I have to take care of the money, you see. Can't face an impoverished old age. Not likely.'

Perdita reached across and laid a sympathetic hand on Katherine's knee. 'Are you sure? They won't be your class of people at all, on the ward. Can you not change to private, even at this late stage? I'm sure that darling boy of yours – Jimbo, isn't it? Wouldn't he help? He would, wouldn't he, Harriet, dear?'

Harriet, just returning from the kitchen, said rapidly, 'Jimbo has offered but Katherine is determined to do as she wishes, so NHS it is. That right, Katherine?'

Katherine nodded. 'My decision. I'm not senile yet, Perdita.' There was a sort of sneering sound that came out when she pronounced Perdita and Perdita recognised it.

'There's no need to be rude. And if that's what you want, then so be it. But I know what I would want: *private* with *all* the trimmings. That's what I'm accustomed to back home. In Brazil we have standards. My boys wouldn't want me to suffer any more than need be. They'd pay straight away, no question, not that they need to, of course, I have plenty of money of my own. I'm surprised Jimbo doesn't insist.'

'He tried to. But fortunately I am still in command of all my faculties and NHS is what I have decided, so NHS it is. Such interesting people you meet on an NHS ward. Salt of the earth they are, I'm told. Now, Harriet, my dear, is this lunch ready? I'm starving.' Katherine stood up at this point and missed the horrified look on Perdita's face as she said, 'Well, if you like mixing with the riff-raff . . .'

It was so delightful to be shocking Perdita that Katherine wouldn't have gone private to please Perdita for anything. Trouble was, she did have a point . . . but no, Katherine was determined. NHS or nothing. She wholeheartedly wished it were nothing and that she didn't have to go tomorrow for the operation, but she did. And making a bad day worse, Perdita informed her that she would be staying on another week so she could visit Katherine in the hospital and make sure she was getting the best the NHS offered. Patting Katherine's knee Perdita added 'I'll make sure you get the very best – you wait and see. I shall be there every day to make sure.'

Katherine didn't know which was worse, the operation or Perdita coming every day to visit her. She sincerely hoped that the woman would be struck down with something ominous and not be able to visit at all.

★

The last thing Katherine remembered before the anaesthetic took over was hoping to God she didn't die during the operation. She'd not said any goodbyes to anyone at all in case she tempted fate. All she'd done was make sure her copy of her will was laid on the kitchen table ... just in case. All her money to her darling Jimbo, except for five thousand pounds each to her grandchildren, and her house to Jimbo too. Would have been interesting to know how much it had increased in value since she bought it. No, now she was getting morbid and that was no way to face an operation. What mattered most was the outcome.

The following night in the Royal Oak Grandmama Charter-Plackett was the subject of conversation at most of the tables, none of them having heard a word of the result of her operation. But no one from the family was in there and although, almost inevitably, there was someone in the bar from the hospital because so many local people worked there that it was always possible to find someone full of news in there, that wasn't so tonight.

Sylvia and her usual group of friends, who by tradition always sat at the table placed alongside the ancient settle, were chatting about everyone and everything imaginable.

Someone remarked in passing, 'If this table could talk, wouldn't it have a tale to tell us? Apparently it was put here in this very spot the first night the pub was open for business in the seventeen hundreds so it's three hundred years old at least.'

'How old do you reckon Grandmama Charter-Plackett is? Jimbo's coming up to sixty, though you wouldn't think so, him still thinking up new ideas for his business faster than ever.'

'So she must be eighty. Old to be going through a major operation like she is. Hope she's OK.'

'She must be ninety, I bet,' said Marie Hooper.

'Easy ninety. She once remembered something she'd done as a child and I reckoned if she was there at that time she must be ninety-two now. At least.'

Willie exploded. 'Ninety-two! Don't be daft! She's a sight lot less than that. You're not as sharp in the head as she is at that age. Eighties yes, but not nineties. No. Never.'

'You might not be but she is. I hope she lives on as an example to us all, of how to be in old age. Lively, active, on the go. I just hope me and Maurice are like that in our nineties,' said Dottie, patting Maurice's hand as she spoke. 'She told me once she didn't intend dying, ever.'

'Well, not even her can avoid that,' said Willie rather grimly.

Silence fell while they all thought over this truism. The outside door was flung wide open with an enormous crash and there stood Jimbo and Harriet along with Fran, Fergus, Finlay and Flick.

No one dared to ask if Grandmama was OK; they waited silently until Jimbo addressed them all. 'Well, my dear mother has survived the operation and we've been sent round by her to buy everyone in the bar tonight a drink – and she's paying.'

'Wonderful!' An outburst of applause from everyone there greeted this statement and there was an outbreak of cheers and laughter and relief.

A few shouted, 'Give her our regards.' 'Wonderful news!' 'Say thank you to her, please, for us!'

'Well, what a relief! Maybe she *is* going to live for ever!'

Willie ever ready to pour cold water on anything hopeful said, 'Now, that's not likely is it? I say, it isn't likely.' The kick he got on his ankle from Sylvia hurt him more than he let on. It was still true though, what he'd said ... she couldn't live for ever.

Katherine, lying in her hospital bed connected to more tubes and wires than she could count, was filled with gratitude. All right, she knew she couldn't live for ever as she'd always said she would, but at least here she was, awake and snug and cared for; if she'd paid a thousand pounds for living through today she couldn't have been better looked after. And as she fell asleep a wicked

44

thought came into her head: 'Stuff Perdita, and her private health. The sooner she goes back to Brazil the better!'

But Grandmama was not rid of Perdita as easily as that. Perdita had set herself a task and she was nothing if not determined to see it through. The first three days Katherine was too drugged to appreciate her calling; she wasn't allowed anything to eat by mouth, and kept falling asleep despite her determination to stay awake and be an interesting patient. But by the fourth day Perdita found a very different patient, one who was protesting at the rigid regime she had to follow and one who kept asking when on earth would she be allowed to eat something? On the fourth day she was allowed a bowl of soup. 'A bowl of soup?' Katherine hated nondescript soup, but held back on complaining in case they decided she shouldn't eat it. Did one eat soup or drink it, she asked herself. She didn't care so long as it went in her mouth and she could swallow it and relish the flavour.

It proved to be the most delicious soup she had ever tasted in her life. 'Is there another bowlful do you think?' she asked the nurse. But she got a shake of the head. 'Better let that go down first and if you're very good, I shall bring a cup of tea round shortly. Milk? Sugar?'

'Milk, no sugar, thank you. Thank you very much.' It proved to be the most wonderful cup of tea she had ever drunk and she fell deeply asleep as the last drop went down. Her deep sleep was disturbed by, of all people, Perdita who came loaded with fruit and sweets and chocolate and muffins. By the time the nurse had gone through the elegantly wrapped packages most of it had been banned.

'Surely,' pleaded Perdita, 'all this is of the best quality and you should know her son owns the smart Store in Turnham Malpas. If you haven't shopped in there you should have done, it's simply wonderful, everything they sell is quality, isn't it, Katherine?'

But the nurse was adamant. 'She hasn't eaten anything solid by mouth at all for five days and she has to take care. This, this, this and this will all have to go home. I'm sorry, but the consultant will have my guts for garters if I allow her to eat these things. And a consultant does know best.'

Perdita, unaccustomed to being denied her pleasures, rose magnificently to her feet. 'And where is this man? I want a word.'

'Five minutes to consultant rounds.'

Grandmama suggested Perdita took the rejected items back to Turnham House. 'Those little boys will love all of that, you know, and it's so long since I've eaten anything I doubt I could manage them anyway.'

'I did tell you not to have it done on the NHS, Katherine. I did say. Saving money, that's what it is, saving money. I warned you and it's not often I'm wrong, in fact, I'm always right. I shall give that consultant a piece of my mind. If he comes, that is.' She glanced at her watch, her best diamanté one as it happened. 'Late he is, two minutes late.'

'You won't. I'm just glad to be alive. This kind of attitude will not do, Perdita. Not here.'

'That's the trouble with you English, always afraid of your own shadow. You should live in Rio. They wouldn't be allowed to starve you like this. They want to get rid of you. Wholesale murder. Wholesale murder! That's what it is. Help!'

Katherine groaned and Perdita called out, 'Quick! Something's going wrong.' There wasn't anything wrong but Perdita, having set her foot on a path, was determined to have her way.

A slip of a young woman appeared from behind the curtain, quickly listened to Katherine's heart, spoke to her about where the pain was, and then turned to Perdita, saying, 'There doesn't appear to be anything untoward, what made you think there was?'

'She went a funny colour. I thought she was dying.'

'Mrs Charter-Plackett is far from dying! In fact, she's making a great recovery and I'm very pleased with her progress. She has listened to our advice and tomorrow will be eating everything put before her. Just as we planned.'

'*We* planned? What can a slip of a young woman like you know about it? Are you qualified in any way?'

A nurse standing beside the slip of a young woman said quietly, 'Miss Felton is the consultant who I mentioned would be here in five minutes. You can rely on her completely; she's very well thought of.'

The wind completely taken out of her sails, Perdita felt behind her for a chair. She'd have to eat humble pie and no doubt about it. But humble pie she would not eat, never had and never would. 'Huh! I told you, Katherine, the NHS is *not* good enough. You should have done as I said and *paid*.'

'Miss Felton would have been in charge of her treatment even if Mrs Charter-Plackett *had* paid.' Looking rather smug after making this comment, the nurse added, 'Now, could I possibly ask you to leave? The consultant needs to examine the patient.'

Thoroughly put in her place, Perdita snorted angrily, picked up her handbag from the floor, and stormed out of the cubicle muttering comments under her breath that were not fit to be heard and she repeated her tirade word for word later that day to Johnny and Alice particularly emphasising her anger at the cavalier treatment she had received from the nurse. 'I tell you, that consultant wasn't old enough to be changing dressings never mind being in charge of starving an old lady to death. You should tell Jimbo to go up there, because that's exactly what they are doing, starving her to death to save money. It's disgraceful, and I'm going back home immediately to Brazil, where Perdita Templeton will get well looked after should she be taken ill. Never in all my life have I heard such a thing.' Perdita imitated the consultant's voice superbly well. 'Part of her recovery! And we're very satisfied with her progress! She'll be eating tomorrow, believe me! Well, in my opinion tomorrow never comes and Katherine has completely lost her marbles! NHS indeed!'

Johnny remonstrated with his mother. 'Mother! I know Katherine Charter-Plackett very well indeed and so does Alice and we both know she will be fine. She has not lost her marbles, believe me. At the moment they'll be feeding her intravenously, you know, all those tubes and things.'

But Perdita was still lit up with anger. 'You're getting as bad as all these other English people allowing this. I like Katherine very much indeed, even if she is English. Book me a plane ticket, Johnny, I'm leaving tomorrow.'

Alice, glad to have Perdita leaving the house so soon, felt compelled to say, 'There's no need to go so soon, Perdita. Stay here a while longer because you have been enjoying yourself so much and ...' She was about to say, 'and we've enjoyed your company and so have the boys...' when she knew that then she would be telling absolute lies and Perdita would know immediately because Alice was hopeless at lying. She glanced briefly at Johnny, begging to be helped out of her predicament.

Johnny rose to the occasion magnificently. 'See here, Mother. By all means leave tomorrow if I can get you a flight, if not the day after. You're most welcome to stay with us any time and I do believe there's a little bit of you which really loves the English because all three of us boys have English blood in our veins, haven't we, and you love us. And Grandad is, or rather *was* English and you liked his forthrightness and his kindness, didn't you?'

Perdita sat down again. 'You're right. I did, and I loved him for it. Yes, but I'll still go home tomorrow if I can get a flight. See to it, dear. Please. I'll be back sometime, obviously, with Chris so much more settled. Deborah has improved him no end, hasn't she?'

Alice agreed. 'She has, you're right. We get on really well with her and I'm glad you do too. Best day's work Chris has ever done.'

Perdita, leaned forward very confidingly, saying, 'Do *you* know where she goes when she disappears without a word?'

Both Alice and Johnny shook their heads.

'Oh! I see. Do you know, but are sworn to secrecy? Is that it?'

It was Johnny who answered. 'Neither of us know and what's more I don't believe Chris does – and he's her husband.'

Perdita shrugged. 'Oh! Well. One day I suppose. It *is* mysterious though. Ticket! Ticket! Ticket! Johnny, please.'

Chapter 6

A great sigh of relief swept through the village when the news that Perdita was leaving reached everyone. It was Alice who told Grandmama the welcome news and a sigh of relief was felt in her ward when the other patients realised that Perdita would not be interfering in their treatment as she had tried to do with Grandmama. They were all rather fond of Grandmama, in fact, because if anyone had a complaint such as their ward being missed out on the bedtime hot chocolate round it was Grandmama who rang her bell and took the brunt of any flack from the staff who brought round the trolley, and it was Grandmama who engineered two biscuits with their bedtime drink instead of one, though there'd been a close call with a revolution when the other wards found out about it and wanted the same privilege.

As Grandmama remarked, two biscuits made a big difference to patients who were in desperate need of emotional sustenance as well as medical. She even organised it so that she paid for her bedside TV to be on all evening and suggested that anyone who wanted could bring a chair over and share it with her, thus saving them from paying for their own.

But the best contribution she made was noticing who was depressed and encouraging them to make the best of their predicament by sitting beside them and talking for as long as it took to cheer them up.

As for herself, she knew that when she left hospital she had an open-ended invitation to stay with Jimbo and Harriet and she looked forward to that immensely. The food was always tempting,

Harriet being a cordon bleu cook; their house in winter was always warm and, best of all, she would have the company of the people she loved.

Fran had decided that Grandmama should sleep in her bedroom so that she had her own en suite bathroom and for that Grandmama was very grateful. 'I really appreciate that, Fran. It wasn't necessary, because walking to the bathroom might be the very exercise I need; I've been in bed such a long time it seems, but I'm still very grateful. Now be an absolute sweetheart and bring me up a tray with a cup of tea and two biscuits, please. I'm going to bed because I feel so ragged with all this coming home and de-hospitalizing myself and I feel very tired.' Fran got a wan smile for agreeing she would do that very thing willingly, and Grandmama shut the bedroom door as quietly as she could. As she checked the bedside clock she was supremely grateful to see that Perdita would be on her way to the airport. Perdita in small doses was bad enough, but spending a whole hour every afternoon keeping her company had definitely hampered Katherine's recovery.

Jimbo stored the gifts his customers brought to welcome Grandmama home in his office so when it was his time to leave he staggered off home with an armful of parcels. His mother was delighted and cheered up enormously. 'I'd no idea people cared about me. All these! Stay with me and help unwrap them. I shall have to make a list for thank-you notes.'

'Mother, they won't expect thank-you notes, not from someone who's only just home from hospital. Writing those will do next week when you're feeling stronger.'

'Well, perhaps by the weekend then. I'm not having my meals in bed, you know. Harriet has enough on without running up and down stairs for me. I shall sit at the table like a normal human being. Right? Perhaps just my breakfast in bed, maybe, that would be nice.'

Jimbo reported when he got downstairs that being in hospital had done his mother a lot of good.

'In what way?' asked Harriet.

'She's more ... more grateful, not so demanding and bossy.'

'That's good then, but we mustn't let her do more than she's capable of just because she's feeling grateful. She's old to have had such a serious operation and will need time. When she does go home, we'll stock her up with food then she won't have to rush about over anything at all. Oh, I understand that Perdita has done her best to find out where Deborah disappears to every so often, but even she hasn't got a satisfactory answer. I do wonder where she goes too, but there we are, if Chris isn't worried about it then ... more gravy?'

'Yes, please. I can't think where you bought this lamb – it tastes wonderful.' He grinned at Harriet, knowing full well she'd bought it from the Store.

'To be honest, and I'm not saying this because it's ours, but this lamb is perfect. Your supplier knows what he's about. Good choice. How are sales going now you're getting well established?'

'Up ten per cent again last month on the previous one, and so far this month even better unless sales suddenly slump. Can't believe it. I shall have to be getting Vince another helper, some-one to do the heaving about so that releases Vince to look after the organisation and Bob to do the butchering side of the job.'

'You'll have to give Vince a rise, Jimbo, it's all due to him being so good with the customers.'

Jimbo hesitated and then said, 'No, Harriet, it's all due to me. I thought it all up, planned everything, with Vince's approval of course, but it was my brain what did it.'

'Your brain what did it? In that case then I humbly toast the brain what did it.'

At that exact moment in walked Grandmama wearing her dress-ing gown and carrying her dinner plate. 'I would love to have some more lamb, please, it tastes absolutely wonderful and I do need building up. In fact, I shall stay down here and have my pudding too, if that's all right. You've no idea how much better I'm feeling. It is lovely of you to give me special treatment and bring mine upstairs but to be honest I'd prefer it downstairs. I shan't stay long – I've a programme to watch, you see. Started watching it in hospital and now I'm addicted. *Happy Valley* it's called and I love it.' Grandmama sank gratefully into the nearest chair. 'It's lovely to be home again. Well, not home, but you know what I mean and the thought that I shan't have to tolerate Perdita every afternoon is a real blessing. I did contemplate dying one afternoon so as to avoid her, but I changed my mind – she just wasn't worth my sacrifice.'

After she'd finished her dessert, sticky toffee pudding with double cream, she asked quietly, 'Tell me, did Perdita find out ... you know ... about where Deborah goes?'

'No, she didn't,' Alice said.

Grandmama burst out laughing. 'Good! Good. And the longer she doesn't know the better I shall like it!'

Harriet, alerted by Grandmama's delight, commented, '*You* know, don't you? You do! I can tell.'

'Me? How can I when I've been in hospital? I must have missed loads of gossip.'

'You do! I know you know!'

'I do not.' But there was a mischievous grin on Grandmama's face, which she hurriedly smothered. 'After this delicious meal I shall retire to bed with a novel I intended reading but never found the time to do so, after *Happy Valley*.'

Jimbo stood up to open the door for her and give her a goodnight kiss. She held him briefly to her, returned his kiss and thanked him for having her, adding, 'I shan't pester you for long, just long enough to know I can cope by myself. Goodnight, Harriet. Goodnight, Fran, and thank you for letting me use your bedroom. So kind.'

The three of them waited until they were sure she had well and truly disappeared upstairs and Harriet said quietly, 'I believe you are right, Jimbo, darling, she *has* softened a lot. This stay in hospital has done her good, despite Perdita driving her round the bend.'

'I did say. She's a brave old stick really.'

'All we need to know now is how successful the operation has been,' Fran said.

'Only time will tell,' said Harriet.

'Indeed.'

'To turn to more cheerful things,' said Fran, 'on Saturday, seeing as it is my day off, I'm going to see Jack and Jenny. Apparently the Fitch grandchildren have bought new harnesses and reins for them and they want me to see them and they're making a cream tea too. Three o'clock, they said.'

'I overheard someone in the Store the other day say that they are taking the donkeys up to that children's respite care place and giving the children rides this weekend too. Lovely thought, isn't it?' Harriet said. 'You've certainly done them a good turn with your idea, Fran.'

'I am *some* use then.'

Jimbo protested. 'Don't do yourself down; you are a lot of use to everyone and most certainly to me. How we shall manage when you go to university I do not know. I mean, who shall your mother and I leave in charge when I want to take her to the Far East on holiday next autumn?'

'Far East on holiday! Did you know about this, Mum, and never found the time to tell me?'

Harriet equally as surprised as Fran said, 'First I've heard of it, believe me. Anyway I shall wait and see. I've heard your dad say things like this before, and then when the time comes he's too busy to go.'

'Well, we *are* going. I mean it this time. For at least three weeks. Australia, New Zealand and Japan, maybe even four weeks or five – perhaps that might be better. Long way to go, otherwise, by the time you recover from jet lag. I shall be hunting round for someone to take your place, Fran, and get them well tuned in time for our departure.'

'Dad! I can't think of a single person at this moment in time who could be as versatile as I am. I do accounts, and that's important; I serve on the counter, and that's important because I work hard at customer relations; I order stock for the Store – and that's very important as you know; I collect Greta's stock for the mail order; I come up with new ideas for stock … you name it, I do it – and it's *all* important.'

'Oh, I'm confident I shall manage to find someone. If I book it I shall have to find someone, shan't I? Can't afford to throw money away.'

Harriet muttered indignantly 'Next you'll be taking Grandmama with you.'

Fran burst out laughing when Harriet said that.

Jimbo agreed with her. 'You never know, that could be a good idea.'

'Much as I love your mother, Jimbo, I do not want to take her with us all that way, thank you very much. Tell you what, you take her and I'll stay here and be in charge in your absence. Then at least your mind will be at rest knowing I'm in charge. Anyway, I don't know why I'm bothering my head about it – we'll never go so I can rest easy.'

A challenge like Harriet's, thrown at him with such conviction, made Jimbo determined to carry out his scheme. 'I mean it you know; we both need a complete change. I am determined. Nothing will prevent it. Believe me.'

'Tell you what, Dad, Bel could order the stock. She's worked here long enough, knows every shelf in the Store, and when you decide to move everything to get people confused and therefore buying things they don't even want, like they do in supermarkets, she knows exactly where everything is within a day and tells me which items she thinks need prime position for increasing sales, and it usually works. If someone on TV comes up with a new recipe and all the cooks in Britain get hooked on it, she has the recipe items they need moved, so they can find them all together in one place. Brilliant for business, she is.'

'I thought it was you who did that?'

'No, it's Bel, not me. Sometimes you don't see what's staring you in the face. It's Bel who does the new banners too, to let people know where to find the items they need for the recipe. Honestly, your head is full of new ideas, but you don't see what's happening right under your nose.'

'I shall see her in a new light tomorrow.'

'Never mind letting her work at the Royal Oak in the evenings, she should be working for us full time. Especially when I go. What have I said? Oh my word. Finding someone to replace me at the Store – who would have thought it? I must be mad. No, I'm *not* mad, I'm doing the right thing. Definitely. Should never have listened to myself thinking the Store was the be all and end all for me. I must have been crazy. I should have—' Catching sight of the look of disappointment on her dad's face, Fran apologised. 'Sorry, Dad, so sorry, I shouldn't have said that. I didn't mean it. I've been very happy – no, completely happy working here and it's taught me a lot, but it *is* time I moved on. Economics here I come. In three years time, I shall come back with a whole new attitude to life, possibly even a husband in tow, maybe ...' And suddenly Fran was in floods of tears and hurriedly left the table, unable to carry on talking any longer. By mistake she went straight to her bedroom, pushed the door open and was astounded to find her grandmama sitting propped up in her bed watching her programme 'Sorry, I'd forgotten, sorry.'

'Why, Fran dear, whatever is the matter? Who's upset you?'

'Me!'

'You? I'll switch this off.' She patted her duvet. 'Here, come and sit with me and tell me all. If you want to, that is. That's it. Right there. I'm all ears.'

'Your programme?'

'Don't worry; I know how to get it back when you've missed bits. Now tell me.'

'Well ... it's Alex.'

'Alex? Right.'

'I'm beginning to wonder if I've made a huge mistake.'

'Right.'

'You think I have too, do you?'

'No. I meant OK. You've made a big mistake, you think.'

'I should never have shrugged him off so precipitately. I was a fool. He's the love of my life. That is, I *think* he is. Now when I've finished with him and haven't seen him for ages, or even spoken to him. I do wish I knew my own mind. It's so hard trying to get things straight.'

'Now look here, you do not have to make up your mind right now, not this very minute, you've got time on your side.' Somehow Grandmama saw as clear as day that she hadn't been given the entire picture. 'Do you know he's found someone else? Is that it?'

Fran shook her head. 'He could very easily though couldn't he, he's so ...' Her voice trailed away.

Grandmama smiled. 'He is very attractive, strong but needs hugging, good looking like his dad, charming, charismatic, and so it goes on. What you have to do is make sure you keep in touch. Give him hope. Encourage without being besotted so as to gain some time for yourself. Nothing would please me more than you and Alex making a go of it. And think of the children – they'd be just gorgeous.'

'Grandmama! Honestly! You're getting carried away.'

What pleased her grandmother was the fact that Fran was beginning to laugh at herself and that was a good thing, she always thought. 'Carried away? No, I'm speaking the truth and you know it. Now, off you go and then you and I will sleep on this problem of Alex Harris and see what we come up with tomorrow. I shall revisit *Happy Valley* tomorrow too. Goodnight, my darling Fran.'

★

By the following morning Grandmama had come up with a plan and was in the Store explaining it all to Fran who'd been labouring there since six, and was now sitting at nine thirty in what had been her mother's cookery area until she'd moved to the Old Barn, drinking coffee and eating croissants with gusto.

'Grandmama! I didn't think you'd be so early! Here, plonk yourself down. Coffee?'

'Yes, please, dear. Early for me, but very welcome. Now ... two sugars, Fran, please. Oh ... that's lovely. Thank you. Now, I've been thinking about Alex, and he is lovely, isn't he? Just like his dad. He's not wanting to be something big in the C of E, is he?'

'No, he's not, he's said so outright. Claims he's not good enough ... spiritually, that is.'

'That's a blessing. I'm glad, because I can't see you as a vicar's wife, not you at all. Now, the next big village happening is Bonfire Night. Since Johnny came it's always on a Saturday night so that's convenient for Alex being at Cambridge, so why not, somehow or another, invite him to go to the bonfire with you? By the look of your face I can see you aren't enamoured of the idea, but there are advantages to it. It's cold and dark, everyone's busy and occupied, lots of opportunities for holding hands, lots of places for kissing where none can see you, lots to eat – and he'll take some filling, will Alex, being a big chap like his dad. I think it's an ideal occasion for romance. Well, what do you think? What's more it will cost you nothing, because Johnny always pays for everything.'

Fran, not wishing to hurt Katherine's feelings, didn't quite see the right answer to Grandmama's matchmaking being Bonfire Night. 'A village Bonfire Night, everyone about, keeping an eye on us, wanting a word with him? I don't think that will be fitting at all. No, we'll have to do better than that. Sorry.'

'Oh! Well, I thought it would be an ideal location. Back to the drawing board, then.'

'Sorry, Gran, we've got time anyway.'

'About two weeks, that's all, and you won't come up with a better venue, believe me.' Grandmama got to her feet and stalked out of the old kitchen with indignation positively sparking out of her backbone. All that time she'd spent thinking in the night completely wasted. She almost crawled back home to Jimbo's, let herself in, and made another coffee in Harriet's kitchen that tasted a whole lot better than that rotgut stuff Fran had made for her. She just wished she was well enough to look after herself, but she wasn't, not yet. Making the coffee had tired her and the thought of making a meal for herself exhausted her just *thinking* about it. No, she'd have to stay for at least another week or maybe two. Yes, more like two. Or perhaps even three; by then she really would be capable of being in charge of herself.

Why were the young so able to be so rude nowadays without even turning a hair?

She'd thought the bonfire was a brilliant excuse to get Alex back home and in a romantically conducive atmosphere. Though a common-sense thought did sneak up on her unexpectedly. Maybe it would be better to leave the two of them to find their own way of deciding they were best for each other instead of an interfering grandmother putting her oar in? Yes, that would be best. She'd keep right out of it, pretend she knew nothing at all if the matter ever came up in her hearing. That was the best idea. Yes, then she couldn't possibly be blamed for a failed marriage or something even worse, like an illegitimate baby, or a shotgun wedding. Those were the days. My word, yes, they were. But she still thought that Bonfire Night, especially *Turnham Malpas* Bonfire Night would be the best ever event to encourage romance. Alex was such a catch. His good looks, his charm, his gorgeous eyes ... it was a wonder he hadn't been caught by a less worthy girl than Fran. But then, he was no fool was Alex. He wouldn't make a stupid mistake would Alex, not he. Though Fran might ...

Chapter 7

It was Caroline who was busy making stupid mistakes, not Fran. She had, much against her better judgement, suggested that if ever Morgan wanted to she would be delighted to have him stay at the Rectory for a few days, thinking in her own mind that Peter might feel better if he saw Morgan for himself and realised that there was nothing whatever left between them. Lo and behold, two days after Fran had disagreed about the Bonfire Night romantic episode her grandmother had thought up, Peter answered his phone to find Morgan addressing him as though they'd been buddies for years. They had met just a couple of times and all Peter really knew about him was that he and Caroline had been lovers until Peter himself met her at her surgery as a patient. The memories of the dreadful cold and cough he had that had prompted his visit to the surgery returned with vigour and the sound of Morgan's voice, with its pseudo-American accent, caused him to feel almost as bad as the cold he'd had then.

There ensued a jolly, hail-fellow-well-met talk which left Peter feeling in a mood for strangling him rather than saying as he did, of course this weekend would be fine for him to visit and they'd be delighted to see him. He immediately rang Caroline and the tone of his voice made Caroline wonder if she'd made a sensible decision with her casual invitation. Too late now, she thought. Oh, this was being ridiculous! She wasn't a teenager and if Morgan did have any lingering ideas about their past relationship, one word from her would put an end to the matter. But as for Peter ... she couldn't believe her cavalier treatment of him, yet she did not feel guilty. For once in his married life he would have to put up with her behaviour, like it or not. This opportunity to go to the States and do research, with a man so well thought of, was an opportunity she was not going to miss. At this stage in her life she needed the association with Morgan's fame, needed something more than being a treasured clergy wife, a hospital doctor, a well-respected person in the community. She needed more, much more than that and while Peter revered her to a point where she felt she could do no wrong in his eyes, it simply did not satisfy her need for a different life at this exact moment in time.

A whole year in the States. A whole year away from Turnham Malpas, a whole year meeting new people, making a worthwhile contribution to medical science. *That* was what she needed, what she wanted, what she was going to do, no matter how distressed Peter would be about her absence. Dottie would be a reliable assistant: she'd clean and wash and iron for him, shop for him, even garden for him, well, Maurice would anyway, he'd lack for nothing. He'd survive and when she got back home she'd make it up to him, his sacrifice would not be in vain.

Friday evening came round all too quickly. Caroline had a very difficult day at the hospital – one problem after another that tried her patience to its very limits, the food she'd ordered from the Store in the village came only at the very last moment so she spent a considerable amount of time before its arrival feeling certain the Store had let her down and now what could she do? She rang three times to make sure they hadn't forgotten her and each time was given the same reply: they'd promised it for five o'clock and five o'clock it would be. They were incredibly busy and Tom had had to go home taking his severe sickness bug with him, so they were shorthanded too, but never fear the food would be there in time to be cooked by seven as promised.

Before the food arrived Morgan came, having taken much less

time than he'd estimated to drive up from London. He thrust a huge bouquet of expensive flowers into Peter's arms added a bottle of champagne along with a box of exceedingly expensive chocolates and turned to Caroline. While he embraced his wife, Peter was left to deal with the gifts. Then Morgan turned to greet Peter. It was the slight hint of amusement in his eyes at Peter's obvious discomfort at meeting him that angered Peter. But true to form he greeted Morgan with apparent pleasure and the three of them went to settle down in the sitting room with drinks in their hands that Peter had organised.

Caroline, Peter saw, was lit up by Morgan's presence and responded enthusiastically to everything he talked about. Animated by every little piece of information he could give her about the research they would be involved in, she glowed with enthusiasm.

'You mean that penicillin is not a final solution and it's running out of time?'

'We've always known that, haven't we? No drug, however good, can be el supremo for ever like penicillin has been, and testing this new one is vital – the sooner the better. It looks very promising, believe me, and we shall be at the forefront of medical science if we prove it is. It's so exciting and I can't wait to begin!' Morgan leaned forward and patted Caroline's knee as he said this.

Peter reprimanded himself for the shock of jealousy that roared through him. He'd always known that Morgan and Caroline had kept in touch all the years he'd been married to her but such was his confidence in his own relationship with her that he'd never felt wary about it. Today, at this moment, he did. Very wary indeed. Where had he gone wrong? Why did she have this intense need to go to the States? Where had he failed her? *Had* he failed her? Or was it a restlessness that just didn't get satisfied here in Turnham Malpas?

Now they were talking about where they would live.

'It would be ridiculous for us to rent two flats – surely it would be more acceptable to the company that's paying us for doing what we're doing if we just rented one flat. A two-bedroom flat, that is,' he added hastily. To assess his reaction, Morgan flicked a quick glance at Peter. But Peter was smiling happily so Morgan assumed the chap didn't mind. In this day and age, of course, husbands had to be broadminded. Not that he cared whether or not Peter was broadminded; what Caroline decided was more important to him. In fact, he'd been stunned by Caro's agreement to his research plan, and had joyously encouraged her decision. After all, what was there here in this dull little village to give her satisfaction? Nothing. Nothing at all. Then he looked again at Peter and wondered ... he didn't strike him as an amorous lover. That clerical collar just about said all there was to say about him. She should never have married him.

He looked up at the photographs on the wall of their two children. Children? Well, offspring because they were obviously in their teens at the very least now. The boy so like Peter it could have been him in his teens, but the girl like neither Peter nor Caroline. They looked seriously profound kind of people though. Like Caroline for that he imagined. She'd always been deep thinking. He looked at her and was lost in his thoughts, so lost he didn't hear exactly what Peter was asking him. 'I'm sorry?'

'I asked if you will miss being in England again?'

'No, not particularly. Been abroad such a lot I almost have no connections with England now, except for Caroline of course.'

'You've never married?'

'No. Liaisons, I suppose one might say, but nothing as serious as marriage.' He laughed but Peter didn't. Whoops, Morgan thought that was a mistake. 'You took the only one I wanted to marry, but when she met you, I couldn't compete.' He smiled generously at Peter and then glanced at Caroline. She was obviously very uncomfortable at his words and said, in no uncertain terms, 'I think it's time I showed you your bedroom? I need to get on with our evening meal.'

She got to her feet and led the way immediately upstairs with every intention of showing him into the other big bedroom on the first floor but half way up the stairs she changed her mind and took him on up to the attic. 'This room has its own shower so ... here we are – and look! Splendid views of the countryside.' She stood by the window looking out across the fields belonging to the big house. 'Beautiful view, isn't it? Dinner will be about an hour, but come down whenever. Use this wardrobe, plenty of hangers.' And abruptly left, leaving him feeling abandoned. Still, twelve months in the States ... He could feel her dissatisfaction with her life pulsing from her in waves. What she needed was a real man, not that hidebound do-gooder, handsome though he might be.

Although Saturday was Peter's day off he almost always had something to do involving the church. This Saturday it was two weddings, an annoying coincidence but whichever weekend Morgan had chosen to visit there would have been something afoot to keep Peter busy.

He came down to breakfast dressed, apart from his white cassock, ready for church as the first wedding was at eleven. 'Good morning, Morgan, sleep well?'

'Yes, thank you. Lovely room. Very comfortable bed. And you?'

'Yes, thank you. It's cold out though today, definitely a hint of real winter in the air.'

'You've been out already?' Morgan checked his watch. 'Half past eight? An emergency, was it?'

'No, I go for a run every morning. Done it so often I could run with my eyes shut and still not lose my way! Makes for a good start to the day. For me anyway. Do you run?'

Morgan spread more marmalade on his toast before he replied. 'No. I don't.'

'Each to his own. I find it gives the mind time to get into gear.'

'Mine gets into gear without needing a starting handle.'

'Lucky you.' Peter sensed the snub delivered in the tone of his voice, but left his reply hanging in the air. Damn the man.

Caroline placed Peter's two boiled eggs in front of him, saying in his defence, 'Good for the heart, though.'

'Possibly, possibly, but those two boiled eggs won't help your heart, Peter, will they? Definitely detrimental those.' He smiled in a teasing manner at Caroline and she couldn't resist returning his smile. Briefly, something of their old association seemed to hover in the air and Peter recognised it. It wasn't in his nature to be uncivil but he was very tempted and only just managed not to reply. He smashed the tops of both eggs with the bowl of the spoon harder than usual and Caroline got the message that he was fast losing his temper.

'If we're going to get to that stately home you want to visit, Morgan, we'd better be making a move. It's about an hour and a half away, you see. They open at ten.'

Morgan pushed back his chair and got up. He saluted Caroline saying, 'Yes, sir. Teeth to clean, then off we go. Sorry you won't be coming with us, Peter.'

'Not to worry, I've been several times over the years. We were at Oxford together, the owner and myself, and that fun-loving, hard-drinking student I knew has become sombre, introspective and dull while struggling to make a success of the house, which he has, and it's very impressive. He'll like it, won't he, Caroline? It's very beautiful even if you're not into stately homes. He's spent thousands and thousands on refurbishing it, improving the facilities, making a big children's adventure playground ... believe me, you'll enjoy it.'

'He will. Hurry up, Morgan. I'm ready. Now! Go on! Peter, will you clear the table for me? I've left you lunch out. Hope the weddings go well.' Caroline, knowing how upset Peter was by Morgan, put her arms round Peter by standing behind his chair and resting her cheek on the top of his head and then kissing him.

'You've no need to worry, you know, no need at all.'

'I know. Have a good time. I went to the bank yesterday when I was in Culworth, so have you plenty of cash? I got plenty out. Here.' He held out seventy-five pounds to her. 'Don't want you to be short of money. More?'

'No, no. I've got plenty. Be seeing you. I've booked for us to go out tonight for a meal. At the Fortescue.'

'What are we celebrating?'

Caroline shrugged. 'Nothing, just don't want him to think we've turned into country bumpkins.'

'Which we haven't! Well, not quite.' He kissed her just as Morgan arrived in the kitchen doorway.

'Not interrupting anything, am I? Should I go back upstairs and wait for you to shout? You did say be quick.'

They drove away from the Rectory in his car, a flashy sports that amused Caroline. 'This is a far cry from that Ford you used to have when we first knew each other.'

'That was a long time ago, Caroline.'

'It was. You were much more humble then. By the way, before we go any further I will not tolerate you attempting to humiliate Peter. Sly remarks that are innocent but hurtful are not on the agenda in our house. I won't have it.'

'You noticed, then?'

'Of course I did.'

'So ... he needs looking after. That figures. That clerical collar—'

'What about it?'

'Well, he seems weak ... kind of. Too gentle for this world. Kind of. Just not tough.' Morgan did think of saying, 'Can't think what you saw in him compared to me ...' but bit the words back quickly. He really mustn't antagonise her, not with the plans he had in his mind for her.

'Weak is the very last word I would use to describe Peter.

He is admired and loved by everyone who meets him. Wait till tomorrow when you hear him in church—'

'Hear him in church? You mean you expect me to go to church? No, thank you very much, I am not going to church. Haven't been to church in years, can't even remember when I was last in one. Sorry and all that.'

For some unfathomable reason Caroline insisted. 'Either you go to church or I don't go to the States.'

'You are joking, aren't you?'

Provoking him right at this moment seemed a very good idea. 'No, I'm not. I mean it. One hour in church in exchange for a year in the States with me. Fair, isn't it? Don't you think?'

'To what good purpose?' Morgan was puzzled, and it was rare to find a woman who could puzzle him, because he was a man who believed he knew women and their motives through and through.

'It's what I want. I want you to listen to Peter's sermon – it might do you good, you never know.'

'You are being ridiculous, absolutely ridiculous.'

'No, I'm not. You're staying as a guest in our house and it's only polite to agree to go to church. A small thing to ask of you, surely?'

Morgan resisted arguing with her because it wasn't part of his master plan, so he pretended to capitulate. 'All right, then. Of course you are quite right. I should attend out of good manners. I will go to church just as you ask. It's not some ghastly hour like seven in the morning, is it?'

'No, it's civilised. There is one at eight o'clock but I've gone to the eleven o'clock ever since the children were born.'

'Thank God for that. The sat nav says I should turn right at the next roundabout – is that right?'

'Of course it is. Do you question the sat nav? I never do. I keep mine thoroughly up to date.'

Morgan pulled in, braked, switched off the engine and turned to look at her. 'You are a fabulous woman, Caroline. Married all these years to a man I sense is not entirely yours because he considers he belongs to God, two children neither of whom look like you at all – the boy is just like Peter but that's it and the girl is so entirely different she *couldn't* be yours. Do you feel neglected? In your circumstances *I* would.'

'As you are a man I find it difficult to understand where you're coming from, Morgan. It's none of your business, anyway; they're not all coming to the US with me. It's only me you're getting, you know, everyone else will be at home here in England so ... I do not feel neglected not at all, the children love me and I love them and, most of all, I love Peter and he loves me. End of discussion.'

'In that case why are you wanting to go to the US? Mmm?'

'For a complete change. I've been stuck here in this village for more than twenty years and it's time I did *something*. Actually *did* something and this is the best opportunity I've ever had. It's not you; you're just the means by which I escape for a while. At the same time I know I shall eventually be back where I really belong.'

Caroline looked out of the car window for a moment and then looked Morgan full in the face. 'Satisfied?'

He smiled disbelievingly at her. 'For the time being, but there's more to it than that. I *know*. And time will tell.' Morgan switched the engine back on, satisfied that he was on the right track. She had secrets to hide and he would know them all before long because he was that kind of person. And what's more, he wouldn't have her doing research with him day in, day out without knowing. He had to know. Had to know where he stood with her.

The two of them spent a wonderful day visiting the house. It was classically Georgian and had been in the same family for three hundred years. The tea rooms were immaculate and the menus amazing and suddenly, out of nowhere, the two of them were back to the days of their earlier acquaintance before Peter. Before

Peter ... Morgan believed they were and briefly so did Caroline. She turned to face him, saying, 'Morgan, we did have a good time together didn't we, you and I, all those years ago? Sometimes I wonder ... Only a matter of weeks – but what weeks they were!'

'But *you* finished it all. Why?'

'Oh, I knew you weren't right for me.'

'And Peter was?'

The hint of scathing sarcasm in his voice angered Caroline. 'Yes, he most certainly was, and don't you forget it.'

'I think, my dear Caro – remember when I always called you that, Caro? – you are the one in danger of forgetting that, not me.' He took her elbow and moved her slightly so they were looking at each other, their faces only half a metre away. He leaned forward and placed a modest kiss on her cheek then grinned. 'Better give you a chaste kiss in case any of his parishioners are watching. You never know, so close to home.' His grin was wicked, this time and she had to laugh. He was fun; no cares burdened the shoulders of Morgan Jefferson, whereas Peter carried everyone's cares on his shoulders. Greta and that strange incident of the trunk in their attic; Ford Barclay and Merc as they always called her, still labouring under the suggestion of his guilt in the theft of the lead from the church roof, no matter how much money he spent on the youth club; poor Dottie, though less of a worry now since she'd married her cousin Maurice. Endless cares for Peter every day of his life, and yet ...

'Time we thought about going back to the Rectory. We're going out for a meal tonight and you'll need a tie and a jacket.'

'That posh?'

'That posh.'

They wandered back to the car park through the rose garden, still a delightful place to linger, even though the season for them was long past. Here and there a stray rose bloomed, and for some silly reason Caroline likened her love affair with Peter to them. It was just, but only just, blooming. And here was Morgan, bursting with laughter, full of fun and obviously making tentative and not-so-tentative attempts at reawakening her love for him.

For one wild, uncharacteristic moment she laid Peter aside and chose Morgan.

Chapter 8

By the end of the weekend Peter was in torment. He was only on the fringes of their lives now; he knew none of the people they laughed about and talked of and felt so excluded he spent hours in his study over the weekend, pretending to have work to do, a sermon to write, emails to answer, anything rather than sit there being totally ignored. Caroline's normal behaviour pattern was conscientious and considerate and would never make him nor anyone feel so isolated, but here she was ignoring him and, deliberately it seemed, making his life unbearable.

Yes, Morgan went to the eleven o'clock service but sat with a patronising smile on his face that made Peter feel momentarily entirely pointless. Did he actually get his message across plainly and simply as always? The congregation to a man guessed that it was that self-important, wealthy-looking guest sitting beside the rector's wife that was the root of it and when the news was passed round and they found out he was the one whisking Caroline off to the States for a year perhaps ... the muttering behind their hymn books and the order of service sheet escalated.

Standing outside the church after the service, Jimbo engaged Morgan in conversation and those nearest to the two of them made desultory conversation so as not to miss a word.

Morgan shook Peter's hand as he said, 'Well, Peter, excellent sermon. Not heard your interpretation of that verse before. Very apt I thought and very thoughtful.'

'Didn't know you went to church frequently. It's not a common verse to use as the base for a sermon, very rarely used, in fact.'

Morgan hastily recovered himself and suggested he might have been mistaken in thinking he'd heard it used before then tried to fill in the silence but, at a loss for words, was grateful to be rescued by Caroline suggesting she should go home to start lunch and did they mind?

Struggling, unusually for him, to regain the upper hand in the conversation, Morgan suggested lunch out in a typical country pub. 'How about it? My shout! You'll say yes, won't you, Peter?'

Peter nodded.

Caroline didn't.

'Come on, Caro, please. Peter, you tell her we're going out for lunch. If we go straight away we'll be there before the crowds arrive. Come on.' As he finished speaking he patted Caroline's arm. 'Say yes. I'm sure you must get fed up cooking, especially when your ...' He appeared to pause purposely, 'your children are home.'

Caroline capitulated with good grace. 'You make going out sound very tempting. Yes. Let's. Where shall we choose to go, Peter?'

'Not the Royal Oak, we'll get no peace in there – half the village will be in there, you see, Morgan.'

'I know, Peter! The Wise Man. Beautiful old village pub, good food. Yes, we'll go there.'

'Better be quick then. I'll get my cassock off, be with you in a tick.'

They managed to get a table close by the big window with a lovely view of Myrtle's beautifully kept garden. Morgan was aware that it was only because they had Peter with them that the table was theirs and he felt like a spare part as it was normally he who was allocated the best table due to the depth of his charm. The landlord, known to Peter as Billy, made sure their pre-lunch drinks came quickly and it was he who took down their orders for food.

As soon as they were left in peace Morgan commented, 'You must come here often; good customers, are you?'

Caroline opened her mouth to reply but Peter beat her to it. 'I did him a favour a while ago, you see.'

Morgan laughed. 'Must have been some favour and not half.'

Caroline's face lit up with delight. 'He got prosecuted for an assault and Peter spoke up for him. It was definitely the story of the week as far as the village was concerned, believe me. Go on, Peter, tell him.'

Peter declined.

'Oh, please darling!'

'Absolutely not. Sorry.'

To say Caroline sulked was not strictly true but she came very close. 'I don't see why not.'

'What he did was not acceptable but it caused *him* a great deal of distress. It's not fair for me to disclose my part in it.'

'I'm not going to find out then?' Morgan cocked his head to one side as he pleaded with Peter to tell him about Billy's court case.

But Peter ignored his plea. 'No way. When are you leaving for the States, Morgan? Soon?'

This complete redirection of the subject of their conversation rather shocked Morgan and momentarily he was speechless. Eventually he replied, 'Very soon. If Caro is still of the same mind I'll take copies of her credentials with me and get moving on her being accepted as my assistant. I know the chap who makes the final decision so it shouldn't be difficult. He's a great guy.'

Peter waited for Caroline's reply. Yes? No? But it was yes, an eager yes that put those who heard it in no doubt that she was heading for the States as soon as. 'I hope so, Morgan, I've already given warning of putting my notice in. Always having been on a temporary basis, never as permanent staff, I can just give the hospital one month's notice. So job effectively done.' She smiled brightly at Morgan, less so at Peter, who, taking a long drink of his home-brewed ale as she answered, decided he was being poisoned because it tasted uncommonly foul.

Slightly startled by her being free to go almost immediately Morgan said, 'I haven't actually got official permission, you know, but don't worry, I will by the end of this week, believe me.'

'Doesn't matter if you haven't, though I'd be very disappointed not to go. I shall find something else more interesting to do than Culworth Hospital day in day out. *Anything* to get out of my present situation.' As Caroline listened to herself saying what she did, she grew in stature and knew more than ever that if she didn't do something very different she would be tearing her hair out in Turnham Malpas. This time, this day, she was doing what *she* wanted and not what everyone else, including Peter, thought she should be doing. *She had to escape.*

When finally the news came that Morgan Jefferson had lived up to his words and got Caroline the job as his assistant, Caroline's twins were horrified. Both still at Cambridge, they phoned each other and planned to go home the next weekend together to talk to their mother. What was she thinking of, leaving their dad for a whole year all alone in the Rectory? It was such strange behaviour on her part, and the two of them couldn't understand it. So they arrived home about four in Alex's car to find Peter by himself, which they expected and wanted, hoping to find out from him what was going on if they could.

'Was Mum expecting you? She never said,' Peter asked as he and Beth hugged each other.

'No, she isn't, but we both wanted to come home to see what on earth Mum is thinking about, didn't we, Alex? Leaving you on your own.'

Alex was now too grown-up to hug his dad, though he would have liked to, because his father looked so unhappy.

'I am old enough and wise enough to be left and I shall have Dottie coming four mornings a week, shopping and cooking for me and cleaning and answering the phone when I'm not here, so I shan't be bereft, shall I? After all, I am a grown-up, believe it or not. In any case, your mother needs something fresh to do, something vital, something new, and this just fits the bill. She'll feel much better, much more settled, when she gets back. Believe me, she will. Tea?'

'Round the table in here, like we used to when we came home from school, and toast too, with raspberry jam,' Beth suggested. 'I'll do it, you sit down, Dad. Come on, Alex, no laggards round here. Get a move on. Do your bit!'

So they sat, the three of them, round the table and, when Beth looked at the clock, she found it was half past four just like it used to be when the school bus dropped them off from school, and it comforted her. That was until Alex brought up the name of Morgan Jefferson.

'Oh, he's someone she met before we knew each other; nice chap, been here to stay. Great fun. Another slice of toast, Alex?'

'Don't you want it?'

'No, one's enough, thanks.'

'You like him?' Alex asked.

'He's all right, but he would try making me think he was a churchgoer, which he patently wasn't, and you know how I hate that. If you go to church, fine; if you don't it's still fine by me, it's up to the individual. It's their choice.' Peter stared into the distance and fell silent. Beth didn't like the look in his eyes and Alex thought his dad was sad.

'Interesting research, though, she'll enjoy that, something to get her teeth into,' said Beth, trying to put a bright side on the matter when she didn't feel happy at all. 'A year will soon pass and Dottie will love being in charge; she thinks the world of you, Dad, you know. Your opinion counts for a lot as far as she is concerned so you'll get well looked after, believe me.' Inside herself she was saying why? why? why?

Dad wasn't exactly speaking the truth about this Morgan chap, she knew that. What on earth had got into her mother? To be doing this silly, stupid thing. The risk she was taking!

Unbelievable! Alex was keeping his own council but she knew he was as concerned as she was. So out of character for Mum to be teaming up with a man she'd known before Dad. She just wished she'd known he was coming for the weekend last week; she'd have been home like a shot with Alex in tow, like it or not. Alex had first of all tried to persuade her it was perfectly normal nowadays what Mum was doing, but in fact he was as worried as she was. So out of character. And her parents still loved each other, very much indeed. She, her mother that is, had once explained what real love was about, complete honesty, passion, adoration, longing, caring, being there for each other whatever crisis they had to face. And the other plus was the two of them had survived the birth of her and Alex in a way no other couple on God's earth would have been able to. Their survival after that must count for something. No wonder Dad looked crushed.

'You see ... I – I understand how trapped she feels, stuck here, small village, always the same people, the small-minded gossip. I should have moved years ago, taken her somewhere interesting like Salisbury or Durham, a happening kind of place, or London even ...'

'Dad!' Alex swore so Beth knew he was worried. 'You always say you can't stand church politics and that's what that would have been, all the time. That's not you.'

'Selfish, that's what I've been. Selfish, thought only of my own needs not hers. This would never have happened if we lived somewhere more—'

Alex shouted, 'Nothing's happened, has it? What are we expecting, the three of us? We're talking as though Mum will jump into bed with this Morgan at the first opportunity. But she's not that kind of a person. I'm certain that is the furthest from her mind. We're being ridiculous.' He banged his fist on the table, his toast bounced, and his tea spilled into his saucer. 'Drat it!'

At that moment Caroline came in through the front door, calling out, 'It's me! Home early for once. All right, darling?'

She stood in the kitchen doorway totally amazed to see them enjoying toast and tea just as they used to after school. 'What are you two doing here? You should have let me know.' She stood, as they'd seen her do so often in the past, one arm around Peter's shoulder, her head bent so she could kiss him on the top of his head, smiling at the two of them in turn. Suddenly all was right with their world.

'Tea! Please, get me a mug, Alex.' She kissed the two of them and sat down on her particular chair where she'd always sat as long as they could remember. 'Right! To what do we owe this unexpected visit? Mmm?' She knew all right what it was about but she needed them to bring it out in the open while all four of them were there.

'Nothing doing at college this weekend. So I rang him and he rang me and here we are.' Beth was so relieved that things were back to normal that she leapt up and kissed her mother knowing how grateful her father must have been when Mum decided to adopt his twins so she had the children she would never have had otherwise. 'Love you!'

'And I love you.'

Alex, never as demonstrative as Beth, squeezed his mother's hand and gave her the smile so like his father's. 'Anything planned for this weekend? Anything special, I mean.'

Caroline laughed. 'Still needing to know what's happening, just as always. You never change.'

'Why, should I, Mum? Do you think I should?'

'No. Stay as you are.'

'Same boring old Alexander Harris, reliable, strong, a shoulder to cry on etc., etc., etc.,' said Beth.

'*You've* cried on it often enough. How's the romance going with what's his name?'

'There *is* no romance with what's his name! How's yours with Fran?'

'I told you before, mind your own business.'

Beth, always quick to read Alex's mind, said sharply, 'You've finished with her or has she finished with you? That's it! I'm right, aren't I?'

Alex took her astute deduction as calmly as possible by not replying at all and addressing his father. 'How's things with you, Dad? OK?'

'See, he can't answer me. Tell us the truth, Alex. Please.'

Caroline, not really into truth at the moment, said, 'Beth! That's very *private,* say no more.'

'In that case tell us more about this Morgan chap, Mum. Will you?'

Alex, deciding there was no point in trying to keep the news to himself, and also relieved the news hadn't been flashing round the village in six metre high letters and, above all, needing to prevent his mother having to reply, said, 'Fran and I are finished. Finito.'

Beth was disappointed. She'd always liked Fran Charter-Plackett who would have fitted the bill very nicely as her sister-in-law. 'I suppose it might be for the best – after all, you were probably her rebound after Chris Templeton. Yes, you've made a good decision there.' She leaned towards Alex and patted his cheek sympathetically. 'You've done right. Give me a shout if you need help with dinner, Mum. I'm going upstairs to my room for a snooze – had a very late night last night.'

Alex left the kitchen too. 'Peter, did you know they were coming for the weekend?'

Peter looked up at her, 'No, I didn't know. I'm just as surprised as you.'

'They've very neatly managed to say not a word about me and what I'm doing.'

'They do know.'

'I know. But it would have been nice of them to say something about their mother striking out from her usual routine. Taking life by the scruff or whatever they call it now.'

Peter did not reply, so Caroline had to ask, 'Don't they approve?'

'What do you expect? Their mother going off to the States with an extremely attractive man – and he is very attractive, even I can see that. They might be bright young things with all the latest take on everything, but you are their mother and therefore they don't approve. Sometimes, Caroline, I don't understand you, I really don't. I shall be in my study if I'm needed.'

Caroline watched him as he disappeared out of the kitchen. She was tempted to follow him and have the whole subject out in the open, here and now, in his study where other momentous decisions had been taken over the years. But something held her back. He needed time, that was it, time to realise she wasn't tied to the church in the same way he was. Time to learn that she wasn't tied by her apron strings to him, not now. Once she was and she wouldn't have had it any other way, but not now. So ... what was different now compared with the past? Morgan's name sprang into her mind as it did so often now; whenever she had a moment to spare, there he was. Yes she still cared about Peter, but after all these years she cared in a different way ... comfortably, quietly, gently. Not passionately, powerfully, consummately, as in the past.

She was a grown woman and knew exactly what she was doing: taking a breather, stretching herself, testing herself, plus being desperately in need of change. Surely the children didn't think ... but they did. That was the reason for the unexpected coming home. They really thought she was going to the USA purposely to have an affair with Morgan, out of the way, where Peter's integrity wouldn't be affected. But that was absolutely not the case.

Caroline took four lamb chops from the freezer and set about defrosting them, a culinary adventure she never seemed to get quite right. Of course she wasn't going to assist Morgan in order to have an affair – it was the intellectual challenge she was after.

She'd never forgive herself if she had an affair. Caroline Elizabeth Harris wasn't that kind of a wife. Never! The chops had defrosted patchily as always. She groaned. Gazing out of the window on to the back garden she had created from a wilderness, she thought to herself that here at least was the one beautiful thing she had created. Well, there was Alex and Beth, both beautiful people; she'd created them, in one sense. As she slapped the four chops into the sizzling heat of the grill she remembered, of course, that she'd had nothing to do with their creation, that had been Peter's big mistake – but how thrilled she'd been to get the chance to bring up the children she knew she could never have conceived herself. So although he was guilty, heaven alone knew the price he'd paid over the years for that temptation. Therefore if she did go to America with the intention of ... Beth came into the kitchen. 'Can't get to sleep, I'll set the table, shall I?'

'That would be lovely. I'm glad you've come home this weekend; sometimes the house is so very quiet with just your dad and I.'

'Best get used to it, I can't see either Alex or me coming to live at home once we get our degrees, can you? All the Charter-Plackett children except Fran live away, and Dean Jones and Michelle even. We'll have to go where the jobs are, won't we?'

Caroline nodded. 'Of course.' Should she say something about Morgan? No. Best keep away from him; she might let something slip and that would never do. Something slip? But what, for heaven's sake? There was nothing to let slip. Was there? Had she not faced the truth? Not yet. No. But what *was* the truth? She didn't know any more. As she sliced the beans neatly, methodically, knowing they were, at the moment, Peter's favourite vegetable, she smiled in anticipation of his face filled with pleasure. Could she cope with not seeing him every day? For weeks at a time? Should she say no before it got too late to back out. Did she really want to be pinned down to research and figures and graphs?

What would it really be like seeing Morgan every day? Beth went off to the dining room and, rinsing her hands under the kitchen tap, Caroline gazed out of the window again, trying to picture Morgan serious, hardworking, methodical, exact, precise – and couldn't. She could picture him at a restaurant, in the open air, sun shining, fresh green leaves on the trees waving gently in a soft breeze and Morgan toasting her as he'd done the weekend he'd stayed and they'd gone to the Fortescue for dinner, but Peter, though he'd gone with them, somehow wasn't there; it was just she and Morgan laughing together and a waiter bringing champagne to their table.

Caroline was brought back into her real world by Alex coming in. By himself, mug in hand. 'Sorry, Mum, took this upstairs, I'll wash it up.'

'Don't, for goodness sake! Put it in the dishwasher with all the rest.' She turned to look at him, 'Alex!' Did she need to have his approval? Of course not. But somehow the strength he had that he'd inherited from Peter, demanded rather more of her than she had anticipated. 'Am I being a fool? Tell me honestly.'

Leaning against the edge of the sink, facing this mother whom he adored, Alex knew she needed the truth. 'Dad. Have you looked at him lately? That wonderful spirit that beams out from him day in and day out is disappearing at a serious rate of knots. That's all I can say. He's being what he is, a Christian gentle-man doing what he feels he should for someone he loves, but it's crucifying him. On the other hand, I can see why you want to go. More than twenty years in this village for someone like you with a good brain and a passion for life well ... I can see why you jump at the chance.'

Beth found them hugging each other. 'Can I have a hug too?' She joined in saying, 'We should be hugging Dad as well. Not just us.' But they stayed as they were for a while longer, each with their own take on the situation. Finally Beth extricated herself saying, 'I'll go find him.'

'He's in his study, darling. Tread carefully. Dinner's almost ready.'

The rest of that Saturday evening they had intended to spend with a box of chocolates Beth had brought with her watching *Strictly,* but that plan was knocked on the head when Grandmama Charter-Plackett rang the Rectory doorbell.

'Beth! I need to see Peter. I know it's Saturday and you're both home but it's urgent. I shan't stay long.' Before Beth could say a single word of welcome, Grandmama had stepped briskly over the threshold, the purposeful glint in her eyes silencing any protest Beth might have had.

'In his study, is he?'

Beth nodded.

'Right!' Grandmama tapped briskly on his study door and waited for him to say, 'Come in.'

She bounded in, plumped herself down on his lovely cuddly sofa, and smiled benignly. 'Peter! I've come and I shouldn't have done, but I have. Since I spoke to you when you so kindly visited me this morning you've been on my mind and I cannot let the sun go down – well, it's already gone down but you know what I mean – without coming to see you. My dear boy, and I'm old enough to have licence to describe you as a dear boy, whatever is the matter? Your light's been turned off and I need to know why.'

Peter said, 'You've made an amazing recovery from the operation. I thought you'd be resting, not visiting me.'

'No time for resting. If it's something intensely private, then I shall retire with good grace, but there *is* something and we need to talk about it. I know people think of me as an old trout but this old trout is discretion itself when it comes to the secrets of people I love, and I love you. Have done since the first day I saw you. In fact, I told Fran only the other day I would marry you if you were free.' She burst out laughing and her laughter drew a smile on Peter's face. 'That's better. Whatever is it that's making you lose your wonderful spirit? Mmm?'

Peter refused to explain. She could tell from his face he wouldn't disclose his problems. She waited a short while longer and then struggled to her feet. 'This sofa isn't designed for hurried departures. It's designed to keep you here till all is revealed ... but you're not going to tell me, are you? Well, all I can say is talk to the person involved if you can't share it with a stranger. That way you may resolve it. Goodnight, Peter. God bless.'

'Goodnight, and thank you for being concerned; we'll sort it somehow.'

Grandmama left the Rectory without seeing anyone else and was disappointed that her mission had come to nought. Still, it might mean he could make himself tell the person concerned who, Grandmama knew, would be Caroline. Caroline, who wanted to spread her wings. She sighed. These highly intelligent, well-educated women didn't always get things right; often it was the quieter, simpler people who were more emotionally well rounded. Those two children of theirs – well, *his* that is – would be torn apart if anything came about that meant the family broke up. My, but she was tired. Bed, that was it, bed immediately. How lucky she was she had Jimbo and Harriet. She'd have breakfast in bed tomorrow, take a rest.

When she got back to Jimbo's Grandmama put her head around the sitting room door to find these two precious people of hers were sipping whisky. 'I wouldn't mind one of those.'

Harriet looked round and seeing the exhaustion in her face said, 'Get ready for bed, Katherine, and I'll bring one up for you in about twenty minutes. OK? Take your time, don't rush.'

Harriet took the whisky up for her, knocked on the door, and went in. 'Here we are, just as you like it. Let me prop up the pillows. There, that's it. You've overdone it a bit, haven't you, worrying about Peter? Leave them to sort it out, whatever it is that's making her want to have an – well, have an adventure.'

'Do you know what it is?'

'No, do you?'

'Yes. And it all depends on Caroline, the silly girl. Thanks for this. I shall be asleep as soon as my head touches the pillow. Good night, dear, I'm glad Jimbo had the sense to choose you.'

'Thank you, Katherine. I'm glad you're his mother. Goodnight.'

'Well?' said Jimbo before Harriet had even sat down.

'Your mother knows, but hasn't told me.'

'It's the same as I think, I expect,' he answered rather smugly.

Harriet almost leapt from the sofa in a single swift movement. '*You* know?'

'I guess.'

'What then.'

'It's that Morgan chappie who stayed the weekend. He's after Caroline – and she's tempted.'

Harriet laughed, convinced he was only guessing.

'Caroline? She only has eyes for Peter.'

'Not any more.'

'Jimbo! You are being ridiculous.'

'I caught sight of a look Morgan gave her when they were outside church that Sunday morning he was here and I know a lustful look when I see one. Believe me, I've seen plenty in my time.'

Harriet almost fell off the sofa laughing at this silly idea. 'You? Lustful looks! That's the most ridiculous statement. You and lustful looks? Who's looked at you lustfully, then? The Senior sisters? Venetia back in the old days when she looked lustfully at anything wearing trousers, even Ron Bissett?'

'I'm really rather hurt. Of course I've had lustful looks aimed only at me.'

'Oh, come on! Good old reliable Jimbo, married to that woman named Harriet what cooks for a living? Please!'

'The very one.'

Harriet had to acknowledge he was being serious. 'Well, I never. Who, then?'

'Never you mind.'

84

'You said that because there isn't anyone who's looked lust-fully at you, not for years.'

'There is.'

'Is there really?'

Jimbo nodded vigorously.

Still not entirely convinced Harriet demanded an answer.

'If you really want to know ... Deborah Templeton.'

'Deborah Templeton! Now that *is* ridiculous. She wouldn't. The apple of Chris Templeton's eye? Come on! You're mistaken. She only has eyes for Chris.'

'Why do you never believe a word I say? I haven't worked in this precious Store of mine all these years without being able to recognise a lustful look. The faces have changed, but not the looks.'

'I don't believe it. Deborah Templeton! Well, I never. She looks as though butter wouldn't melt.' Harriet, enjoying the fun, pretended to be convinced that Jimbo was speaking the truth and sat back as if to contemplate this very new state of affairs. 'I tell you what, here and now, if anything ever comes of it I shall personally strangle you, closely followed by Deborah. Right? And I mean it. I've stayed completely faithful to you for all these years, borne four children to you, and I haven't done that to end up lost and lone on the scrapheap at an early age. I shall look at her with new eyes, I shall.' She got up from the sofa saying, 'I can't understand why she's interested in you with that marvellous Chris hanging on her every word and I'm off to bed. Goodnight!' She came back into the sitting room, eyes twinkling, to add, 'Next time she comes in to the Store I shall keep a sharp eye on her.'

Jimbo refrained from reminding her that her kitchen was no longer in the back of the Store so she wouldn't know when Deborah came in shopping.

Chapter 9

After the conversation they'd had the night before, Jimbo had chuckled again as he opened up the Store. It was his early morning and he was there on his own for over an hour before any other staff appeared. It was Bel who came in first, ten minutes earlier than expected, and then, to his surprise, not a member of staff, but Deborah Templeton, was the next person to arrive.

After last night and the laughter his comment about lustful looks had brought, she was the very last person he'd thought who would be in at such an early hour. 'Good morning, Jimbo! There's no need to look so surprised, we've run out of milk and I volunteered to come to buy some. Turnham House cannot manage a single hour without a plentiful supply of milk. How we would cope without your store I do not know. Beautiful morning, isn't it? I'm so looking forward to being here when it's Bonfire Night. Chris and I have been asked to light it and I am so pleased.'

'Two litres?'

'Nothing less. Isn't it wonderful news?'

Jimbo swung round from the chilled shelves to ask, 'What wonderful news?'

Deborah looked embarrassed. 'Oh dear, I thought everyone knew by now.'

'I don't know. Tell me, tell me.'

Deborah fidgeted in her purse looking for the money to pay him. 'Here we are – that's exactly right, isn't it? Well, they're expecting again, Alice and Johnny. Isn't it marvellous? They told us last week. I'd imagined everyone knew by now. News travels so fast in this village.'

'That's fantastic! I expect they're pleased.'

'Very pleased indeed. I'm so glad for them.'

'So am I. Give them our good wishes, will you? We have four children ourselves and it seems to have gone out of fashion, having large families, but it is such good fun. Wouldn't be without a single one of them. I can recommend it. Heartily.'

'What are they?'

'What are they? Oh! I see what you mean. Two boys and two girls.'

'Just right that is, two of each.' Deborah looked forlornly into the distance behind Jimbo's head, paused as though about to say something important, changed her mind and picking up the carrier bag into which Jimbo had placed the milk, turned away from the till and left. He was convinced there were tears in her eyes. So it was far from any sort of lustful look he got today but a very sad one. Still, she and Chris had only been married a matter of weeks – surely it was too early to be filling up with tears at the thought of no babies on the way yet?

Willie staggered in for his morning paper as usual, anxious at not having, for once, the correct change to pay for it with.

'It doesn't matter, Willie, I've told you a thousand times I always have plenty of change even at this hour in the morning.'

'How would we manage without you here, Jimbo? I really don't know. Sylvia and me, we've got past being able to shop at the Saturday market in Culworth like we've always done. It's carrying it all, you know. Such hard work for her, because it's as much as I can do to walk, never mind carry anything.'

'Mmm. Yes. I can see the problem.'

'Bye-bye, Jimbo. Thank you.'

'No, it's for me to say thank you to you, Willie.'

'Harriet keeping well?'

'She is, yes, certainly she is.'

'Still cooking and baking for you, is she?'

His question recalled last night's conversation and made Jimbo smile. 'Indeed she is, still at it.'

'There'll come a day when she won't be able to. Sad how life treats you, isn't it?' On that cheerful note Willie went home, leaving Jimbo with an incredibly crushed feeling in his bones. Harriet not able to cook? She'll be cooking at the last trump, will my Harriet, it's her life's work is cooking.

Mercifully another early riser came in at that moment and prevented him from dwelling on Willie's last words, but as soon as they left he went back to thinking about Willie and his doom-laden remarks. Harriet never complained about life being burdensome. Never. Just chugged along, day after day, catering for wedding after wedding, meeting after meeting, party after party, reception after reception. Lapping up all the praise she got for her wonderful food, her choice of menu, her ingenious table decorations, always so appropriate to the occasion. Yes, she loved her work – silly old Willie depressing him with his gloom-ridden talk. But he had to admit he needed to be reminded, definitely reminded, of how hard she worked and how uncomplainingly. Well, their wedding anniversary was coming up shortly. He'd do something spectacular. Really spectacular! Jewellery, well-chosen, expensive jewellery, no skimping. Definitely no skimping. He'd talk to Fran about it; she was good at keeping secrets was Fran.

His phone rang and when he heard Harriet's voice he felt spooky, very spooky.

'Jimbo?'

'The one and only.'

'You sound full of bounce this morning. Just to tell you I've had a phone call from that woman who spoke about her daughter's wedding being a "Society wedding, had I not realised?" Well, she's come up trumps, it's on and we're doing it, everything of the best. Four-tier cake for starters. What fun!'

'Oh! Her. Yes.'

'I've worked the magic, deposit arriving today she says and it's not until June 2016. She'll be a pain in the neck, but the money! Wow!'

Jimbo only half listened to her enthusiasm. 'They could have changed their minds about getting married, by then, you never know.'

'You misery! You out-and-out misery! You've spoiled everything. Absolutely everything. You don't need feeding tonight, do you?'

'Don't I?'

'You don't deserve it. If it was a triumph of yours you'd be expecting me to be shouting from the rooftops, but because it's mine you dismiss it with a snap of your fingers.'

'I didn't snap my fingers. Honestly.'

'You might as well have done. I'm out tonight and Fran is too so you can please yourself. Have a good time!'

'But I'm not going anywhere, am I?' Too late, she'd switched off.

Jimbo put his mobile back in his trouser pocket and gazed at the main window of the Store that he had reorganised that very morning to his unparalleled delight. Only now, looking at it *now,* it had all the appearance of the lowest-priced table at a jumble sale. As if he'd filled the window with all the junk he could find. That band of red crêpe paper, supposedly the bonfire burning and the purple imitation rockets spiking their way up to the turquoise paper meant to be the sky. Honestly! His customers would think he'd had a nervous breakdown. First thing in the morning – no, *tonight* – he'd have to rehash it tonight.

Fran would help. No, she wouldn't, she was going out with Harriet. No, she couldn't. She'd have to help him. She would, he was certain, but when he rang her she said she was going out with her mother. 'Sorry and all that, but you're right, it *is* a mess, not a patch on your usual. You need fairy lights, Dad, and real rockets; those ones you've made are a total failure. It took me a minute or two to work out what they were. You can do much better than that.' And then she switched off. When the women in the household ganged up they made a real job of it and not half. He needed Flick. That's right, Flick was artistic and she'd pop home and help at the weekend. But of course she couldn't! She was in India, now, doing her charity thingy. But she'd have helped ... no she wouldn't, she'd have ganged up with Fran and Harriet, all girls together. He was doomed, he thought which made him remember Willie and how crushed he'd felt after the old man left with his newspaper first thing that morning.

There was nothing he could do but tear the whole thing out of the window and begin again. Proper rockets, three boxes of fairy lights, those red electric lights he'd bought years ago and never used again, real logs for the bonfire. At least his two part-time helpers, who normally did the last two hours to save him having to work late, were at the Youth Club's charity doodah tonight, so no one would see him redoing the window, thank heavens.

He had just finished the lighting requirements of his new design, having cleared out all that terrible crêpe paper and dumped it in the recycling, when he happened to look up at the sound of a car engine going by and there were Harriet and Fran, dressed to kill, roaring past. Neither of them even glanced in his direction and they were going the wrong way for the Wise Man. Where on earth were they going? Surely not to Fortescues'? Well, he hadn't time for jollification, he'd work to do. He was the only one in the Charter-Plackett family who *slaved* for the business, the only one. The hours he put in! No one had any idea how hard he worked. But if he got cracking he might just manage a meal out; after all, he'd been working since six thirty this morning, it being his early turn. He would. An hour's work and he'd be finished, get washed, change his shirt and be off.

Which he did, and at precisely eight thirty he walked into the Fortescue, exhausted but very chuffed with the results of his hard work. The window looked fantastic, better than his Bonfire Night window-dressing efforts had ever been for the last twenty years. Yes! He raised his clenched fist to the heavens. Tonight he was top of the class in window dressing.

'Yes?' queried the waiter a few minutes later.

'A table for one, please.'

'Here by the bay window, will that suffice, sir?'

'Definitely.' Jimbo sat down and ordered a shandy while he studied the menu and, filled with self-satisfaction, he glanced up and saw Harriet and Fran plunging into their main courses with enthusiasm, their plates piled high with delicious-looking food. So he was right, this was where they had come. He leapt up and strolled across, pulled out a chair and sat down. 'Mind if I join you?' There was no reply. Fran was saying 'She can't act, honestly she can't, but somehow she gets brilliant directors and good parts and manages to pull off a good performance. But she still can't act, she's the same person whatever the part, in every film she makes. How does she do it?'

Harriet, his dearly beloved Harriet, carried on talking to Fran as if he didn't exist. 'So it's worth going to see?'

'Oh! Yes. You'd enjoy it. Mum!' Fran leaned towards her mother and whispered, 'Who's this man sitting at our table? Do you know him?'

'Slightly. I have met him before.'

'Funny looking chap, isn't he?'

'I've not really thought about that for years. But, yes, he does look a bit odd. It's his shiny bald head that makes him odd. Shall we ask him to move?'

Fran agreed. 'Yes, definitely.'

Jimbo opened his mouth to protest but began to laugh instead. 'Oh! Very funny. Yes, very amusing. I've ordered steak and *all* the trimmings. The slimming diet can go hang, I don't care. I've redone the window for Bonfire Night and it looks super. Real rockets as you suggested, Fran, and I'm really pleased with it.'

Fran leaned towards her mother again, whispering, 'Window? What window? What's he talking about?'

'Seeing as we don't know who he is, I can't help you there. Ask him.'

'Shall I?'

Harriet nodded as she piled more food on to her fork.

But Fran began to giggle and so did Harriet, which was difficult when her mouth was full of food. And what good food it was too. She was so glad they'd come out for a meal, for there were days when she was sickened with cooking and this had been one of those days.

Before they knew it the three of them were laughing their heads off.

Half cross and half amused at the situation he was in, Jimbo was the first of the three to control his laughter and said, 'Very childish, very childish indeed. You are a naughty pair, you two girls, definitely. Teasing this hard-working man. I've been in the Store since six fifteen this morning and finished at a quarter past eight, so that's how many hours? Fourteen? Doesn't sound much, does it, but it feels it.' The waiter found him and delivered his steak and it looked splendid. He picked up his knife and fork and said not another word until he'd cleared his plate completely against a background of Harriet's and Fran's teasing and lots of laughter. Sitting back, Jimbo said, 'Do either of you desire a pudding? Because I do. Join me?'

They both nodded and Fran said, 'And coffee to round it off. It's been delicious! We're so glad you joined us. And thank you for offering to pay.'

'By the way,' said Harriet, 'who are you? You haven't said. We don't usually dine with strange men, you see.'

'Ha! Ha! Big joke.'

'But good fun, Dad.' Fran smiled at him and he smiled back. He'd forgotten how all this started but he'd enjoyed his evening. He remembered, as his eyes closed tight shut on an exhausting

92

day, that he was about to be generous with a wedding anniversary present for Harriet. Well, perhaps a slightly less expensive gift than he first conceived of ... then he heard a voice say 'Skinflint!' Curiously, it was his own voice reprimanding him. No, this time he would be super gen–er–o–u–s he decided as he fell deeply asleep.

Chapter 10

What Jimbo hadn't noticed that evening in the restaurant was the fact that Chris Templeton and his wife Deborah were in there along with Alice and Johnny. The reason why he hadn't noticed them was because they were sitting at a table occupying an odd corner of the restaurant that allowed those occupying it almost complete privacy. But the four of them looked serious all evening. No bursts of laughter emanated from their table and, worse still, they found the laughter from Jimbo's table aggravating, even though they couldn't see who was causing it.

'You'd think that people who can afford the prices here would know how to behave; it is disgraceful,' said Chris. 'However, back to what we were talking about. Despite what mother has been planning, like moving house and us all living altogether in it, I for one – and that includes Deborah – well, we are not interested. This has become our home and that's how it's going to be. We are definitely not going back to live in Rio permanently. No way. Right, Deborah?'

'Right! I like Rio, but in small doses. England is where I live and will till my last breath.'

Chris took hold of her hand and gripped it tightly. 'Don't say that, please, darling.'

'I mean it. I really do. Perdita likes Turnham House and wants to live in one similar because she thinks it so much more smart than a fashionable apartment in a fashionable street in the centre of town. That's what is at the bottom of it all. If she could move Turnham House to Rio, she would, believe me.'

Johnny visibly shuddered at the thought.

'So,' said Chris, 'we're determined then, here we are and here we stay. If, a year ago, someone had prophesied that I would say that and mean it I would have been horrified. But I do say it and I do mean it.'

'Oh! So do we. I'm not moving, believe me. So it's decided? We stay in Turnham Malpas?' Alice looked in turn at each of them and saw confirmation in their eyes. 'Right! We've sorted it, so we can laugh now as loud as we like, and I shall laugh the loudest. I love it here. Johnny, you being the eldest can speak for Chris and Deborah, can't you? And me. You'll tell your mother, won't you, and make sure she knows that's the end of it.'

'I shall do my best but it will be a struggle because she's so used to getting her own way and can never see the other person's point of view. But as she can't physically drag us across there, I can't see how she can change our minds when we are all set on it.'

'She'll try. She's very determined,' said Deborah who looked as though she had had experience of their mother's determination. Alice, delighted they had all agreed to stay where they were, asked Deborah if she loved living there.

'I most certainly do. Anyway, if Chris wants to stay then stay, we shall.' She gave him such an intimate, loving look that Alice saw just how much Deborah loved Chris and, in a flash, the wary attitude she always had with Chris became much more approving. Deborah added as an afterthought, 'She can come to stay, Alice, whenever she likes, can't she?'

'Of course she can,' Alice replied knowing full well from what Perdita had said to her just before she went to catch her plane home that they'd probably never see her again in Turnham Malpas – and as far as Alice was concerned, that would be too soon. Wanting to have an imitation Turnham House over in Rio! It would look hideous, completely hideous. So inappropriate. But if that was what she wanted, then so be it, so long as Alice didn't have to live in it.

However, a few days after their meal together and the decision having been made not to even discuss the possibility of moving to Rio, photographs arrived in a big fat envelope. Pictures of large detached houses, without the slightest resemblance to Turnham House except size, accompanied by enthusiastic notes penned by Perdita. Deborah saw Chris shudder in horror and marvelled at the change in him. Was it she who had brought this about or was he more sensitive than even she had recognised? One thing for certain; she loved Chris in a way she had never loved anyone in the whole of her life. A life lacking love and affection, for even as a small child her parents neither loved nor wanted her in their lives, and she knew right from her very earliest years that was the case and would never change. All she had left now was a father who expected love where he had never given it and was surprised to find himself unloved by this beautiful child he'd carelessly fathered.

As he was all she had in the way of family, Deborah dutifully wrote to him stiff, awkward letters without a word of love in them, but they were the best she could write. She loathed the conscience that made her visit him regularly, the smiles he gave her that lacked emotion, the kisses she received that meant nothing to either her or him. But she went faithfully and never divulged to any living soul that was what she did when she was 'missing', as Perdita called it. Not even to Chris. One day, perhaps, she would find the courage and the confidence to tell him. Being Chris, all he would do was laugh but others ... if Perdita ever found out it would be the end of Deborah's happiness, for her mother-in-law would make her life a living hell. Deborah paused for a moment while she attempted to give credit where credit was due, but could find no redeeming features in her mother-in-law's make-up that would allow her to do so. So Deborah decided to wait and see where Perdita was concerned, and at least she had the others on her side with this business of moving to South America. All that desperate poverty! She couldn't face living with that almost right outside their door, for there seemed to be no escape from it.

So the fat envelope filled with Perdita's dreams lay ignored on Johnny's desk for a while, till Johnny eventually got rid of it in the shredder.

Chapter 11

Peter, as part of his pastoral duties, regularly did a round of visits in the villages and this week it was the turn of Little Derehams. Some houses he loved to visit, others were a trial. In the category of 'pleased to visit' was Sir Ronald and Lady Bissett's; delightful coffee was always on the menu and home-made scones or a muffin or, occasionally, carrot cake, the making of which was one of Sheila's superb skills and, more importantly, the best of the local gossip was also on the menu and that fact frequently helped him in his pastoral duties.

This morning it was carrot cake. 'This is delightful, Sheila, thank you so much. No wonder you win first prizes at the Village Show.'

'I do try my best and when I know it's your week for visiting I'm only too pleased to make your favourite. Sugar?'

'Yes, please. Just one spoonful.'

'Now, Peter,' she said. 'You don't look yourself this week. What is the matter? Tell me before Ron comes in. Go on.' She'd heard on the village grapevine that Caroline was contemplating going to the States for a year but she wanted Peter to tell her in his own words about it.

'Just a bit of a cold, Sheila, there's a lot of it going about. Are *you* keeping well?'

'Oh, yes! Thank you, very well indeed.'

'You've certainly lost a lot of weight and kept it off – I can remember when you were always endeavouring to lose weight but you don't need to worry about that now, do you? Losing weight, I mean.'

Sheila sipped her coffee and didn't reply.

He suddenly realised that Sheila was avoiding looking him straight in the eye, and a second later he associated her successful loss of weight to the time when her daughter Louise's newborn son died. In one way the baby's death had come as no surprise – he had so much wrong with him physically that it was almost a blessing when he unexpectedly died. Both Sheila and Ron had been much quieter since the baby's death and he had heard that they didn't see as much of their daughter and her husband as they'd once done. He wondered why that should be – and then he and Sheila locked eyes and he saw a truth hiding there. But no, it couldn't be what he thought. Horrified, he tried to dismiss his idea. After all, no grandmother would ... surely not, not Sheila. She hadn't that kind of courage ... no, he'd jumped to the wrong conclusion, of course he had.

Peter cleared his throat. 'I see a lot of Gilbert because he's church choirmaster, but just recently I haven't seen much of Louise. Is she well?'

She was looking him in the eye now, straightforward, honest as always. 'We – we haven't been seeing much of them. The children have been ill a lot just lately. With five youngsters there always seems to be one or another under the doctor for something. It's a big family, you see. Five children. But Gilbert is such a help. He's a wonderful husband.'

'I'm sure he is. Just so long as she's all right.'

'Yes, she's fine. Thank you.'

The two of them munched their carrot cake and conducted a desultory conversation about village news and such and then eventually Peter said he really had to leave.

He stood up to go just as Ron came in from the garden. Peter delayed his departure and had a short chat with him and then said he really must go. Ron went with him to the door, while Sheila busied herself clearing away the coffee things into the kitchen.

Ron said he was glad Peter had called but he didn't try to

detain him and Peter left, happy that Sheila hadn't pushed her thoughts about him not being his usual self. And he wasn't. Alex and Beth might put a modern view on Caroline's needing to have a completely fresh start somewhere for a while but Peter, who loved every single centimetre of her, knew deep in his heart that Morgan was loving the idea of having Caroline all to himself for a whole year. Because there must be dozens of young students who would be better qualified to do the research than Caroline, to whom a year in the States would be paradise. Having thought that, he bitterly admitted that Caroline also found it paradise, simply because she would be with Morgan. There was no doubt about it, he, Peter, had failed her. Failed her badly. Otherwise she wouldn't be so determined to go. He should have thought about her needs, not his own. As if he hadn't done enough damage to their marriage. At the time he didn't see it like that; at the time he simply couldn't help himself. It had happened. And it would happen to Caroline – except there'd be no children because of it, seeing as she was unable to conceive and was now beyond the age of conception anyway.

Two hours later he drove back to Turnham Malpas in turmoil. Before Morgan Jefferson's reappearance Peter would have driven back, glad his visiting time was over but at the same time energised by his contact with everyone. But not today. Oh no! What the blazes was he to do about his predicament? He pulled into a layby, switched off the engine and lay back in his seat to think. He must have slept for a while for when he looked at his watch he found it was already half past twelve and Dottie would be wanting to leave. He sighed. He'd done wrong, so why shouldn't Caroline do wrong? On what grounds could he stop her? He couldn't. The two of them together had survived *his* sin why should they not survive Caroline doing wrong? But maybe ... maybe this time she would leave him. After all, Morgan was free to marry, nothing to stop him. If Caroline felt strongly, profoundly, attached to Morgan then ... No, his, Peter

Alexander Harris's moral stance, meant marriage was for life, so divorce would be impossible. Which it was for him ... He sighed again; time he got home. Home? It didn't mean what it used to.

A car drove past far too fast for a country lane like this. It was Chris in his red sports car. He screeched to a halt, reversed, and pulled up alongside Peter, ignoring the fact that he was completely blocking the lane. 'Hi! Peter! Lovely day, isn't it?'

Peter pulled himself together, cast aside the retrospective moments he'd been experiencing, and cheerfully acknowledged Chris's greeting. 'Absolutely! Just been visiting in Little Derehams. How are you and Deborah, doing well?'

'Always doing well. Best day's work when you married us. Never thought I'd find someone so compatible. She's a dream of a woman.'

'Good! I'm glad, nothing like a happy marriage for making a man feel great. Must press on.' He made to start up his engine, but Chris didn't take the hint so Peter couldn't move away.

'Caroline OK, is she? Saw her the other day and thought she appeared very introspective, not her usual relaxed self.'

'It's this affair of debating whether or not to take this research job in the States, that's why.' Now why ever did he say that? It was no one's affair but their own. Oh, that was unfortunate, using the word 'affair'. Was that genuinely what he was thinking, that it was going to be an *affair*?

Chris started up his engine, ruining the peace of the beautiful day. He shouted, 'Tell her from me to grab the chance with both hands! A whole year in the States? Wonderful. If I were she, I know I would. Bye, Peter!' He roared away, leaving Peter furious with himself. From now on he would treat this escapade as a perfectly normal thing for a wife to do, not behave like a spoiled boy who'd dropped his lollipop in some thoroughly unpleasant filth. From this moment on he'd accept the event as perfectly reasonable. Which it was. Wasn't it?

But he couldn't. The whole problem of Caroline's decision

to go gnawed away in his brain, and worse in his heart, day in, day out, until something occurred that overshadowed the whole Caroline situation more than he would ever have thought possible.

It began in the early hours of the Thursday following his morning visit to the Bissett's, when the Rectory phone rang before dawn had yet streaked across the sky. As he picked up the receiver from his bedside table his heart sank, convinced it would be Morgan ringing from the States and having got the timing wrong. Unless ... it sounded like Ron Bissett's voice except ... but he was unable to understand what he was saying.

'Ron, take it slowly, please, I can't tell what you're saying. Slowly, take a deep breath. Slowly, say it again, that's right a deep, deep breath.' Then he listened. 'Yes, yes. Caroline? You want Caroline? For what?'

Peter listened, horrified. Caroline was awake now. 'We're coming, but maybe an ambulance might be better, no, no, no!' The mention of an ambulance had triggered total panic in Ron Bissett. 'No all right ... don't worry, we'll come immediately. Yes, definitely both of us. Yes. I'll ring off and get dressed and we'll be as quick as we can.' He switched off and turned to Caroline. 'Darling, there's something terrible happened at the Bissetts'; they want you to go there. I'll drive.'

'Oh no! What did he say it was?'

'It was difficult to tell but I thought he said he couldn't wake Sheila and ...' The rest was muffled by him dragging on his clothes.

'Peter! It's cold, put a sweater on too.'

Though it was only a mile and a half to Little Derehams it felt like fifty.

It was easy to see which house to pull up at as all the lights were on and Ron was standing out on the front path waiting for them. They both leapt out of the car and saw as they approached him that Ron was shaking with distress.

'Come in! Come in!' he said, brokenly.

Their bedroom, since Sheila had broken her hip and found stairs difficult, was now on the ground floor and in a trice Caroline had her stethoscope out, listening to Sheila's heart, but knowing as she did so that Sheila had already died.

'I'm sorry, Ron, we're too late I'm afraid. Far, far too late. Has she ... I'm so sorry, we came as quickly as we could. Has she been ill for a few days?'

'No. Right as rain. Honestly, right as rain. I can't understand how it's happened. Can't you press on her chest like they do on the telly? Go on, you press on her chest, start her up again.'

'All right, all right. But Ron, dear, I think we're far too late.' As Ron became even more agitated when she failed to revive Sheila the first time, Caroline, to pacify him, tried again and again until Peter intervened. Taking Ron's arm he tried to lead him from the bedroom. 'Let's go make a cup of tea, Ron, you and me, and leave Caroline to deal with things. Come on, old chap, you've got to face up to things. Sheila's gone, I'm afraid.'

'She can't have! She was all right when we went to bed, told me how much she'd always loved me and I mustn't fret if she went first. All those kinds of things you say when you get older, you know? You say them, but you don't expect you're going to go that very day. I tell you, she was fine. Been out gardening this morning, went to a WI committee meeting this afternoon, then she went down to the post box with some letters and took twice as long as you'd expect 'cos she met a friend of hers and they had a chat on that seat by the pond, came home and made a lovely meal and we cleared up together. She went into the kitchen later and made us a cup of tea to go to bed and we did that and then, after we were asleep, she got up for the bathroom like always, and I woke up just before dawn as I usually do and found her not breathing just before I rang you. I knew the doctor would be able to help, that's why I rang.'

Peter sat him down in what he knew was his favourite easy

chair, and, still holding his hand he said, 'I'm afraid this time she isn't able to help.'

'She has magic hands, has the doctor. She kept old Lavender Gotobed alive that time she collapsed, lived another three years she did, she'll do the same for Sheila I know.' He looked pleadingly at Peter as though asking him to have faith, then saw the real truth in Peter's vivid blue eyes and began sobbing in great gulping gasps. She was dead and he'd known it but wouldn't accept it until he saw the truth in Peter's eyes.

An unexpected death demanded the law in one form or another, so later that day an ambulance arrived to take Sheila's body for a post-mortem to be performed and the village was left swapping stories about Sheila, such good stories over the last twenty years, full of 'remember that time when ...' and they all realised what fun Sheila had provided for them over the years – and aggravation too, of course.

Her crowning glory had been the annual village flower show – no, wait a minute, what about when she organised the WI fundraising for the mission in Africa and they had that afternoon tea party at the big house, everyone dressed in black and white, and the gamble they had on the Arc de Triomphe race and Major Malpas won? And the skinny-dipping in Jimbo's swimming pool at midnight? Now *that* was a laugh! And don't forget the pyjama party when that car slid into the village pond in the dark.

And then Peter received a letter in the post the day afterwards. It was from Sheila, written the day she died, and its contents were dynamite.

Chapter 12

The letter lay locked in Peter's safe for two days while he thought about what to do. Eventually, knowing he had to make a decision sooner rather than later, he confided in Caroline.

'I want you to read it because you are closely involved and I rely on your common sense. I know you won't allow emotion to cloud your vision.'

Caroline, suspecting that if Peter couldn't decide what to do with it, then perhaps she wouldn't know either, was rather more wary than he was. 'Surely the police should have it? They would know best.'

'If I give it to the police they will have, *definitely* have, to take action. They can't avoid it.'

'Can we?'

'Can we what?'

'Can we avoid taking action? Whatever is it, Peter, for heaven's sake?'

'Whatever way you look at it, from whatever angle, it's murder.'

Caroline was astounded. 'You mean someone's murdered Sheila? But that could only be Ron. Surely not! He wouldn't, not Ron; he's too kind to do that.'

'No, no you don't understand. According to that letter it's baby Roderick who was murdered.'

'Baby Roderick? But that was ages ago. And in many ways it was a blessing, he was so physically damaged.'

'I know he was, I saw him. I almost felt relieved when he died.'

Caroline said, 'But Sheila's known all this time and never said anything? How did she find out? Who was it?'

'Sheila.' He pointed at the letter. 'Read it, she did it.'

'Sheila murdered him? How could she? Her own grandson! How?'

'She smothered him with a cushion out of the chair she was sitting in. Then when she was sure he – he had died replaced the cushion and called for help. Read it, I can't bear it. Just read it. Please. She saw it as a mercy killing.'

Caroline took the letter from the envelope and began to read.

Dear Peter,

I am so glad you came to see us last week because I had arrived at a stage when I could no longer tolerate myself for what I did and just talking to you helped me come to a sort of peace with myself so that I knew what I had to do and I have put all my affairs in order so that poor Ron is not troubled by them.

Remember Roderick? Louise and Gilbert's handicapped baby? I know that isn't a word we use nowadays but it is much more the truth than the scientific words they mask everything with now. The fact remained, whatever they call it, he would have had to face surgery of a major kind many times in his life and would, even after all that, not be guaranteed the lovely carefree life his brothers and sisters can look forward to.

I faced that the first time I saw him and I knew that, for his sake, and his sake first and foremost, and secondly, for Louise and Gilbert's sake, and for the other children's sake, that I had to do something. That life would never be carefree again for his brothers and sisters or his parents. They would be facing the horror of his incapacities twenty-four seven, as they say.

On the odd occasion when his sweet little eyes opened he felt to be asking me to end it. No, not asking, but telling me to end it for him. But who would have the courage to do that? Certainly not his mother, Louise, and definitely not his father, Gilbert; they would have shouldered their responsibility for him and cared for him as best they could. But how about the other children? Always, always, the needs of little Roderick would have to come first – and rightly so. Well, I slept on my decision, thought about it sitting in church when no one else was about, and always, always the answer was the same, it would have to be me.

Caroline turned another page.

I have never been brave, never understood anything very much, but what I did know was that if I didn't do what I was called to do then I would regret it for the rest of my life and so would everyone else except they wouldn't say so. So I did it. It was me, when I was left alone with him while the consultant talked to Louise and Gilbert for a few minutes, explaining yet again what little Roderick would need to have done to put him right. Well, as right as he ever could be. I used the cushion in the chair I was sitting in, as I said. Pressed it hard down on his little head and chest. I relieved him of his suffering in such a short space of time, no time at all really. It took nothing, no strength, no nothing, and he was gone, for ever gone. All that pain and suffering he would have had to do, I saved him all that. Thank God I found the courage to do it for him. So little effort it took. So very little. His life so delicately balanced, to finish his pain required only a mere whisper of strength.

But I need your forgiveness, Peter, for doing what I did. Forgive me also for being foolish so often, for being bossy and organising everyone. Let's hope over the years that I've done some good somewhere along the way, but bringing an end to Roderick's life of pain was the very best I have done.

Goodbye, dear Peter, thank you for everything you've done for this village, for the love, the compassion, the kindness, the courage you've always shown us. I'm not clever enough to use big words to say what I have to say but believe me when I say you have always been a wonderful example of a good Christian man to us all.

Do what you have to do about this letter and please make sure Ron is looked after – he deserves it for putting up with me all these years. Tell him what I've done as gently as you can.

God bless, Peter,

Yours,

Sheila Maude Bissett

Caroline, on the verge of tears, slowly folded Sheila's letter, put it back in the envelope and found the strength to say, 'My God! What a letter! I have never read such a one as this. Now, what shall we do?'

'Frankly, Caroline, in my opinion we won't tell a living soul. Not anyone at all.'

'But you can't do that! It was murder! Someone has to know.'

'Really? And who will benefit from knowing? Ron? Louise? Gilbert? Their children? Will they feel all the better for this piece of news? I don't think so. What will the police be able to do? After all, the perpetrator is dead.'

Caroline sat back to think over what Peter had said. Should the children know their Granny had killed their baby brother? Surely not. Should Louise know her mother had done the dreadful deed? The whole situation was blindingly puzzling and unresolvable. That poor baby, his life snuffed out before he'd had a chance to live more than a day or so. What on earth should Peter do? Nothing? Or reveal all to someone? But to who? Surely someone at the hospital must have realised what happened? And if they had, in the circumstances perhaps they had said absolutely nothing too.

The post-mortem had revealed a huge dose of sleeping tablets Sheila had taken immediately prior to her death. But what on earth did Sheila need to escape from, everyone asked. The post-mortem had shown nothing sinister. No cancer. No heart problems. No life-threatening symptoms of any kind. Nothing. Why should Sheila need to put an end to it all? Well, maybe Ron had finally driven her over the edge, after all he couldn't have been an easy person to live with, could he, when he's so dull?

Chapter 13

Ron Bissett – rather Sir Ronald Bissett – had lost the will to speak. If you took him a cake, or a bowl of soup or a whole dinner, which Grandmama Charter-Plackett often did, he never said a word except, 'Thank you.' He went to church but never joined in a prayer or sang a hymn. He never gossiped, and he'd always been good at gossiping, had Ron, spurred on by Sheila. He spent hours in the Royal Oak sitting, if it was available, at that little table nearest to the log fire, saying nothing. The staff knew what he drank so he didn't even have to speak to order his drink. His clothes became grubby because he couldn't remember how to press the buttons on the washing machine that had been the pride of Sheila's life, so gradually over the next few weeks he grew careless about his appearance.

Louise, his very own daughter, mind, was not allowed to help. She wasn't even allowed in through the door, neither back nor front, and was definitely not permitted to give him gifts of food. If she did, they arrived back on her doorstep almost before she got home again. It was a pain him living in Little Derehams, but she'd no room in her own house and he refused to move back to Turnham Malpas so it was status quo whatever she tried. Strangely, the only person Ron would let in through his door was Chris Templeton.

Chris Templeton? Why is that, everyone asked themselves. Chris, of all people. Yes, he had joined the human race since he'd fallen in love with Deborah but why did he find talking to a dull man like Ron, sorry Sir Ron, worthwhile? Not exactly his cup of tea, surely? Chris was allowed to shop for him in the Store in Turnham Malpas, allowed inside the house for hours at a time, and even Deborah called to see him sometimes and was permitted to go in.

After a few weeks of this state of affairs Johnny asked his brother, 'Why?'

'Johnny, the chap is desperate. Lost his wife after fifty-two years of marriage, and his newest grandson was hopelessly damaged and died because of it. That's why.'

'Well, yes, I know. Of course. But what on earth do you and Ron have in common?'

Chris laughed. 'Curious, are you?'

'Yes. Well?'

A broad grin flashed across Chris's face. 'Betting on the gee-gees. Gives him an interest in life when he has absolutely no interest at all. He's very astute where horses are concerned and I've won hundreds of pounds since Sheila died. She refused to allow him to bet, so he gave up, but now he can do as he likes.'

'Hundreds of pounds?'

'Well, four hundred so far, but that's in only four weeks. I make him put the brakes on, otherwise he would be skint, and we have such a good time, you wouldn't believe.'

'But it must be your tips, Chris. You used to win hundreds of pounds years ago in your teens, remember? You've obviously not lost your touch.'

'Partly him and partly me. And he's so lonely.'

'Well, Chris I'm amazed. I never thought you would finish up as some kind of superior social worker.'

'I'm not a social worker, thank you very much! I am simply helping where I'm needed. OK?'

'But you've never helped anyone in the whole of your life. Never. It's always been what Chris Templeton wanted to do and that was exactly it, no more, no less.'

Chris went to stand by the window looking out at his favourite view. 'Changed man, I am. And one day I shall find out what it is Ron knows and no one else knows except Sheila and she's dead.'

Johnny, concerned about a member of his village being in trouble, queried his brother. 'You mean he knows something about Sheila's suicide, perhaps what caused it?'

'Did I say that?'

'No.'

'Well, don't put words into my mouth. You're getting as bad as all these villagers whose welfare is now your deep concern every single day of your life. The gossip flying round the village is unbelievable at the moment. The air is thick with it. They're all gathering in little groups in the Store, at the bus stop, at the coffee mornings, even in the church: there's nothing else on the agenda but Ron and Sheila.' He turned to look at Johnny, his face alight with laughter. 'I wonder if Sheila knows she's the number one topic of conversation absolutely everywhere? She'll be delighted if she does. Right, must go. Promised Deborah I'd go for a walk with her this morning. She's leaving this afternoon for a few days.'

'Right. You are very tolerant of this disappearing act she does, Chris. Where does she go?' Johnny had longed to ask him this question ever since it first happened and today he dared to ask simply because Chris seemed a very different person than he had been all the rest of his life and he presumed he now knew. But Chris just gave him a long, penetrating look and walked out without answering.

Johnny shook his head in disbelief, realising as he did that Chris still didn't know the answer. Johnny and Alice were totally open with each other; no secrets set them apart from each other, yet Chris was apparently perfectly comfortable with the idea that Deborah had a secret she could not share with him.

Later that morning Johnny walked about his farm inspecting his veal calves, his dairy cows, his small Gloucester Old Spot herd of pigs, his chickens now producing so many eggs they had regular orders on their books from people who loved the rich flavour of an egg for breakfast and the glorious deep yellow sponge cakes they could make with them. Johnny smiled to himself, remembering his lifestyle before he inherited Sir Ralph Templeton's title and came to live in this idyllic place. He gazed up at the winter sun streaming down on to the thatched roofs of the farm buildings and tried to imagine a thatched roof in Rio. Totally out of place, of course, but his mother was determined to thatch the roof of the house she intended buying. He hoped she would come to her senses before she'd actually *bought* the blessed thing, because the whole idea was idiotic, to say nothing about the complete lack of good taste.

Johnny rested his forearms on the gated entrance to the chicken run while he reflected on the big changes in Chris since he had married Deborah. He guessed he'd be over at Ron Bissett's right now. They always met on Thursday mornings.

And Chris was. 'All right, Ron?'

'Yes, thanks, Chris, as well as can be expected … just put my garden boots away, she hated me leaving them out in the kitchen. I've switched the telly on so it's warming up nicely. I never say thank you for you wasting the morning with the gee-gees so I thought about giving you—'

'Oh no—'

'Well, I am, Sheila would have insisted if she were here, which she isn't and I wish she was.'

'You're not giving me anything, Ron. I enjoy coming as much as you like me coming; we have a good time, we make money and what's wrong with that? Nothing. You need the company and I've got Deborah going away for a few days so I shall be glad to have someone to talk to. So shut up, put your boots away, get the kettle on – and remember I like two sugars – and then we'll sit down and sort out our bets for this weekend's race meetings.'

Ron, unaccustomed to patting anyone's arm except Sheila's, did just that to Chris and then fled into the kitchen to put his gardening boots away. He returned with the coffee for the two of them, two mugs, no silver coffee pot with its matching sugar basin and cream jug that Sheila would have used had she been alive, and the two of them settled down to planning their strategy. An hour later Chris checked his watch and realised he would miss Deborah leaving if he didn't hurry back. He shot to his feet. 'Got to go. I'll miss Deborah if I don't, this instant. Right now. You place the bets exactly like we said.'

He left Ron's cottage at speed and, as he drove up to the big house he contemplated his strategy with Deborah and this question of disappearing once a month and not telling him why. The first time it had happened he vowed he wouldn't ask but since they'd married the need for him to know had become more acute. They shared everything but this. There she was! About to leave. He'd only just made it in time.

'Darling!' Chris shouted. 'Just in time.' He slurred to a halt, leapt out of his car, and flung his arms around Deborah. 'Have a good time and ring me whenever ...' He knew, though, she wouldn't, because she never did. 'Love you.'

'I thought you'd forgotten.'

'Never! Only organising our weekend betting schedule as usual. Got absorbed, you know how it is.'

Deborah checked her watch. 'Must go, mustn't miss the flight. Take care while I'm away. I love you so much! Bye, darling.'

Chris felt her withdraw from him and go wherever she was going; as usual he was already alone before she'd even put the car in motion. Where the blazes did she go? She, being wealthy in her own right, had her own bank account as well as the one they'd set up for the two of them when they married, so he couldn't even look at her bank statement for clues. He kicked the gravel where he stood in temper. One day, he swore, he'd ask her outright where she went. It was absurd to be in this situation. Completely absurd. What if something happened to her? A car accident, serious illness? Would anyone know how to communicate with him? Would it mean he'd never see her again? Never know the end of her? Had she ever contemplated that?

The thought of losing Deborah caused him horrendous pain all over his body and that was the moment when Alice walked out of the front door with the two boys. She was horrified when she recognised his pain.

'Chris! Whatever's happened? What is it?'

Nothing could make Chris be disloyal to Deborah; he loved her too much for that. He hesitated for a moment and then said, rather apologetically, that he always felt like this when Deborah wasn't with him. 'Silly, really, I think I must have fallen in love.' A rueful smile crossed his face and then he cheered up. 'I need a coffee can I make one for you? Mmm?'

That he cared enough to offer to make them coffee cheered Alice too. She could remember the time not long ago when he would do without rather than offer to make one.

'Lovely, yes, I'd enjoy that. I was going to take the boys for a walk but it's too cold for me this morning, I hope it will be warmer on Saturday for the bonfire or no one will turn up for it.'

'Don't you fret about that. They all talk about nothing else; they'll turn up in droves even if it's ten degrees under and snowing like mad.' Chris took her arm and turned her round to go back inside.

'I do like this new Chris we've got,' she said. 'You're so much nicer than you were. I shall sit in the kitchen while you make it. The boys will have hot chocolate, please.'

'OK. Sit down boys, won't be long. Sugar?' Charles and Ralph both nodded agreement.

Alice remarked, 'Must be wonderful to be so young that you can have sugar without bothering about your weight.'

Charles asked, 'Deborah gone away?'

Chris answered him. 'Yes, Charles, she has. But she will definitely be back in time for the bonfire.' He sounded totally convinced she would be and the boys cheered.

'I like Deborah. Do you like Deborah, Chris?'

'Definitely.'

'*We* do. Both of us. Don't we, Ralph? We love her stories. She tells us about when she was a little girl.'

'Does she? She doesn't tell me,' said Chris in reply.

'About her daddy,' said Charles.

'Not nice,' said Ralph.

Alice, afraid Charles might come out with an explanation on Ralph's behalf, hastily said, 'I think you must have got it wrong. She's nice so I expect her daddy is nice too.'

Charles, curious to have a further explanation about daddies in general being nice, asked 'My daddy's nice and we are too, aren't we, Ralph?'

Ralph nodded, now more interested in the biscuits Uncle Chris had given him than who was and who wasn't nice. Charles, however, further advanced with his talking than Ralph eighteen months younger than he, said, 'She just said he wasn't kind like our daddy is. I love my daddy. I do. All boys love their daddy. Our new baby will love her daddy.'

Alice laughed. 'Our new baby is going to be a girl then?'

'Yes, of course. It must be our turn for a girl when we've already got us boys.'

Alice smiled at Charles. 'Some people have more than two boys. I know someone who has five girls.'

'Who?' asked Charles.

'A girl I used to teach the piano. She had four sisters.'

Charles tried counting on his fingers but gave up when he mixed up his fingers and became confused. Ralph laughed and a row broke out, silenced by Uncle Chris volunteering to take them both swimming that afternoon.

'You're nice, just like my daddy, Uncle Chris. Say thank you, Ralph.'

But Ralph's mouth was full of biscuit and he couldn't reply.

Chris decided he was a fool and that he should never have

volunteered to take the boys swimming. He, Christopher Templeton, squeezed into a cubicle trying to get not only himself but
two small boys dried and dressed. He must be going soft in the
head. He handed them their hot chocolate and admired their polite
thank you's. He and Deborah had never discussed having children
before they married, nor since for that matter. Now he knew he
was truly going soft in the head. Chris with children? Was that
because Deborah didn't want them or because she did and thought
he didn't? He never used to be troubled by questions of this sort,
now he was. Idiot.

But in fact as he struggled to sort their clothes out later that
day, and make sure everything was on correctly, he discovered
himself to be enjoying life as a substitute dad. He found the cup
of tea he had in the café in the swimming pool reception area
before they left just about the very best he'd had in years. Maybe
it was because he needed it and the company he was keeping was
so pleasurable.

Ralph was delighted because he'd used float discs successfully
for the first time.

Charles was thoroughly pleased with himself as he had, for
the first time, managed to do *three* breaststrokes before he sank.
'Three times I did it! When will I be able to swim right the way
across, Uncle Chris?'

'A lot depends on how hard you work at it.'

'Shall we come every day for a swim, you and us, then I would
go right across by next week, wouldn't I?'

'We'd have to wait and see. Ready to go?'

They all stood up ready for the off but not before Ralph had
stuffed another two biscuits into his pocket to eat later. He loved
biscuits.

As Chris listened to them telling their mother how much they'd
achieved when they got home, it dawned on him how much
he'd enjoyed himself this afternoon. Maybe this was what gave
life a boost as the years passed along, watching one's very own

children growing up and turning into pleasant, companionable adults whose company one enjoyed. He'd talk to Deborah when she got back. See what she thought about the parent situation. Why had they not talked about children before? He knew it was he who was at fault because he'd never appeared to like children. Not like them? When they were such unexpected fun, so unpredictable, so amusing, so outright honest, so frank? That, he had to admit, was what he found he liked about children; they were so open about things. Well, Charles and Ralph were anyway; maybe they did lie sometimes, but perhaps always for a good reason. He thought about being sixty with no children to follow on. What an empty life that would be. He'd be proud, would this new chap called Chris, so proud, especially if they were bright. No, that wasn't right; he'd be proud if they did their very best and, let's face it, you can't do more than that, do no more than your best. Wasting one's talent he considered a sin. Had he wasted his? Yes, he had. He could have done equally as well as Nicholas and Johnny if he'd applied himself, but it had all seemed too much for him to do as they did. It was easier to do just enough to keep the teachers from complaining and his mother compliant. He'd done only just enough. But they all liked him as a person and that had counted for a lot to Chris in his earlier days.

He ambled off to his room and stood for a while gazing out at the land that surrounded Turnham House. He imagined Deborah wandering home up the drive, perhaps with one of Johnny's dogs accompanying her. Where was she now? She could be anywhere in the whole wide world because she had the money to go anywhere at all, no doubt about that. In his bones he guessed she wasn't here in England, somehow he was sure of that. He kept meaning to sneak a peek at her passport but his innate honesty forbade it. He mustn't, absolutely not. He had to learn where she went from her own lips. This situation demanded bold honesty. So this time that was what he would do. *Ask.*

Chapter 14

In bed, alone, nearly a week later, sleeping fitfully, he sensed rather than knew her presence. She smelled fresh and slightly damp, but welcoming, and as her hands reached to feel for him his heart throbbed with anticipation. It was always like this: a wonderful getting together before a word was spoken.

They rolled apart. Chris switched on his bedside lamp the better to indulge his need to see as well as feel. 'You're back.'

'I am. Been all right?'

'No, not all the time.'

'Worried?'

'Of course, I always am when you're away. I should be there to look after you.'

'There's no need. I am grown-up, you know.'

'I know you are.'

'Good! Then there's no need to worry.'

'Alice and Johnny share everything. They have no secrets. Same with Nicholas and his wife.'

'I know.'

Chris propped his head up on his hand, his elbow crooked to support its weight. Looking as closely as he could, straight into her eyes he said, 'I love you with every bone in my body, every inch of me adores you and I know it's the same for you, so why?'

'Why what?'

'Why is your going away kept from me? Why not tell me where you go?'

Deborah sat up. 'One day, when I know the time is ripe, I shall tell you. But it's not yet right. I never thought you'd change so much that I would feel confident enough to marry you but you did. You did change into a beautiful man, beautiful in every way, but how do I know you won't change again and be unreliable and crazy and unlovable? Like you used to be.'

'With you, married to you, I shan't change back. I can't. So tell me, please. Just spit it out. There's nothing in this world that could turn me away from you. Honestly. No matter how ghastly or unsavoury or peculiar.' He waited for her reply but recognised from the look in her eyes he wasn't getting his answer, not tonight anyway. Chris lay back down again and turned his face away from her. 'I see. Glad you're back. Goodnight, darling.'

Within five minutes he was out of bed dragging on the clothes he'd worn that day and leaving the bedroom before Deborah, exhausted by travelling, was aware of what he was doing. 'Chris! Chris! Don't —' She was too late; he'd run two at a time down the staircase and out of the front door. Would he ever come back? His wallet wasn't on the bedside table where he normally put it when he went to bed, so he very probably had his credit cards with him which, being gold standard, would take him any-where in the world except ... except, he was without his passport presumably. So he couldn't leave England.

A quick search of the drawers where Chris kept his belong-ings revealed his passport. She touched his photograph with gentle fingers, smoothing over his face, his deadly serious face, as required by the Passport Office. The love she felt for him overwhelmed her but though one half of Deborah knew she could trust him, the other half remembered the old Chris and she knew she couldn't. He was capable of doing absolutely anything at this moment in time. And that was why she couldn't rely on him to remain silent. If that old battleaxe of a mother-in-law ever found out it would be the end of Deborah Templeton. She'd be hounded out of the safety of Chris's protection and banned forever more from communicating with or seeing him. And that would be unbearable, completely unbearable. She threw on her clothes, which only an hour ago she had joyfully dropped on the bedroom floor, and rushed after him. She caught him up as he was reversing out of the garage, revving his engine, far too fast and far too dangerously in his fury and disappointment. Deborah snatched the front passenger door open and thrust herself on to the seat only just before he had the wheels spinning. Where they were going she had no idea and she didn't care, so long as she was with him.

He had no time to even glance at her for a moment; in fact, she began to wonder if he even knew she was sitting beside him. That didn't matter though. Having managed to fasten her safety belt she clung to the seat with both hands and prayed he'd slow down soon. She daren't say a word of caution in case she made his temper flare even more and by the time they were on the Culworth bypass, his speed had slowed and briefly, for one second, he glanced at her, snarling, 'You've come with me, then?'

'Of course.'

They drove for another hour, not speaking. He turned the classical music channel on as loud as he could and then finally he slowed and turned into a service station just as dawn was on the brink. 'Breakfast?'

'Yes, please. My God, Chris, you're a dangerous man when roused. Don't ever do that to me again. If you do, that will be the end of our marriage. How we managed not to have an accident I shall never know. I need the loo first.'

'So do I.'

Finally they sat facing each other, drinking coffee and eating a motorway service station fried breakfast followed by toast and marmalade. By the time every scrap was consumed Chris looked more relaxed, for which Deborah was relieved. 'Chris. Do you feel able to listen to me?'

'Of course.'

'I meant what I said. If you ever do this to me again it will be the end of what you and I have – if we haven't been killed, that is. I will *not* ally myself to a man so angry that he loses all sense of what is right. You went completely crazy and I won't tolerate that. I love my new Chris, desperately love him, but the old Chris is still there only just below the surface of the new one, isn't he? Time you got rid of him completely. Even your own mother couldn't tolerate the old Chris any more.'

'She'd tolerate anything I chose to do, you know that. The sun shines out of me, didn't you know?' Chris looked her full in the face. 'Has done all my life.' The wry, mocking smile on his lips didn't win her over.

'More fool her then, because I won't. Don't spoil what we have, Chris.' She forced the tension out of her voice as she added, 'I need more coffee, please? Will you join me?'

He nodded and got to his feet, heading for the coffee counter.

Deborah wiped her mouth on her paper napkin and prayed that something of what she had said had finally convinced him she meant it. She found that her hands were shaking with fright, and there was no way she was going to be frightened of her own husband – that simply was not right. She watched him coming back, balancing two huge mugs of coffee on a small tray. He looked to be more reasonable now, not the demon any more.

Halfway through drinking her coffee Deborah decided to ask him, 'What next?'

'I don't want to go back to Turnham Malpas just yet. We'll buy a change of clothes and such and take a couple of days off somewhere. Somewhere quaint and quiet where no one knows us. Time to breathe, if that's all right with you, Deb?' He paused briefly and then continued. 'I'm so sorry Deb, so very sorry. You're right, darling, the old Chris is only just beneath the surface.'

'This is my promise to you,' she said quietly, 'when I feel confident, completely confident, of your love – and it's taken a battering today, you don't need me to tell you that, you *know* it has – I shall tell you everything there is to tell. I promise on my honour.'

Chris took hold of her hand and kissed it. 'Thank you for saying that. My promise is that I will not frighten you ever again. I saw your hands trembling. I'm sorry.'

A deep silence fell between the two of them during which they couldn't take their eyes off each other. Eventually it was Deborah who broke the silence, 'Ron will wonder where you are tomorrow because it's Thursday. He'll be putting all the bets on by himself.' She smiled.

Chris smiled too and the divide between them felt to clear a little. 'Let's hope he gets it right, then! I might just send him a list on my mobile.'

At Turnham House the doorbell rang persistently next day. Alice flew to the door, thinking it would be Chris and Deborah, back home without their keys.

But it was Ron Bissett looking agitated.

'Good morning, Alice. Is Chris in? Is he not well? Usually he comes to see me every Thursday morning but he hasn't come and I don't know what to do.'

'Come in, Ron, come in please. Got to be honest with you, he isn't here and we don't know where he is. Deborah's back and we've tried ringing them both but they've left their phones here at home. I expect they've decided to have a couple of days on their own. Can I help at all?'

Ron shuffled about on the doorstep, not knowing if Alice knew about their betting.

'Well, it's about … well, we have a little arrangement, he and I, on Thursdays and he comes to see me and—'

'It's about the betting on gee-gees, isn't it?'

'Well, yes, that's it. We always make money: he's very good, is Chris, about racehorses, very good indeed. Loses on some but wins on lots. They always say it's the bookies who do the winning but believe me—'

'Come in, Ron. Please do. Johnny's just back from the farm and I'm making coffee for him – would you like some too?'

Ron's face lit up at the mention of Johnny. 'Does he bet on horses?'

'No, he's not as clever as Chris at it, so he doesn't. Almost always loses, you see.'

'Won't stop then, must press on.'

'But you're most welcome, Ron. We haven't seen you for ages, not since ... not since the funeral. Please come in.'

'No, thank you. Very kind, but no.'

'It must be lonely all on your own. Please?'

'No thanks, I'll do it by myself. But what will he say if I lose it all? I wouldn't like to get the wrong side of him. I should imagine his temper ...'

After seeing what she'd witnessed during the early hours of Wednesday, Alice quickly agreed with him. 'You'll have to be extra careful with your choices. But I'm sure he won't be too cross, not with a mate.'

Ron cleared his throat. 'Don't know about *mate*. More *comrades in arms* than mate. I'll be off then. Thank you, Lady Templeton. Good morning.' He hurried away from the doorstep, glad to have escaped. He already knew what Chris's temper was like and hated the thought of being on the receiving end of it.

Ron got back in his car and drove home – and there on his computer was an email from Chris with a list of possible bets for him to refer to. So he hadn't forgotten! Wherever he was he'd remembered and it cheered Ron immensely. So maybe they were mates after all. He breathed a sigh of relief. He'd have loved to tell Sheila about their success, but of course he couldn't. He was missing her more than he ever thought possible. At first he'd imagined he would be glad not to be getting nagged every five minutes, because that was Sheila all over, do this, do that, all the time. But he did miss her. No other way to explain how he felt. He missed her being about the place, always busy. He knew she was bossy with him and he'd in the past often wondered why he tolerated her, but tolerate her he did, day in, day out. Now here he was standing by her grave yet again, in the dark. Was suicide the only solution to anything at all? It left one's relatives tearing themselves apart, *'If only we'd noticed it was about to happen we could have ...'*

But you couldn't, could you? He'd never thought for one moment that Sheila was that kind of a person. Poor Sheila. Poor, poor Sheila. He heard footsteps coming towards him.

'Ron? That you, Ron? Yes, I'm right. It *is* you. It won't bring her back, you know, standing here in the blessed cold. Get back in your car and go home! It's too cold for a man your age to be standing about in a graveyard, this time of night.'

'Oh! Hello, Zack. Just thinking about Sheila and why she did what she did when she did. Unanswered questions always nag.'

'What's done is done, Ron. It won't do any good, you know, standing here catching your death of cold, so just get off home. You have got your car, have you?'

Ron nodded. 'Of course. What about you standing about in the cold at your age, never mind me?'

'I'm here in my capacity as verger of this church. I am doing my duty making sure everything's locked up for the night. See?'

'Wish I had a purpose in life, but I've nothing. Just nothing.'

'Then find something, Ron. Locking yourself away, not talk-ing to people, that's not good. That's no life now, is it? I ask you? Find someone who needs help. Your Louise with all them kids, she could do with some help, I'm sure.'

Ron made to leave. 'I might. I might. Goodnight, Zack. Goodnight.' He turned down the path towards the lychgate and disappeared into the darkness. Zack watched him till he could see him no longer. Poor Ron ... used to be so cocky with his title and that and his trade union backing him up at every turn, on the radio a lot and *twice* on the TV. Sheila had been so proud of him. What it was to be needed. Whatever was it made her kill herself? Now Ron was just the same as every other widower, desolate and lonely. Zack called out extra loudly, 'Take care, Ron!' and chuckled to himself when he recalled how Sheila always referred to Ron as Ronald. ''Spect she thought Ron was a bit common, just like Sheila to think like that,' he said to himself. 'Take care!' he shouted again.

Ron's answer floated back to him. 'I will. I will. And you.' Poor Sheila, thought Ron, killing herself like that. Oh, if she'd known what he'd done ...

Chapter 15

Unknown to Deborah and Chris, Alice had been aware of their hurried departure, having been disturbed by Charles an hour before they raced away because he was suffering from one of his stomach episodes. She'd cleaned up the sick, put his pyjamas and the sheets in the washing machine, and gone back to his bedroom to wait and watch until he slept.

'I'm back, darling, try to sleep, it's the middle of the night, you see.'

'Give me a big hug, Mummy.'

'OK.' And Alice sat there puzzling why Deborah, who'd arrived back at the house only a couple of hours before, had rushed out to throw herself into Chris's car and disappear with him. Judging by the speed that Chris was driving he was plainly very angry. No suitcases with them, though that had never stopped Chris from doing what he wanted; he soon solved that problem by buying more clothes in the first smart gentleman's outfitters he fancied. But why go now, in the middle of the night?

Slowly Charles's grip on her hand relaxed and Alice was able to go back to her own bed. She rolled into bed and Johnny offered a mumbling question about Charles and was he asleep now? And after she'd answered him, Alice applied her mind to sleeping, with their new baby flicking round her womb like a being possessed. They'd decided not to know what sex this baby was and all Alice knew was that everything appeared different from when she was expecting the boys. Was there anything significant to be deduced from that? No. No. No. And another boy would be a delight. Wouldn't it? Yes. It would. And she already had a name for him. James. For some reason it felt to be just right. If the baby was a girl then she'd be called – no, she didn't know what. Possibly Victoria or Alexandra or Emily.

Yes, perhaps Emily. Strong but pretty. She smiled to herself and fell asleep, hoping Chris and Deborah were safe. They must have had a terrible row, the two of them. Something enormously important. Chris, driving the way he did, was obviously tremendously angry, rather like he could be sometimes in the days before he had begun to care seriously for Deborah. She guessed it was probably this business of Deborah disappearing for days at a time every month. When they got back she'd have a word when it was opportune to do so and talk to Deborah about keeping secrets. It never did any good in a marriage. Keeping secrets.

The two of them returned in the middle of the afternoon of Friday, the day before Bonfire Night in Turnham Malpas. From the window of their bedroom it would have been difficult to avoid seeing the massive, yes, massive bonfire waiting to be lit the following night.

By long tradition the estate maintenance staff were always in charge of building the bonfire and this year it appeared they'd found more old furniture and more dead trees on the estate than ever before. Barry Jones stood about twelve feet away, admiring his handiwork. How many years had he been in charge of doing this? Twenty? Surely not. Twenty? It must be. How time flew!

He felt in his bones that this bonfire was somehow very special. It was bigger, for one thing, and somehow Barry felt extra proud of it. He had two drums of petrol kept specially for the purpose which he would spray on the bonfire an hour before the ceremony of lighting it. He'd seen Sir Ralph light it, Muriel light it, the son of Ralph's cousin light it one year, three years Sir Johnny had lit it, and tonight Chris Templeton's wife, Deborah, would be performing the ceremony. Lovely lady. A really lovely lady she was. They'd all taken her to their hearts. Lady Alice – oh, he knew fine well, just as everyone else did, that she shouldn't really be called Lady Alice, because she wasn't a Lady in her own right, but it was like Princess Diana, wasn't it? – she was extra lovely with her beautiful looks and her kindness and those two delightful boys but ... there was something very special about Deborah. He just hoped and prayed that he'd get the petrol in the right places in the right amounts so that suddenly and almost unexpectedly the lighting of it would be spectacular. He liked it best when it lit up in good order, not a bit here and a bit there but more regularly than that, more like the guns firing in Green Park for the Queen's birthday. In succession, one after another, regimentally, in order. That was how he liked it.

He was surprised to find Chris standing beside him. 'My word, Barry! This bonfire is huge! And so beautifully built. What crafts-manship! A master bonfire builder, you are. Do you get extra in your pay packet for doing this? You should.'

Barry laughed. 'Not round here, you don't. All I get is a big thank you, but I don't care because it gives me such pleasure to build it. I think I can honestly say it's the best and the biggest ever and that's enough for me.'

'You've never spoken a truer word. I'm looking forward to it very much indeed and so is my wife. She feels very honoured to be lighting it.'

'And we all feel honoured she's doing it. You're very lucky, sir, to have such a lovely wife, if you don't mind me saying so. Very lucky. We're all very fond of her. Now, must get on. I've been on the go since six, still got a lot to do. See you tomorrow evening, six o'clock prompt. Don't forget!'

'I most certainly won't. Bye Barry!'

'Bye! Mr Templeton.'

As it always was in Turnham Malpas, if there was a big event on they all arrived early. So if you didn't count the people who were working to make it a success the crowds were already arriving by five thirty to make sure of a good spot to stand to get the best view of the lighting of the bonfire and the splendid fireworks that would follow. What seemed like years ago, when Jimbo used to organise the fireworks and provided the finance for them too, they'd all thought the bonfire and the fireworks were the best in the county, but now, with Sir Johnny's vast fortune behind it for the last five years, it had been classified as the best in the country and some people, besotted with the splendour of the display, were convinced it was the best in Europe till they were reminded Europeans didn't have a Guy Fawkes Night, now did they?

At exactly five minutes to six the special guests invited by Sir Johnny emerged from the main door of Turnham House and a great burst of applause started up supported by wild cheering as the volume of applause escalated. As Deborah Templeton stepped forward alongside her husband Chris, Barry Jones carefully handed her the flaming torch with which she was expected to light the bonfire. There'd been a lot of ooohs and aaahs when the crowd had realised just how huge the bonfire was this year, but when the flames caught hold, in regimental order as Barry Jones had planned, the noise of the crowd filled the sky. In fact, the Little Derehams' crowd, holding their own celebration, could hear the huge cheer, could see the glow of the flames and, try as they might to ignore it, they could feel envy creeping through their veins. It was always the same, no matter how they tried, Turnham Malpas always did it better.

The beer tent was already doing business; not for them waiting till the flames lit the sky. They'd been selling beer since half past five and, judging by the way the cash drawers were filling up, would definitely exceed last year's takings. Dicky Tutt was on top form and as he pushed another ten-pound note into the till drawer his blood pressure soared. What a night it was going to be. What a night! Things were getting better and better for him and Georgie. He waved across to her where she was serving soft drinks for the children on a seperate counter. The queue at hers was long and winding but not to be compared to the queue for alcoholic drinks that wound right the way round the tent and out into the darkness. If you weren't caught up in the excitement before you arrived in front of Turnham House, then you very quickly were enveloped in the thrill of it all.

Sir Johnny couldn't move away from where he was standing when the bonfire was so successfully lit. It seemed everyone felt the need to thank him for hosting such a wonderful evening. There was always an hour with nothing happening immediately after the bonfire was lit to permit the refreshment tents to do good business and also to allow time to stand and admire flames and enjoy the terrific heat they gave off. You certainly needed thick gloves and woolly hats because, being November, the air was so cold you felt as if you'd left your overcoat at home by mistake. Ten minutes before the hour was up the refreshment tents began to empty and everyone except the killjoys reassembled where they knew from experience they would get a good view of the fireworks. And they did.

The ooohs and aaahs, the shouts of glee, the screams of the children, the applause – it was all magnificent. The faces of the crowd, upturned, watching the rockets, were lit with glowing admiration. It didn't matter that a large number of the crowd were already drawing their pensions, this was the best the very best of any Bonfire Night display, and everyone became a child again and loved it.

Barry Jones stood quietly by knowing that was what they would be saying. The best ever. And it was. After all, he was the best judge; he'd built the blasted bonfire, hadn't he with his own hands? Well, with help from the others in the maintenance team, of course. Then Barry spotted the reverend, difficult not to seeing his height, and even Barry Jones, a man not particularly in tune with the church like some of the villagers were, could recognise

Peter was not his usual compassionate self. He was standing beside that chap they all said was whisking the reverend's wife off to America for a year. But he didn't believe it. Not her. Not the doctor. But the very moment he had that thought someone moved and he could see her face, illuminated by a gigantic Catherine wheel, standing between the reverend and that chap, and she was laughing obviously at something he'd said that had delighted her.

If a man had delighted his Pat so much that she'd laughed like the doctor was doing right now, he'd have killed him on the spot. There was much more to it than laughter at a joke of some kind, it was too intense, too obviously ... well, Barry, didn't have the vocabulary to explain what he meant, but he knew it wasn't right. He deliberately moved through the crowd though progress was slow because everyone who noticed him wanted to congratulate him and shake his hand, but eventually he arrived beside the reverend, who immediately turned and, seeing Barry his face lit up. 'Barry! I know everyone is saying the same as me, but I've got to say it too. Wonderful bonfire, the way it lit up, not haphazardly but all so theatrically, it is thrilling, how you do it, I do not know.' He shook Barry's hand, but when Barry looked into the reverend's face what he saw was not joy but a deep deep sadness.

He felt like saying, *'Shall I fetch him one on your behalf? Knock him to the ground? Smash his teeth in?'* Instead he pointedly reached across to shake the hand of this Morgan chap. 'Good evening, Mr Jefferson. Enjoying Guy Fawkes Night, are you? We have a big celebration every year. Being English you must know all about it.'

'Of course I do, but I have lived abroad for more years than I've lived here, you know, one forgets, but yes, I've enjoyed it.'

Peter interrupted their conversation. 'This, Morgan, is the chap responsible for the bonfire. How many years is it now, Barry?'

'Twenty, I think.'

Morgan worked hard to pay attention but he failed miserably to show genuine interest. Peter tried to keep the conversation going but Barry didn't help, he remained silent and sceptical. Caroline turned to ask Morgan something about the States so the conversation broke up. Before he disappeared into the crowd, Barry said out of the corner of his mouth, 'What he needs is a good kicking. I'll oblige any time, Reverend.'

'Now, Barry.' Then Peter forced a smile and immediately became a conspirator alongside Barry. But deep down inside himself Peter knew Barry was right. Morgan had turned up unexpectedly and all too obviously had expected a great welcome. Neither Peter nor Caroline were in the right mood for joyously welcoming an unexpected visitor; for one thing they already had a college friend of Peter's staying and, as it was Bonfire Night and that figured highly in the village social calendar, they had friends like Jimbo and Harriet, Johnny and Alice and Chris and Deborah coming for the rest of the evening.

Caroline found herself putting on a welcoming act for which she had no enthusiasm, but it being Morgan she made a tremendous effort, and gave him the impression that he was the one person in all the world she really, really wanted to have to stay. Morgan, so full of himself, found her welcome very genuine and mentally rubbed his hands at the prospect of having Caroline all to himself thousands of miles away from this dull, parochial little village. The major fault with every single one of those who lived here was that they were utterly convinced the very best place in all the world to live was Turnham Malpas. Well, he knew better ... it most certainly wasn't.

If he never saw it again it would be too soon. No wonder Caroline was panting to get away for a while. He'd give her the time of her life while she was with him, and he knew for certain she'd fall in with his plans with no problems of conscience on her part and certainly none on his.

Morgan turned to glance at her, hoping to catch her eye but

she was speaking to someone he didn't know, an elderly woman with a hint of good breeding about her. He edged nearer to catch what they were talking about. Caroline was saying, 'It's lovely to see you out and about, Katherine, just don't overdo it.'

'Couldn't if I tried, I'm still living at Jimbo's, and Harriet and Fran make sure I don't do too much. But I am determined I shall go home by next Saturday or I shall become a permanent fixture at their house and that will never do.' Rather wistfully, Grandmama added, 'But they've made me so welcome.'

'It's not often you call upon them for help, you know, so don't go before you feel able.'

Morgan admired the lovely sympathetic smile Caroline gave the old lady then found himself on the receiving end of the old lady's sharp eyes. Oops!

'So, young man, I've been hearing about you. Glad to meet you.' Morgan found his hand being grasped firmly. No fragile old lady stuff about her, whoever she was.

'I'm Morgan, a friend of Caroline Harris and Peter, and you are ...?'

'I'm Katherine Charter-Plackett, Jimbo's mother. Pleased to meet you. I've heard all about you even though I haven't been circulating as I usually do. Had cancer. Had the operation and so far everything seems fine. Nasty thing cancer, very alarming, but I've *mastered* it. But then we have a very good hospital here, no waiting weeks and weeks for an appointment. How long are you here for then?'

Morgan found himself momentarily intimidated by this Katherine Charter-Plackett who was, as she said, capable of mastering cancer. 'Just the weekend. Very pleased to meet you. Wonderful evening here, thought the fireworks and the bonfire were perfectly splendid.'

The old bat put her head slightly to one side and examined him closely. 'That sounds more than a little patronising. Thought it would be rubbish, did you? Little village full of doddery, gormless people who don't know how to do anything well, or clever, or outstanding? Is that what you thought? Hang around a little longer and you'll find out how good we are at doing spectacular things extremely well. Just because it's an old village doesn't mean we're all gaga, you know.' She grinned wickedly.

By the end of her speech Morgan felt uncomfortable because that was exactly what he'd been thinking earlier in the evening, so he felt distinctly put in his place.

'By the way,' she turned away so only Morgan could actually see her face and only he could hear her say softly, 'we all know what you're up to, even if Caroline doesn't realise. Just you watch your step, young man, we've got your number and don't you forget it.' She tapped the side of her nose with a beautifully manicured finger, then turned to Peter, saying in a completely different tone of voice, 'Another wonderful Bonfire Night, Peter, it comes round again so quickly, doesn't it? Take care, you dear man, never forget how much we all respect you and Caroline, I don't know where we'd be if we hadn't got the two of you at the helm.' She glared at Morgan and then moved off, waving to someone passing by to get them to pause for a moment for a word with her. Morgan could just hear her saying, 'About helping with the refreshments next Saturday, Maggie, I'll gladly . . .'

Morgan, his feathers ruffled more than he cared to acknowledge, paused a moment to reflect on Jimbo's mother. She was tough and not half. Mastered cancer and still firing on all cylinders. What a woman. He didn't like the idea that she was well aware of his plans for Caroline. He'd never told anyone his thoughts on that matter and never even hinted at them to Caroline, though surely she must *know,* she was no fool. Not Caroline. He looked at her and she was immediately aware he was looking at her. She smiled and for a moment she and he were the only two people in the world. All those years ago he should never have accepted her statement about meeting Peter and that it meant their own affair was at an end because of him. He should have hung around and fought harder to keep her. Morgan Jefferson was worth twice the value of Peter Harris. In every possible way. *Every* possible way. He half raised his hand in greeting to Caroline and she did the same and the world stood still except for Peter who walked rapidly away as though on a mission of some sort.

He took the liberty of escaping everyone by finding his way to the stables and the two ponies that belonged to Johnny's boys. Johnny had taken him to see the ponies the day after they'd taken up residence and over the last year he'd become familiar with them.

The ponies were pleased to see him and welcomed him enthusiastically. He liked the smell of them, and the warmth of their breath on his hands as he greeted them, and he welcomed the simplicity of their reaction to him, nothing complicated with them at all.

Leaning over the stable door, stroking the ponies and being able to talk to them relaxed him considerably, and for the moment they were all he wanted. He understood Barry's impulse to give Morgan a kicking because that was exactly how he felt. The man was a continuous irritation to him and nothing Morgan said or did inclined Peter to change his opinion of him. He also knew that without doubt that Caroline had a strong fascination for Morgan. In all the years they'd been married he'd never felt so far away from her. Their closeness had been the greatest joy to him but now he felt abandoned, as though all the support he had enjoyed during their time together had been savagely dragged from him, leaving him badly wounded. Several of his parishioners had hinted that he appeared to have lost his faith in God. But it wasn't that he'd lost his faith in God: what he'd lost, for ever he felt, was the love of his life ... Caroline. Nothing he said or did appeared to bring her close. She was so distant, so absorbed in looking at a future that didn't include him, and without her love he simply didn't exist.

'Well, you two chaps look comfortable and happy, so I suppose that's something to be thankful for. Goodnight then, Laurel and you, Hardy, goodnight to you. Sleep tight.'

Peter closed the stable door, envious of their companionship. He checked his watch and saw he would be missing out on one of Caroline's celebrated suppers, and hurriedly left for the Rectory and chatter and friendship.

The supper party was in full swing when he finally arrived which made him feel guilty but he pushed that idea to the back of his mind and joined Harriet and Jimbo. They were both thoroughly enjoying themselves eating Caroline's food, drinking that wine Morgan had brought which he declared cost a fortune and Jimbo was saying that very thing as Peter joined them. 'Peter! Try the wine. Morgan paid a lot for it so you'd better approve! Brought it for you, he said, so you'd better have a glass. Go on, Harriet, pour one for Peter. Hurry! Or it'll all be gone!'

'I don't usually do what he tells me to but because it's you, Peter, I will. It *is* good, but I don't approve of paying a fortune for wine. I think that's exceedingly indulgent and quite unnecessary. Here! Let's toast our host. To Peter and many more Bonfire Nights.'

'To wish you good health and happiness, Peter! Cheer up! It's Bonfire Night. Enjoy!' said Jimbo enthusiastically. 'Well, what do you think to it? Good! Eh?'

'It is. Very good. But, like Harriet, I don't approve of excessive amounts of money being forked out for wine. Money has much better uses,' Peter replied.

Jimbo felt Harriet dig a sharp elbow into his ribs, and he knew, just knew, he'd said the worst thing in the circumstances. Turning his back on the rest of the company, Jimbo said quietly, 'You've got to fight for her, Peter. Really fight, you know.'

'Too late, I'm afraid. Far too late.' Peter raised his glass to Jimbo, as though Jimbo was uttering pleasantries and not desperate advice.

Harriet knew full well she shouldn't kiss him, but she did. On his cheek, whispering so that only he could hear, before she let go of his arm, 'For her sake, Peter, you must. He's no good for her. It can only end in tragedy. Believe me.'

Someone cheered her action, someone laughed, Harriet blushed and Jimbo applauded. 'That's enough, Harriet, thank you. I know he's a very charming man but there is a limit.' He said his bit sounding full of approval and passed the gesture off as normal in Turnham Malpas society.

Peter looked embarrassed and had eyes for no one but Caroline, who hastily began sorting the buffet food and suggesting people take second helpings of everything. 'Please, do eat it all.'

Morgan began offering slices of delicious quiche round, and a large bowl of beautifully fresh salad that looked too tempting to refuse. He followed this with fillets of salmon dressed with mayonnaise, but not the out-of-a-jar kind from a supermarket, it was one of Jimbo's specialities and it gleamed with good breeding. Morgan loved it. That's what he cared about, good food from the best of establishments. In fact, he cared about everything that was quality; he surrounded himself with good things and Caroline would be the very best in his collection. So good looking, so well spoken, her bearing, her style! Yes, she was top class and together they would stun the students and the staff at the university. How he looked forward to it all. They'd be a sensation.

By mistake he looked straight into Peter's face and saw honesty and truth and compassion – but above all, sadness, and for one brief second he didn't like himself for what he was about to do, and then thought damn it! Why not? The reverend should strive to keep her but he just doesn't care enough about her. Not like Morgan Jefferson did. She should never have married a vicar or rector or whatever he was called. She wasn't his kind. Not he! He turned round to put the serving dish with the remains of the salmon on it on the buffet table, and there stood Katherine Charter-Plackett looking straight through him. She knew him for what he was. Damn the woman! He winked, and she winked back. Maybe she was on his side. She was certainly intrigued by him, no doubt about that; on the other hand, she had threatened him and that he didn't like. Was she one of those people who is ultra-sensitive about the vibes others gave out? Perhaps that was it. Well, he'd better have her on his side.

'Katherine! How are you tonight? Enjoy the bonfire and the firework display? I certainly did. What it is to have money – and not just money, but loads of it.' He leaned towards her, whispering confidentially, 'It's a blessing that Johnny has all that money from his hotel business, otherwise he wouldn't be able to throw money at every problem, and the village certainly benefits from that fact, doesn't it?'

Katherine never talked money in any circumstances and Morgan's reference to it in such an obvious way really angered her. 'This village has *always* had money available, even Craddock Fitch benefitted the village until his company collapsed. It is such bad taste to mention money in the way you have just now. Such very bad taste. I would have thought you would know better. Not good manners, you know.'

Morgan laughed. 'You wicked woman, you're pulling my leg, aren't you? I thought we were friends ...'

Grandmama, not wishing to alienate him and sensing she'd gone a step too far, pretended he was right. 'You're right, of course you are. You and I are friends.'

'I hope to see a lot more of you when I get back from the States.' He fondly massaged her elbow in a supplicating way.

'You're coming back here afterwards?' Was he completely mad?

'Of course, with Caroline, before I tackle my next project.'

'You'll not be welcome, believe me.'

'Not welcome? Why ever not? I love it here. I've made friends here.'

Grandmama knew why not and anyone with their head screwed on properly knew why not too. The whole of the village would probably join in his murder. Breaking Peter's heart without caring about the damage it would do? How could he? He was clever enough to know the consequences of his actions in this matter. Oh, in one way she couldn't blame Caroline: *she* was an innocent going to the slaughter. At least, that was what Grandmama thought until she caught the expression on Caroline's face as she watched Morgan still grasping her elbow. There was a hint of something there. Was it jealousy? It was! Caroline felt jealous about him spending time with her, an old lady well past her sell-by date ... Matters were more complicated than she'd ever imagined.

Hurriedly, Grandmama said her goodbyes to Peter, thanking him and Caroline for being so generous with their time during such a busy weekend and left before her face gave her away. Once in bed it was almost three o'clock before she fell asleep. But at least she'd made a plan. Well, a kind of plan, but she'd need an ally.

She wasn't the only villager unable to sleep. Peter couldn't either. His life, instead of being full of light and love and passion, was in shreds. And worst of all was losing Caroline. Not yet actually, *lost*, but slowly slipping away from him. The wonderful understanding they had had, despite him fathering the twins, was shrinking rapidly and he no longer made any effort to retrieve it. What the twins' response would be if he and Caroline finally broke apart, Peter could only conjecture.

Chapter 16

Alice Templeton had suffered a poor night's sleep too, but on Sunday night. Firstly, Charles had had another restless night complaining of stomach pains and the expected baby had been thrashing about almost all night. Well, a large part of it. Why was it when she went to bed the baby frequently decided it was time for athletics? It simply wasn't fair.

Johnny slept through it all as usual and she hadn't the heart to wake him to share her burden of being a mother. There was nothing he could do anyway. This one would have to be the last. No way was she going to have four children. Three was plenty, more than plenty. Her mother had only had her and declared one was enough although Alice would have liked to have a sister or a brother – she hadn't minded which.

She turned over and began to settle into sleep but Charles had woken again. She swung her legs out of bed and called at the same time, 'I'm coming. Hush! You'll wake Ralph.' Then she heard the sound of someone being sick. 'Oh no! Not again.'

As she dashed into Charles's bedroom Alice thought this sickness business had to be faced. Doctor, that's what, no more messing about. Take action, Alice Templeton, *this morning*, not next week, not waiting till he's sick again, do it *today*.

Consequently she wasn't at home when Peter called.

But it was Johnny he'd come to see because of Johnny's position as Church Warden.

Peter entered the old familiar study, which in his mind he always associated with Craddock Fitch. Poor chap was no longer the bustling, active businessman they all remembered him being: handing out money whenever there was a need for it, providing money for the village children if they showed talent and needed to go to college or university. How he'd loved being able to do that. Now he was crouched in a room at Nightingale Farm, living with one of his sons and his family, needing help every time he moved from chair to bed or bed to bathroom. So sad, and Kate dying so suddenly ...

'Ah! There you are, Johnny. Shan't keep you long, just brought the correspondence I promised. Here we are.' Peter heaved a thick pile of A4 out of his briefcase. 'Shall I put it here? No need to hurry, this is your copy to keep. OK?'

'Yes, that's just where it needs to be. I can't work in a mess, everything has to be in the right place. Sad, isn't it?' He grinned at Peter.

'I'd call it very sensible and very organised. Wish I were the same. How is everyone?' He gave Johnny a beaming smile.

'We're all fine. Thanks. And you. How are you?'

'I'm fine thank you, Johnny. Absolutely fine. Planning Christmas of course, at the moment. I want to make it the best ever, so if you have any bright ideas, let me know. Be glad to have some input.'

'Caroline looking forward to her US adventure?'

'She is.'

Johnny saw a kind of shutter come down over Peter's face and decided to say something. They all knew now, so Johnny didn't feel he had to hold back. 'Pity you can't go with her on some kind of trumped-up excuse.'

'Well, that's not possible, is it, and I don't want to anyway.'

He said that sentence so firmly that Johnny began to wonder if they'd all got the wrong idea about that Morgan fellow.

'You know Morgan from before, then?'

'Only met him a couple of times before that first weekend

he stayed with us. He's someone Caroline knew before we got together and they've kept in touch.'

'There's something he's hiding, isn't there? Just an instinct I've got about him, probably wrong.'

'I'm sure you're right, Johnny. I think the same, but I thought it was just me. The man actually ... Anyway I most certainly will not be going to the States. I shall be here, doing what I do best.'

'I've rarely said anything at all to you about the wonderful job you make of being rector here Peter, but everyone thinks the world of you, you do know that, don't you? If ever you should move away ... well, just make sure you stay here where you belong.' Johnny not only shook his hand but put his other hand on Peter's shoulder as he did so. 'I want you to stay. OK?'

'Thank you for that. Look, I haven't seen Ron Bissett lately, Johnny. Is he all right, do you know? Is he willing to have visitors now?'

Johnny nodded. 'Just make sure it's not Thursday morning when you go, that's when he and Chris get together to put the bookies out of business.' Johnny was laughing as he spoke. 'Did you know?'

'I do. And I think that's kind of Chris, spending time with him.'

'I don't know about kind, they make a lot of money together the two of them. However, if they enjoy it ...' He laughed and shrugged at the same time. 'Poor Ron misses Sheila. Apparently he didn't think he would, but he does. Not the nagging she used to do, but misses *her*.'

Peter laughed too but avoided further conversation as soon as Sheila was mentioned. 'Must go, got a lot to do today. Thanks, Johnny. Bye!' He still had Sheila's letter hidden in the secret drawer in his desk and he knew he must be careful not to let on about it till he'd decided what the best course of action was for him to take. Somehow, at the moment his mind wasn't clear and sharp as it usually was. When he got back Caroline's car was parked outside the Rectory and in front of it was Morgan's flashy sports car. So he was still here then. Lunch would be yet another contest of wills and Peter was growing weary of it all. He braced his shoulders and marched inside to find Caroline in the kitchen and Morgan in his study, running a curious eye over his bookshelves.

'Hello! Hope you don't mind, Peter, but Caro said you'd had a couple of books published and I thought I'd take a look. Whereabouts are they?'

'Please, Morgan, do not profess an interest in books written by me just to curry favour with me and shut me up! It won't work. And that's Caroline saying lunch is ready.'

Peter began to leave his study but Morgan had other ideas. 'I'm disappointed that you think that of me. I have better things to do than curry favour, as you put it. I am genuinely interested.' He looked quizzically at Peter, awaiting a favourable answer, sure he would get a favourable one when he'd laid on the charm.

But Peter wasn't having any of it. 'You may think I'm a fool and can't see a sham when it's there, but to be honest, Morgan, I am sick and tired of you trying to get me on side so I won't kick up a fuss about you and Caroline being in the States together. I may appear to be a gentle, pathetic, feeble country parson to you, but I am far, far away from that. I know what you're after, I know you think I'm an idiot and not a patch on you with your money and your sophistication and your charm. I know your plans and I despise you for it. The sooner you leave the better it will be as far as I am concerned. Right now before lunch would be a good time. Caroline is *my wife* and I would commit murder to prevent the loss of her.'

Morgan stood transfixed. He was unaccustomed to people telling him the truth and listening to this man, living as he did in a god forsaken dump like this village, most certainly was not part of his plan. What did he know of the goings on in the world in which Morgan Jefferson lived? Nothing! Go before lunch? 'Me going now wouldn't be fair to your wife when she's taken a long lunch hour from the hospital and cooked a lovely meal for us. Come on! Peter! Play fair!'

'Play fair? You don't know the meaning of that phrase. Just pack your bags and go. Now! I've had enough of you.'

They heard Caroline call out again that lunch was ready and waiting. When they didn't spring into action she came to the study to find out why. She stood in the doorway, appalled. The husband she'd grown weary of was standing with clenched fists raised to chest level, ready to strike the man she'd love to have change places with him.

'What's this? What's happened? Have you had an argument?'

There was no reply from either of them.

'Peter! Why are you so angry with Morgan? You're forgetting he's a guest in our house.'

'Not any longer. He's leaving before lunch, darling, and I'm glad he is. He's all pretence to suit his own ends. Pretending to be interested in my writing. He isn't. He couldn't care less about me and the things that matter to me. Why are you still standing there, Morgan? I told you to get out. Now.'

Morgan asked Caroline if she wanted him to go.

'Of course not. Morgan, go into the kitchen and eat your lunch, there's a good chap, while I speak to Peter.'

The way she phrased it made Morgan feel like a small boy being given a dressing down by his head teacher. That wasn't right for a man of his calibre. He still had some dignity left.

'No, Caroline, it will be better if I leave; Peter obviously needs time to calm down. Thank you for all your hospitality this weekend, the food has been wonderful. Cheese soufflé, you said? I shall be sorry to miss it. I'll leave immediately but I'll be in touch.' Morgan smiled at her and then closed the study door very gently as though to illustrate what a well-behaved, gentlemanly person he was.

Caroline, knowing how physically fit Peter was with his weekly games of squash and his three-mile daily runs, wanted Morgan out of the way before Peter thumped him, which she knew from the past was very likely the next move on his agenda.

The two of them stood silently, looking at each other neither of them knowing what to say next. When they heard Morgan revving up his sports car they both began speaking at the same time.

'It is cheese soufflé and it'll soon be ruined . . .'

'What you see in that man—'

'You leave that man to me! How dare you treat him like that? You would have hit him if I hadn't come in.'

Peter almost began to apologise but changed his mind. 'In all the years we've been married I have never—'

'I'm still going to the States to do this research, and don't even begin to think you will stop me, because you won't. I am going, believe me. *I am*. If I don't, I will definitely go raving mad living here in this so-called idyllic village. Idyllic my foot. Petty, parochial, mean-minded, cruel, pathetic, stick-in-the-mud. And that description fits you exactly. Yes. All those things, and I shall be glad to leave it and you. Believe me. Cheese soufflé? For what it's worth right now.' Caroline turned on her heel and left him.

The lunch she had prepared finished up down the waste disposal and both of them stormed out of the Rectory without speaking.

Peter wished, oh how he wished, he'd punched the blasted man and sent him off with a black eye, possibly two black eyes. But he hadn't and Caroline had told him in no uncertain terms exactly how she felt about *him*. It was all out in the open at last. He felt sick with the despair of it all. He was not the man he had been. How had he arrived at this appalling point in his life? He, a pacifist, delighting in the idea of punching a fellow human being. But worst of all was losing his beloved Caroline. He examined his feelings for her and knew whatever she did he would love her to the end of his life.

As for Caroline, she couldn't understand how she had arrived at the situation she found herself in. Peter was the man she'd loved despite his major sin of fathering the twins with another woman ... She remembered how eagerly, how gratefully she'd taken on being their mother, how much she loved them, how much she'd loved *him*, how she'd gladly forgiven him. But right now ... now, not even Peter's shattering desperation would stop her. She was going to work with Morgan and damn the consequences.

Chapter 17

That night the bar at the Royal Oak was packed. Georgie and Dicky couldn't pull pints fast enough to please all their customers. As fast as one crowd got served the queue had already lengthened right round the bar again. If it had been summertime, the outside tables would have been packed too, but as it was every table in the bar was full and people were also standing, or had decided to occupy an empty table in the dining room.

The old table with the long settle down one side of it was fully occupied by its usual customers. Zack and Marie, Dottie and Maurice, Sylvia and Willie, Greta and Vince, and Pat and Barry. They were all squeezed in elbow to elbow but were glad to be in their favourite place to sit.

'So, I told the rector that if he wanted to give that chap a kicking I'd be willing to help.'

They were shocked, every one of them. Horrified.

'Ah!' said Willie, 'but I bet he didn't agree, not the rector. He wouldn't, being a good Christian man. He'd be more likely to say, "Now, Barry", and wag a finger at you.'

Barry chuckled. 'You're right about 'im saying "Now, Barry" but he looked as though he agreed with what I'd said.'

'He never!' This from Willie who always thought, no matter what, that the sun shone out of the rector, day in day out. 'Mind you, there's something not right about that Morgan chap. He's hiding something.'

'Exactly!' Barry was delighted to have his opinion confirmed.

'Just what I think. Don't know what it is but you're right, there's something he's not letting on about.'

Dottie, knowing much more about the Rectory comings and goings than she ever let on about to her friends, agreed. 'Not seen much of him but there's something not quite straightforward about him. But, having said that, I can understand Caroline needing to get away.' She nodded convincingly. 'Time she moved on.'

Greta, who'd always known that Dottie knew a lot more than they all did, asked, 'So why should she? Want to get away? What better place is there to live than here in this village? We've no drug problems like they have in Culworth, no late night carousing due to drinking too much, no kerb crawling . . .'

'Is there late night kerb crawling, then? I didn't know that. Sounds like a den of iniquity, does Culworth.' This from Merc, who had just managed to squeeze another chair in at the end of the settle. 'First I've heard of it. In Culworth?'

'Well,' said Marie, 'I wouldn't live in Culworth, not for anything. It isn't safe for a woman to be out on the streets after dark. I mean, round here you can walk where you like any time and you're safe. That bus station, it's just as bad as London for picking up women.'

'The bus station? For heaven's sake, the last bus leaves at ten o'clock nowadays,' said Willie.

'So where are these women you can pick up?' asked Zack.

There was a moment of amazement and then Willie, being as awkward as only he could, suggested that Zack must want to know for future reference. They all had a laugh about that till tears ran down their cheeks.

'Zack? That's a laugh,' someone said.

Marie was furious. 'Are you inferring that my Zack goes looking for women in Culworth? Well, I can tell you I know where he is every waking minute and it isn't the bus station in Culworth, believe me.' She folded her arms and looked round the table, trying to catch everyone's eye to make sure they believed her.

'Every waking minute? Are you sure?' asked Barry, keen to make everyone laugh.

Marie hesitated then said, in order to convince herself as much as anything, 'Every waking minute.' She patted his hand as he picked up his glass and he almost spilled beer on her coat sleeve. 'Mind out, Zack, it'll ruin my coat.'

Zack, though he wouldn't have admitted it, was quite chuffed that someone thought he might have a secret life. 'You don't know every minute, I'm sure. Do you, love?'

Marie nodded confidently. '*Every* minute. Believe me.'

Zack thought furiously for a moment or too and then decided that yes, Marie did know where he was every single second and to himself he made up his mind it was time he led a more exciting life like when he caught the thieves who'd stolen the lead off the church roof. So just to be provocative he said, 'Doesn't matter what time the last bus goes, you don't go kerb crawling in a bus, now do you?'

A roar of laughter went round the bar and it seemed everyone present was listening in.

Marie went bright red. Zack's eyes twinkled wickedly and the general consensus was that Zack was leading a double life.

'Come on then, Zack,' a chap from Penny Fawcett shouted above the hubbub, 'give us a few tips.' That was a remark typical of a man from Penny Fawcett and for a moment no one responded, but then they did and a roar of laughter made its way round the bar and some people from the dining room wished they knew what was being said because it sounded a lot more fun in the bar tonight.

Dicky, as joint landlord of the Royal Oak, realised someone needed to take charge or there could be a fight. So he stepped forward and told a joke about bus stations.

They loved it! Then another, and another, and he had control of the bar back in his hands in seconds. That was the fun thing about Dicky; he could take control in the nicest possible way without anyone taking offence.

Under cover of the companionable laughter brought about by Dicky's jokes Marie asked Zack, 'You've never been to the bus station, have you? Ever?' She paused and then added, 'To look for a woman? Yer know?' She discreetly nudged him with her elbow.

'I wouldn't tell you if I had. Anyway, I haven't, so don't worry. It's all a bit of harmless fun.' He dried his eyes. 'You have to agree Dicky is a brilliant teller of tales.'

Zack had a private chuckle to himself and it made Marie doubtful of his declaration of innocence.

'But you're laughing! If I ever found out it was true, that you had been to the bus station, I'd kill you and I mean it.'

Zack turned towards her and, looking her straight in the eye, he declared to her and those nearest that he had never been in the bus station late at night, not any night.

Then it occurred to her there was that time when he was very late when the trains to and from London had been on strike and he'd arrived at the bus station in Culworth too late to catch the last bus. 'What about that time when—'

'Shut up, Marie, you're making a mountain out of a molehill. Have done. I mean it. It's gone beyond a joke now.' Zack was obviously very upset and Marie had the sense to stop pulling his leg, but Barry and Willie were enjoying themselves and were reluctant to put a stop to their fun.

Barry nudged Willie. 'He'll be going late to make sure the church is locked up but instead he's off into Culworth hanging about at the bus station with Marie asleep in bed and him on the loose.'

Willie agreed, taking a slightly vicious pleasure in upsetting Zack by saying, 'Good little job that, being Verger, gives yer excuses for all sorts of goings on.' He laughed rather cruelly and Zack, furious that he couldn't shut them up and angry on Marie's behalf, stood up and going round the table he stood behind

Barry's chair and threatened to strangle him. 'Sick of it, I am. None of it's true as you well know. How many years have you lived in this village?'

'Born here.' A fact of which Barry was proud.

'Same here, so we should be brothers not enemies, stop it here and now, if you please.'

'All right, all right. Friends?' Barry held out his hand but Zack was too furious to notice and gestured angrily, which dashed Zack's hand aside and his thumbnail jabbed rather forcefully into Barry's eyelid. Blood began to flow and Barry snatched at a handkerchief he found in his trouser pocket to catch the blood.

Dicky, a head shorter than both of the protagonists, intervened, and put an end to the fight immediately. He wagged a cautionary finger, saying as he did so, 'That's enough. Finish it. Immediately.' When he caught sight of Barry's hand about to punch Zack, Dicky lost control. He grabbed Barry by the scruff and, despite the difference in their height, he hauled Barry out of his chair and put him outside the door. Came back and tried to do the same to Zack.

Marie was furious and, totally uncaring about the impression she gave to the packed bar, hit Dicky over the head with Zack's tankard.

Tankards in the Royal Oak were exceptional weapons, intensely heavy for their size and on more than one occasion had proved their worth when the recipient of the blow had to go to hospital to get stitched up. Tonight was no exception.

Dicky's forehead gushed blood; it ran, not trickled, down his face and the front of his white T-shirt was drenched in seconds. Dicky went as white as a sheet, which only intensified the effect of the blow on everyone. Marie had never intended to cause such a terrible scene and begged for forgiveness from Dicky. 'I'm so sorry, Dicky, so sorry, I never meant . . .'

She inhaled a huge breath to calm her nerves and then burst into a flood of tears.

Georgie, who always stepped into the breach whenever discipline was needed, stood between the two of them, desperately trying to stem the blood with a brand new tea towel she happened to have in her hand. Dicky hated being coddled and pushed her and her tea towel away. 'Leave me alone!' he shouted as loudly as he was able because fresh blood had begun filling his mouth each time he opened it. 'It hurts too much.'

Willie, considered an expert on wounds, though he didn't know why, said, 'Hospital, he needs taking to hospital. Right now. I mean *right now*. He's losing so much blood.'

More angry than she could remember being for years, Georgie asked, arms akimbo, 'You taking him, then?'

'No, can't, never passed my test, but I'm right about what I say, he needs professional help, he does. Right away. It's his forehead, you see.'

'We're none of us blind, Willie, we can all see.' She rushed to the outside door hoping to catch Barry before he left. Luckily she found Barry still standing outside the door where Dicky had left him, laughing himself helpless.

'Barry! Come in your car tonight?'

Barry nodded as best he could.

'Dicky needs to go to hospital. He's hurt. Now, right away. Will you oblige? I can't leave here, you see because there's no one on except me and Dicky tonight.'

Getting no reply she asked him again and this time he answered her. 'I will. I will. It's the thought of little Dicky hauling me, the size I am, out of the door. Oh dear! It won't do my image any good will it? Wait till I tell Pat! She won't half laugh. I'll bring the car round to the front. Not so far for him to walk. Got something big like a tablecloth to catch the blood, otherwise . . .'

It took two hours just to get attention to stitch the wound and control the bleeding. Two hours in which Barry and Dicky did a lot of laughing, feeling more comfortable now they were in a place where professional help was right on hand. The effects of it began to tell on Dicky, though, and the doctor in the emergency department insisted he stayed in for observation. 'If it was his arm that had taken the blow,' he said, 'I wouldn't worry so much, but his head, that's a different matter.'

Dicky began to protest. 'No, I want to go home. Back home where I belong, thank you very much.'

'No, I insist, Mr Tutt. Talk some sense into him, Mr Jones, will you? He needs to stay – just in case. Must have been one hell of a tankard to do so much damage.'

'The Royal Oak tankards are renowned for it,' said Barry as he peered intently at Dicky's forehead. 'It has swollen a lot, hasn't it?'

Dicky gave a shuddering groan as though the pain was unbearable.

The doctor persisted. 'Yes, better if he stays. Is there a Mrs Dicky Tutt?'

Barry answered on Dicky's behalf. 'There is. She saw it happen because the two of them are the licensees of the Royal Oak pub in Turnham Malpas. I'll make sure she knows about him staying in for the night and that. Thank you for everything, doctor. Right then, I'll go tell Georgie face to face, better than the telephone. Take care. Dicky, you're in good hands. I won't alarm her, Dicky, I'll tell her gently.'

'Good. And don't tell Georgie how swollen my forehead is now. Give her my love, won't you and tell her that I'm doing all right, I am. It's nothing really. Awwww! I've got one hell of a headache though!'

As it turned out, Dicky stayed in hospital two whole days before he was allowed home and in no time at all he was back in hospital having collapsed unconscious at the top of the long flight of stairs down into the cellar.

'I *told* him not to begin work, but would he listen?' Georgie said. 'No, he would not. Doctor, he's going to be all right isn't he? I mean . . .'

'I did say *rest*.'

'I know, but anyone who knows Dicky knows he can't. He doesn't ever rest.'

'I'll have him tied to the bed if he doesn't do as he is told, Mrs Tutt. Use your influence please and tell him he must rest. Or else . . .'

'What's "or else" mean?'

'I refuse to say. Suffice it to say that *rest* is what will save his life, not galloping down into the pub cellar to carry crates of beer up. Right!'

Georgie nodded. 'Right. So he's to go home and lie in bed doing nothing at all?'

'Exactly. *Nothing*. I want to see him in three days' time, and if he worsens in the meantime then bring him in and make sure the nursing staff let me know you've brought him. Goodbye, Mrs Tutt, I don't envy you your task, but I mean it. Goodbye, Dicky, be a good chap and *behave* yourself.'

Georgie did not enjoy looking after Dicky. He claimed he was as fit as a flea but Georgie knew he wasn't. Agreed the swelling began to go down but his memory was poor and he'd no appetite and kept dropping asleep in the middle of a sentence, even in the middle of telling a joke.

As for Marie, she didn't show her face anywhere in the village because she felt so ashamed of losing her temper. She'd never hit anyone over the head ever before and certainly not in a pub brawl. She'd hated the idea that Dicky intended to throw Zack out, just as he had thrown out Barry. Could there be anything so shaming as that? She felt as though she could never show her face in the village again. Fortunately she had people clamouring for rooms for her B&B business for a couple of weeks and in fact was too busy to go out and she even asked for her weekly groceries to be delivered from the Store so she wouldn't have to go in there and probably meet someone who knew the whole story.

The idea that someone could hit Dicky over the head with one of the heavy tankards they used in the Royal Oak shocked everyone. Dicky! Such a nice chap, always so friendly, so kind. And his jokes, they're always brilliant. Who hit him?

'Marie did,' said someone in the queue at the till in the Store.

'Marie Hooper? But she doesn't do things like that, not Marie. You must have got the wrong woman. No, not Marie. So unlike her. Now, if you'd said Greta Jones, I'd believe that,' said Connie.

'Well, it *was* Marie,' Greta said, laughing. 'She hit Dicky with a tankard for dragging – or, I should say, *trying* to drag Zack out for being involved in an argument with Barry.'

'Surely you must mean Georgie? When it comes to it she's always the one in charge of discipline.'

'No, it was Marie, she was so angry.'

'And Dicky how did he fair?'

'Well, Willie said he had to go to the hospital and they kept him in *two* nights, so close to his brain you see, and the blood! Oh! My word! Georgie gave Barry, who took him to the hospital, a *tablecloth* to mop up the blood on the way. It poured out of him. Never seen anything like it. Them tankards should be banned. I was there. I saw it happen! She hit him on his forehead with one of 'em and you know what they're like, half as big but twice as heavy as anyone else's. The Wise Man tankards are twice as big but half as heavy.'

'Well, I never. Poor Georgie, she must be upset.'

'Oh, she is.' Greta, glad to have a piece of prize gossip to tell, added, 'They say that Georgie is thinking of giving up the pub and that they've already got a buyer. She says the licenced trade is not what it was.'

'Over-charging is still on the menu, though. I bet they're making a fortune out of the Royal Oak.'

The two of them trundled out of the Store still muttering about the charges in pubs nowadays. Greta nodded. 'Well, even if this buyer is just someone's imagination, they'll sell it easy enough though, you know, smart pub like that with all the latest gadgets in the kitchen and the food much improved since they got the new chef – not that it was poor before he came, it was all right – but he's come and transformed the menu, transformed it is. Do yer know, he wouldn't move from his last pub unless he got *twice* what he was paid where he was.'

'No! Twice? Fancy that! Amazing! Twice!'

'Plus a rent-free cottage down the bottom of Shepherd's Hill included, right opposite where Dottie Foskett that was lives with her Maurice. All newly decorated plus a brand new bathroom.'

'No! Well, I never! He must be a good chef. I might very well go in for a drink there tonight, find out the latest.'

'It'll be packed, believe me, they'll all want to know. Bye, Connie.'

'Bye, Greta. I'll let you know if there's any more news about Dicky or anything at all come to that.'

Connie didn't get to the pub that night because a friend of hers rang up and suggested she went over to Penny Fawcett for a drink at their house. Had she gone to the Royal Oak she would have found that Greta was right. It was packed. They had Dicky and Georgie working, Alan Crimble, and, lo and behold, Linda Crimble. Now that their Lewis was in his teens they felt free to leave him to his own devices so Linda could earn extra money as the three of them were passionate followers of Formula One around the world. Lewis always had plenty of homework to do, or rather prep, now he was attending Prince Edwards' Grammar just outside Culworth.

They weren't standing idle behind the counter hoping someone would want a refill, either. Oh no, tonight the till never stopped ringing and Dicky and, in particular, Georgie, were filled with delight. How everyone knew that they were selling the Royal Oak as soon as possible, already had a buyer, Georgie couldn't understand, but know they did, and the questions about who was buying came thick and fast. But they'd been asked by the secret buyer not to let on until the contract was definitely signed.

'You'd think they'd have the courtesy to tell us. After all, it's our money that fills the coffers tonight and every night, so why shouldn't we know?' asked Willie Biggs. He stared grumpily into his tankard, thinking of Dicky as he picked it up for another sip of his home brew. Every night of his adult years he'd had a pint or two or three of the Royal Oak's special home brew and he knew more than anyone how it had always kept him in good health. His mind contemplated the possibility that the home brew might not exist if some idiot bought the pub and determined to modernise it. Then every drink would be just fancy this and fancy that and nothing would ever be the same again. Indeed, if the regulars didn't watch it they'd be serving cocktails in no time at all! He could be heading for a speedy demise. Surely not! He wasn't ready for that, not yet; he still had the world to put to rights, hadn't he? Barry and Vince and Zack brooded on the very same problem. Would the Royal Oak ever be the same again? Where else could they go where they felt relaxed and happy and had Dicky's jokes to look forward to? Where they met the same people any night they came in?

Barry said, 'I'm not going to that dump in Penny Fawcett that they've called the Slug and Lettuce since that new landlord took over.'

'What about that daft chap that's started up the wine bar in Little Derehams?' asked Vince.

'What about him? He must be daft to try it. Full stop. I'm told you can go in there some nights and there're more people serving behind the bar than there are buying drinks. They lose money every single blinking night they open. You can't go on like that for long, now can you?' Vince looked gloomily into his ale.

Barry had a more cheerful attitude to the problem they were all facing. 'If we could just find out who's buying it, then we could perhaps influence 'em a bit. Persuade and cajole, as Sir Johnny says.'

Willie leaned forward and their three heads all came closer so no other person could hear. 'Who do you reckon, then? It's only five days since Dicky was inca- incapacitated, so I reckon it's someone close to home.'

'Well, no one lives close to us and above all there's no Jones's with money, believe me. Except our Kenny and our Terry. They're rolling in it, over there in Canada.'

'Could it be them?'

Willie scoffed at the idea. 'There's not been enough time for letters to cross the Atlantic. No, it can't be them, how can it?'

Barry reminded Willie about emails and texting and that. 'Letters is old hat, nowadays. The whole world has speeded up. It has, you know. They could have emailed, and then Dicky emails back, and before you know it, it's all signed and delivered.'

'It could be them, couldn't it?' said Vince. 'Do you really think it is your Kenny and Terry, Barry?'

'To be honest, no I don't. Neither of them have a clean enough record to be a landlord, they're that particular, they are, nowadays. It isn't any Tom, Dick or Harry that can get their name above a pub door, believe me. Clean as a whistle their character has to be nowadays, and those two brothers of mine ain't as clean as a whistle, though give them their due they seem to have done well in Canada.'

'So who else could it be?' asked Willie.

There was a long silence at their table. None of them could come up with an answer, try as they might. 'In any case, whoever buys it,' said Willie, 'there's no one can tell jokes like Dicky so we shall miss all that, shan't we?'

The atmosphere at their table grew gloomier and gloomier until Barry suddenly said, 'I know! I've got it. Plain as the nose on your face. It'll be either Jimbo or Tom who does the Post Office counter, I bet. Or ...' His face lit up with the excitement of his theory ... '*both* of 'em. Jimbo with the money and Tom with the know-how. Good character reference, too, him having been a policeman before. I bet I'm right. You wait and see. He'd be all right, he would, for turning 'em out when they're misbehaving. Aren't I right? I am, I know I am.'

Vince was immediately won over by Barry's reasoning. 'Considering how Jimbo's always looking for a new idea to make money you could very well be right. He's got the meat under his belt now with Vince working like a slave for him, and that Bob the butcher cutting up meat like crazy, so he'll be ready for a new scheme, will Jimbo. Right, I'll buy the next round in. We've solved it. My turn. Give us the empties.'

Chapter 18

Barry desperately wanted to find out if his theory was right, so when Pat said she fancied some of Jimbo's real mint sauce to go with the lamb chops she'd chosen for their evening meal, Barry immediately offered to go down into the village and buy the exact brand she wanted.

Luckily for him, Jimbo was in the Store and not the part-timers as they both had exams to sit that same night.

'Evening, Jimbo. There's three beautiful lamb chops waiting at home for me and Pat and Greenwood, and Pat's begged me to come into the village and buy a jar of mint sauce. She says you know which one she likes best.'

'I certainly do. You don't usually do the shopping – in trouble are you? Trying to put things all fair and square with Pat?'

'Me? No. I know just exactly how to keep Pat in a continuous state of approval where I'm concerned.' He dug vigorously into his wallet while Jimbo went to find the mint sauce. 'Business good, is it? I hear your frozen meat website scheme has taken off brilliantly. What's your next money making scheme? The Royal Oak?'

He waited for Jimbo to reply, convinced he would be proved right. While he opened the cash till and accepted Barry's five-pound note, Jimbo ignored Barry's question, but the moment Jimbo slammed the cash till drawer shut he replied. 'I was hoping *you* would know who it is with enough money to buy the Royal Oak, because I certainly don't. I'm too well committed for any hare-brained scheme like buying a pub. I put in enough hours running the Store, I certainly don't want to add on all the hours a pub would need.'

Barry looked him straight in the eye and was surprised to find himself believing Jimbo.

'I was sure it would be you.'

'Well, believe me it most definitely isn't James Charter-Plackett. When you find out, let me know. Right?'

'Right!' Barry came out of the Store very disappointed. So, after all that boasting he was wrong. Or was he? Jimbo could play his cards very close to his chest when he chose. Even so, he wasn't a liar and the look in his eyes when Barry challenged him had convinced him that Jimbo was speaking the truth. But who was there in the village who would (a) have the money and (b) be capable of all the complicated business doodah that would be needed to run a pub according to the law? He arrived home with the mint sauce just in time for Pat and Greenwood to be ready for sitting down to their evening meal.

Greenwood asked him if he'd proved right.

'Actually, no. According to Jimbo, I've got it all wrong; he claims it isn't him who's offering to buy it.'

'Come on, Barry, you know Jimbo, he can lie faster than a donkey can trot if it suits him. He's pulling your leg. Got to keep it all under cover till it's signed, sealed and delivered. You wait and see – I wouldn't be too downhearted.' Greenwood put the first forkful of lamb in his mouth and sighed with pleasure as he chewed it. 'My word! This is grand and not half.'

'They're all complaining, saying whoever buys it will never make home-brew ale like Dicky can, that the tankards will be replaced with lightweight ones so they won't be good enough to kill someone, but we all like those tankards, kind of satisfying to pick up and drink from, they are. They belong to the Royal Oak like the inglenook fireplace does and that little table for two, right where you can feel the heat from the log fire. We're losing a lot with Georgie and Dicky leaving.'

'They might not be leaving,' suggested Pat. 'Perhaps they'll manage it for someone who can afford more staff, then they won't have to work such long hours.'

Barry nodded in agreement. 'You could be right.'

That evening Harriet and Jimbo kept a low profile. Jimbo went to his bell-ringing practice at the church and Grandmama, who was now back in her own house, kept Harriet company. She'd given Harriet a ring first to make sure she wasn't up to her eye-balls with a wedding or something and then bobbed across the green. There was a glass of whisky awaiting her arrival and she and Harriet settled down for a good gossip. Her first words were, 'So he's done it, then?'

'Done it? What? What's he done now?' Conscious she sounded more like an idiot than a sensible businesswoman, Harriet asked again: 'What's Jimbo done?'

'In the village they're saying Jimbo is buying the Royal Oak. Is he?'

'If he is he hasn't discussed it with me.'

'Oh! Right. I'm glad, really, it isn't the sort of business a man of Jimbo's standing should be dabbling in.'

'Where did you hear that?'

'At the cancer sale in the church hall this afternoon. Thought I should go in recognition of my life being saved from cancer and they were all guessing who it was who was buying it from Georgie. None of them really *knew*; it was all guesswork.'

'All too often, Katherine, their guesswork turns out to be true and if he has I shall kill him on the spot. So you'd better go if you don't want to see your nearest and dearest slaughtered in his own sitting room.' Harriet stood up and began pacing about. 'I will, I'll kill him. The meat business needs twice the staff he's got because it's just exploded into success and I don't mind that, that's wonderful, but who the blazes is going to manage a pub as well I simply do not know.'

They heard his key in the door.

Harriet turned to face him.

He looked surprised by her anger.

She said, 'Well, is it you?'

'Is what me? What have I done now?'

'Bought the Royal Oak.'

Jimbo was lost for words.

'I'm telling you here and now, if you have, you'd better start saying your prayers, because I have had enough.'

'I haven't.'

'You haven't what?'

'Bought the pub. But it *is* a good idea. It'd be a real money maker with me behind it.'

Seeing Harriet's intense distress Katherine opened her mouth to protest at his foolishness, but she was beaten to it by Jimbo. 'But I've not bought it and I have no intention of doing so. It's a mug's game, believe me. Barry's been in and was convinced it was me buying it, but I told him it isn't, and isn't going to be, so you can calm down. I wouldn't do it anyway without discussing it with you, now would I? We've enough on with what we've got. Now, I need a whisky. Join me, anyone? Oh! You've got one. Right. Nothing on the TV?'

Harriet asked, 'Will you promise me you won't?'

'Here and now, I promise. In the presence of my mother, I promise I am *not* buying the pub.'

Harriet stood up to emphasise her point. 'There's a twinkle in your eye, Jimbo. I mean what I say. I shall *murder* you if you do. I will, God help me, I will. A few years in a prison cell would be paradise compared to what I put up with now.'

Jimbo began to laugh. He almost spilled his whisky on his trousers and on the armchair, then he laughed even louder at the look on his mother's face, and then, when he finally dared to look at Harriet, he sobered up. 'I mean it. I faithfully promise I am not buying the pub. Honestly, it's never even crossed my mind. I'm flattered, though, that people think I have so much money to spare. Where do they get their ideas from?'

Having had the idea put there by other people, Jimbo did wonder momentarily about buying it; after all they wouldn't have had time to advertise it, never mind sell it, and it must be a money spinner and then he saw Harriet's face, and he knew he mustn't, for her sake, even dream about it, never mind ask how much they wanted for it. He did pause to estimate how much they would expect for it, though. Be amusing to keep them all guessing though, wouldn't it? Them thinking he was loaded with money, which he was, though he never let on he was. Best not in a place like this.

Which made him think of Caroline leaving the village. OK it was only for a year but ... would she survive? Did she want to survive? Did she want that creep Morgan? What a name. Jimbo had convinced himself the chap had changed his name from something unsuited to the impression he liked to give about himself. Probably called Albert or Cyril if the truth be told. He pictured himself calling Morgan Cyril and was rather taken with the idea. 'I reckon it's not his real name.'

'Pardon?' said his mother.

'I'm just thinking that Morgan isn't his real name.'

'You could be right, dear. There's something he's hiding. Anyway, what's a glamorous man like him doing not married? By all the rules he'd be married, wouldn't he?'

'He could be divorced,' Harriet declared.

Her mother-in-law nodded her agreement. 'He could indeed. I can understand Caroline getting fed up with her situation, but must she be so dramatic about it all? Surely, with her qualifications, there's something different she could do apart from floating off to America with that man. And leaving Peter, the poor lamb.'

Harriet found that last statement hugely amusing. 'Poor lamb, indeed! With Dottie coming in virtually every day, shopping for him, cleaning for him, washing and ironing for him, what more does a man need? For heaven's sake, Mother-in-law! Get real!'

Grandmama, who'd so recently come to the conclusion that Harriet was a wonderful daughter-in-law, found herself furious with this harsh criticism. Get real? She *was* real, she was an up-to-the minute grandmother, a proud, tolerant mother, and what's more, au fait with the daily goings on nowadays of all the grandchildren. This was too much. She heaved herself out of her comfortable chair, picked up her bag from the floor and stormed out, leaving Harriet and Jimbo looking at each other with amazement, both so shocked that neither of them tried to stop her.

'Oh dear!'

'Harriet! You shouldn't have said that.'

'I'm going after her. Hells bells! I'm an idiot. I'll be back shortly.'

Jimbo had every intention of going across to his mother's cottage after Harriet had had time to heal the breach, but he never got there because it was one of those nights when each of their four children decided that phoning home was an essential part of their lives. As fast as he closed a conversation from one, another was on the phone complaining they hadn't been able to get through and who on earth was needing to talk to him for so long? By the time all four of them had rung in such quick succession, Harriet was home. She went straight into the kitchen and eventually appeared in the sitting room carrying a tray with their hot drinks and a pile of biscuits on it.

'I thought you might come across and help me.'

'That was my intention but, believe it or not, all four of the children have rung us in quick succession and I have only just finished speaking to Flick. I *was* coming to rescue you, but she obviously hasn't murdered you as you are here speaking to me. Everything all right now?'

Harriet flopped down on the sofa saying, 'All right? Just about. My word, was she cross. I should never have said what I did. But it's true; he *is* going to be well looked after, and I can understand why Caroline is eager to go. She is sick, absolutely sick with her life, and is desperate for a change before she goes totally crackers. He should be glad she's found an opportunity to escape. You'd let me go, wouldn't you, if I needed to?' She raised questioning eyebrows at him and waited for his reply.

Rather hastily Jimbo changed what he'd intended saying. 'Of course, yes, I would. You're not thinking of going anywhere right now, are you?'

'You should see your face!' Harriet began laughing uproariously and finished up clutching her sides, the pain was so bad. Jimbo began to laugh too. They sat together on the sofa clutching each other, laughing so hysterically that neither of them could speak.

Eventually Harriet pulled herself together, saying between howls of laughter that soon the tea would be too cold to drink and she'd pour it out right away.

'There you are, darling, your favourite tea and I'm going to try it too. Biscuit?'

'One please. No, two, please ... please?'

'Very well, here you are, the slimming diet ignored yet again. I wish you were as athletic as Peter is. He keeps his weight absolutely right with his squash and running every day.'

'Some of us are made that way and I am not. My dad was so thin he always looked as though he was about to waste away.'

'Considering he had two wives to keep happy, it's hardly surprising. Did you, as a boy, ever suspect things weren't quite right?'

'No. He went away on business and then came back, so it was normal for me, I never questioned it. To be truthful he was a good dad – when he was there. He loved fishing and we had some brilliant days catching fish for our evening meal. He used to say "we can't go home until we have enough fish for our dinner tonight" and I imagined sitting there in pitch black waiting to catch a fish, but we always did catch some in plenty of time. He was brilliant at fishing, really brilliant.'

'You don't fish now, why not? If you enjoyed it so much.'

Jimbo didn't answer for a while then he said, 'When eventually I found out what he was up to I felt so cheated, so betrayed. It's funny, isn't it, that children require absolute truth from their parents and nothing else will do, but they in their teens can fib about girls they've had, or getting drunk, without batting an eyelid and think it's all right.'

Jimbo stared for a long time at the flames leaping up in the wood burner and then said, 'But once you've found out about your dad's unfaithfulness the innocence of childhood is gone for ever and things are never the same.'

Harriet said softly, 'I have never understood why your mother put up with his unfaithfulness. She has such a strong will, so why didn't she put her foot down?'

'No idea.' Jimbo was still watching the flames. He shrugged and added, 'Loved him too much, I suppose, and was thankful she had him part of the time and made do with that.'

'I wouldn't tolerate it, believe me. I definitely would not. He must have had plenty of money, though, to keep two wives and four children *and* two houses.'

Jimbo laughed at the prospect of all that to support. 'Indeed. When he died every penny of his money came to my mother and me, you know. All his second wife got was the house she lived in.'

'No! That wasn't fair, now was it? His three boys must have still been in their teens when he died. How did she manage? They eat such a lot in their teens.'

Jimbo shrugged again. 'Don't know. Tell you one thing, though, I'm glad I'm married to you and that it's all fair and square between us and we love each other and you're not thinking of running away for a year like Caroline's doing. Thing is, with a taste of freedom like she'll have, will she ever come back?'

'Jimbo! That has never occurred to me! She will – won't she?'

'I don't know, and perhaps she doesn't either. Or maybe she does know and it's all part of a plan.'

They both heard the doorbell ring but it was Jimbo, seeing that it was late and dark, who went to answer it.

Harriet could hear talking, then in through the sitting room door burst her mother-in-law.

'I've got up out of bed to apologise. I can't have us going to bed without the truth being said. Look, I try very hard to be up to-the-minute with everything and I do believe I am, but this be-haviour of Caroline and that – that *blasted* man is just too much. She must be so mixed up. I know, you see, what a marriage that isn't all fair and square like yours is like. It eats away at you, things not being straight and equal, eats you away till there's nothing left. I know. So we've got to stop her. Got to.' She sat down on the chair she'd occupied before she left in such a temper and immediately burst into tears. Harriet, without a word, went to Jimbo's drinks cabinet and poured her mother-in-law a whisky. 'Here, drink this, slowly mind.'

Katherine smiled weakly at her, said a quiet word of thanks and began sipping her lifesaver.

Harriet remarked, 'She's not a fool, Caroline; she knows ex-actly what she's doing, believe me. I've known her twenty years and I know she knows exactly what the consequences are but ... leaving the love of her life! Hells bells! Peter has been able to be what he is because of her common-sense approach to life, the support she's given him, the shock and horror of the twins being his. I mean, life has thrown her some difficult cards but she's come through it all and how she survived him having twins to that floozy Suzy Meadows I will never know, but then blow me she took them on as her own! If that wasn't brave I don't know what bravery is.'

Jimbo heaved himself from his easy chair and went to warm himself at the burning stove. 'When you take into consideration that she couldn't have children and knew it when she married Peter, and he did too, taking on the twins was *almost* an easy thing to do; it solved a lot of things for her, don't forget. A gift from God?'

Harriet was stunned by Jimbo's reaction to Caroline's decision. 'You've never said that before. I didn't know you thought like that.'

'Jimbo's right though, isn't he?' suggested her mother-in-law. 'It did solve a lot of things.'

'Yes, but all the same she had to face the fact that Peter strayed into another woman's arms.'

'Hardly surprising, Harriet. He's so utterly attractive it's a wonder they're not all queuing up still, even though he's in his sixties now,' Katherine reminded the two of them.

This remark of hers silenced Jimbo and Harriet. So she really was an up-to-the-minute grandmother then, thought Harriet. 'I think I'll join you and have a whisky,' she said.

Jimbo got up to get one for her and one for himself. How on earth were they managing to discuss something everyone in the village had kept secret all these years? He thought about the tabloid papers and what a sensation they could make nowadays of the fact of Alex and Beth's birth and he shuddered at the prospect. 'Fact nevertheless remains that she is going with that creep Morgan thingummy and going for a year and leaving Peter in our care.'

Katherine had downed her whisky in one go, felt slightly unsteady for a moment, and then said, 'Anyway, we're all right, aren't we, you and I? We're still friends, aren't we, Harriet dear.' Harriet nodded and Katherine smiled. 'Right, I'm going home now I've sorted that out.'

Harriet and Jimbo turned out the lights, put their whisky glasses into the dishwasher and went to bed, relieved they hadn't got a big family row on their hands.

Chapter 19

But that night, in the delightful Rectory sitting room, looking if anything more beautiful as the years passed, Peter and Caroline were still talking long after the Charter-Plackett household had made their peace with Jimbo's mother. Caroline had just said that nothing on earth was going to stop her going to the USA.

'Darling, please! I have said time and again that I am willing to move anywhere in Britain that will give you more variety, more life, more excitement than Turnham Malpas, that you can choose. I don't have to be a Church of England rector. I can write, teach, whatever, and you can do what you need to do ... whatever makes you happy. I want to see you smiling and vigorous and positive as you have been ever since I've known you.'

'Why do you still persist in trying to prevent me from going to America with Morgan? I'm not disappearing for ever, you know.'

Peter knew if he said what he sensed was beneath it all, it would be the end of their relationship for ever.

Caroline persisted with her declaration. 'There's nothing between him and me, nothing at all, I'm simply going as his research assistant and that is *all*. You're not an idiot, Peter. Why do you not understand? Surely you can take my word for it. I mean what I say.'

Before he could stop himself Peter answered her with the truth; it blurted out of his mouth and lacked discretion and understanding. 'He wants *you*.'

His blunt statement shocked her. 'Me? Now you really are being ridiculous. Of course he doesn't.' But at the same time as she said those last four words she knew Peter was right. Was it also obvious that *she* wanted Morgan? God in heaven, she thought, is it as plain to see as that? She was appalled, fingers tightly clenched, face grim, knees trembling with the shock of it all. She should have known. Peter had always been intensely sensitive about people's emotions; that was why he was so good at understanding people and their deepest desires. Had it come to this, then, that she was as guilty as Morgan in her needs? Was that why she so desperately wanted to get away from Turnham Malpas? It was boredom, wasn't it? It wasn't that she needed a complete and utter change. It wasn't that she was weary of the small place that had been her comfortable, blessed home, rich with life and totally rewarding all these last twenty and more years. She was blaming it on that and not on what it truly was: a sudden and tremendously unexpected desire for someone other than Peter. How could she? How could she? Whatever would the children think of her? Alex, high-principled and so like his father, would be appalled. Beth, well she was Beth, and she was beautiful in every way and still so innocent. Caroline knew she had to struggle to completely understand her own feelings. No more pretence. No more hiding her intentions. First and foremost, did she really want Morgan as her lover?

Looking intensely at Peter, Caroline could see the adoration in his eyes. His arms reaching out to hold her, willing to give his love to her so generously despite her waywardness at this moment. So here was the love of her life, offering her all he had to give, actually *begging* for her love. But she knew she had to be totally honest with Peter, because he would know instantly if she were pretending.

She slowly shook her head, refusing, for the first time in their lives to allow him even to touch her.

Chapter 20

The next evening in the Royal Oak the conversation, though subdued, was all about who would be the next owner of this pub which was the centre of their village life and had been for four centuries. The landlord was a prominent and very necessary ingredient of their pleasure. A few of the older ones reminisced about the ones they could remember.

'I can remember one landlord who dropped dead behind the bar one icy cold night,' Willie Biggs muttered. 'It was only the second time I'd been old enough to come in and order my own drink. Very strict they were in them days. He handed me my ale, I gave him the money, he opened the cash till to look for some change for me – and in two seconds flat he just collapsed. Dead as a doornail he was.'

Silence greeted this memory until Zack asked him if he ever got his change.

A roar of laughter lightened the moment, but the reply came back quick as a flash.

'No. It was clutched in his hand and no one had the courage to get it for me. I know I certainly didn't.' Willie stared into his glass of home brew. 'Nice chap he was. His wife was foul-mouthed, though, and nobody liked her for it.'

'Not surprised. I wouldn't want to be served by someone daft enough to think it a good idea. Not good for business that.' Those sitting on the old settle nodded their heads in agreement.

'Remember Bryn? Bryn Fields? Kept a lovely pub, he did, just such a pity he couldn't keep his hands to himself.' Willie recollected one or two landlords before his time that his dad used to talk about and had them in hysterics about their antics. 'I wonder who we'll get next.'

'Exactly,' said everyone gathered at the old table that could tell a tale or two if it could speak. Their conversation was halted abruptly when in walked Sir Johnny and Chris Templeton, ushering in front of them their wives. It was so unusual for the four of them to come in together that Sylvia, covering her mouth with her hand and averting her eyes from them, whispered, 'Surely it can't be them, can it? Them who want to buy it?'

Subdued laughter greeted this whispered comment and talking stopped completely while everyone present listened to them ordering drinks at the bar. Georgie and the new girl they'd temporarily employed because Dicky was still under doctor's orders and thus unable to do a long day behind the bar, scurried about to ensure they got good service and would be pleased by their visit.

The four of them squeezed on to the table by the huge log fire, Johnny and Chris pulling up two extra chairs from another table. All four of them waved or nodded towards people they knew and to anyone who offered them a greeting. They toasted each other and Chris gave Deborah a kiss on her cheek and she thanked him, they noticed, by gently resting the palm of her hand on his cheek for a moment. Anyone able to see this loving gesture smiled indulgently. How he'd changed, that Chris. So different from the chap who'd first come here, thinking the world admired his every misdeed. That Deborah had been brave marrying him! What a risk she'd taken and not half, but now . . .

Soon the four of them were allowed to converse without constant supervision from almost everyone present in the bar. Then, after about fifteen minutes, the manager in the restaurant came through to advise them that their table was ready for them in the dining room and they left the bar, a fact that enabled everyone to discuss them.

'Lady Alice is beginning to show now, isn't she?' said Marie, now allowed in the bar after being banned for a week for thumping Dicky with Zack's tankard.

'Yes indeed – but do they know if it's a boy or a girl then?' asked Pat, here on one of her rare visits to the pub.

Marie told everyone who wished to listen that they had decided not to find out whether the baby was a boy or a girl. 'I understand they want to enjoy the surprise, like back in the old days.'

'Be nice if it was a girl,' Greta stated. 'But I expect it'll be as loved like them two boys are, whatever it is. Let's hope it'll be perfect like what we all want when we have children, eh?'

'Definitely. Remember little Roderick? That was terrible. I don't think Sheila ever got over it. Lost all that weight was 'cos she was sad about him dying.'

'You're right there. His problems were terrible, though. A nurse I know in the maternity unit said it was criminal that such children can go full term in these days of X-rays and scans and whatever.' Greta Jones paused for a moment and then added, 'Yer see, they can work such miracles nowadays, but some kids are born so damaged despite all the technology. Makes yer wonder if . . .'

'What? Makes you wonder what?'

Greta shuffled uncomfortably and eventually said, 'Makes you wonder if someone did for him, like . . .'

Puzzled, Marie had to ask her what she meant. 'You don't mean . . .' she said and gestured as though cutting a person's throat.

Greta, reluctant to put into words what she had always thought, said, 'Well, not that but something. Like . . . you know . . . smothering.' She whispered the last word, hoping no one was listening in to what she said.

'No! But then that's . . .' Marie, shocked beyond belief, whispered, 'murder!'

'I know, and that's what I mean. Murder. Rather than wait to watch everything that modern science can do to help him to live maybe someone just finished him off to save him having to go through all the operations and that, and perhaps still not be all right. At the time I never thought about it, then I watched this programme about handicapped babies and how they can operate on them and that, and that was when it occurred to me.'

Marie was appalled when she fully realised the implications of what Greta was saying and whispered, 'You mean Sheila Bissett, the late *Lady* Bissett, a stalwart of the WI, chairwoman of the village church Flower Club, the wife of someone who's been on *TV* would do *murder*? I don't believe it and don't you talk about it any more. It could be *libellous*. Then it'd be you in prison!'

Greta, in her own head, knew she shouldn't have voiced her opinion, so she shut up quick smart and changed the subject to discussing the weather in Canada in winter and decided she'd keep her opinions to herself from then on. But she still believed there was an element of truth in what she'd surmised, even if it was unbelievable.

At this exact moment, in walked Ford and Merc. They went straight across the bar to the counter and spoke softly to Georgie. No one other than Georgie could hear what they said but in a moment the two of them, Ford and Merc, went into the dining room.

By coincidence, Greta said she needed the loo and off she went through the dining room to see with her own eyes, which was what she intended, that Ford and Merc were sitting at the same table as the Templetons. So ...

When she returned to her seat on the old settle they were deep in conversation about cricket and why Australians were so good at playing cricket and, though desperate to reveal this interesting piece of news she'd just observed, she had to wait, and wait, and wait. Men and cricket! Frankly, Greta didn't know why men found such a lot to say about it. It was tedious, boring, slow and complicated, to say nothing about the absurd rules. Finally, after two attempts at interrupting them, Greta was able to tell her tale.

'And there they are, together on the same table. I ask you why? Now why?'

Stunned though they were by this curious collection of people having a meal together, it didn't stop them speculating.

'Perhaps they're moving away I heard Merc saying the other week that Ford was bored with nothing in particular to do every day. He was used to a busy life, she said.'

Barry said, 'Apparently, though he does a lot of work for the village Youth Club, it isn't enough to keep him busy and that's what he likes. I was talking to her Bonfire Night and she said he needed something to get his teeth into. So I suggested trying scrap metal again, lot of money in that I understand, if you get stuck in with a will.'

'Ha!' said Willie as he banged his tankard back down on the table to emphasise his point, 'maybe a stretch in prison for whatever it was – except it wasn't, 'cos he got let off – has made him wary of trying that again.'

Barry nodded. 'Exactly. But it is odd. Do they look comfortable together? No arguing or nothing?'

'When I went past it was Chris who was doing the talking. I heard the word "experience" but that was all.'

'Mind you, if it's the pub they're talking about Merc would be lovely as a landlady.' Sylvia observed. 'But why should Johnny and Chris be involved? I ask you.'

'Maybe it's a job for Ford they're talking about. That could be it, with all their business interests there might be something for him to do, you never know,' suggested Willie.

'I reckon they'll be off to Brazil before long,' offered Marie. 'Nice cushy job for Ford and Merc with her colourful ideas'll fit in beautifully. Her ideas are brilliant for our embroidery work. Any question about colours and Evie always asks if Merc agrees with what Evie has in mind.'

Everyone sitting round the table decided that Marie was

absolutely right, it could be the only explanation for them having a meal together. Yes. Brazil it was and their house would be up for sale.

Willie, being more than usually alert tonight, then had an even bigger explanation.

'You've got it wrong, I'm afraid. Very wrong. I bet Sir Johnny is wanting to buy houses in the village to rent out like old Fitch did with Little Derehams. You don't need me to remind you that old Fitch owns every single house in Little Derehams now, except for Gilbert and Louise's who've always refused his offers, and Sir Johnny'll intend to be the landlord living in Turnham House like it used to be for centuries. The only change of ownership is that Louise and Gilbert exchanged houses with her dad because his house was larger. Templetons in the big house and us poor critters in the little houses paying rent to him all our lives. Doomed to be slaves, we shall be. Doomed. Obligated to Sir Johnny for ever, us and our descendants. Sir Jonathan Templeton, Lord of the Manor of Turnham Malpas. This is just the beginning of a trend in Turnham Malpas, mark my words.' Willie stared gloomily into his tankard of home brew.

There was silence after this weighty speech by Willie. Could he be right?

'Well, he has enough money to pay whatever price is asked so he won't care if you ask an exorbitant price, he'll buy it. But don't forget all them house owners in Little Derehams got paid a substantial amount of money in the first place by old Fitch,' Barry declared. 'Remember them that lived in that house that looked like a pepperpot, on the corner not far from the old prison that Fitch restored? They had a round-the-world cruise on some of the money they got for their house. They paid rent ever after, I know, but it was a ridiculously low rent.' When he'd finished speaking, Barry spent a moment wishing he didn't live in a tied house that went with his father-in-law Greenwood's position as head gardener.

Having decided that Willie's perceptive explanation was the right one after all, they all of them sitting round the table decided on another round, unsure whether or not they liked the idea of being slaves.

But they did note that the six of them, Johnny and Alice, Chris and Deborah, and Ford and Merc, went to shake Georgie's hand before they left after their meal. Was that significant?

Very possibly Willie was right about the Lord of the Manor idea ... or was he?

Chapter 21

In Turnham House during what was left of the evening Chris and Johnny sat discussing business. 'You see, Chris, you would have something to keep you busy. Being without an objective can make life very tedious. I have plenty of things to be doing, even if it does look as though I sit about with nothing to do, and I wouldn't intend you just having the one village pub, I'd like us to have an empire. Say what they might about them being in decline, the English will always want them whatever anyone in their glossy office up in London might say. They are the life and soul – well, perhaps not soul exactly – but they are the *heart* of the village. Where else would all those people be assembled on a Tuesday night if not in the pub? In villages they need a pub without doubt. Of course there's the youth club once a week, the embroidery group once a week, several exercise groups of one kind and another, but where is there just for socialising? OK, occasionally there is the church hall where things take place, but not *every* night. Pubs are essential to the life of the village. Take that away, sell the premises to be turned into a house, and all that camaraderie has gone.'

Johnny made a sweeping gesture and accidentally knocked a small vase of flowers on to the floor and also a pile of papers that fell into the water spilt from the vase as it tipped.

'Blast it!'

Between them they cleared up the mess, rescued the papers, and settled down to discuss Chris's future.

Chris contributed the comment: 'Until now I've done nothing

since I came to live here. Absolutely nothing, and it's time I got a move on. But do you honestly think that Merc and Ford are the best people for the job?'

'Yes, I do. He has a sharp business brain and he ran a pub for several years before he turned to scrap metal and he's excellent with people. And his big asset—'

'You said it, not me,' declared Chris.

Johnny laughed. 'Well, she *is* big in more ways than one. Lovely temperament for a pub – you agree with that, don't you?'

'Yes. But Johnny, I know he got off that prison sentence but was he really as innocent as he claimed? There's a million ways with scrap metal to make money. I knew a fellow back in Rio—'

Johnny raised a hand to stop a flood of stories about fraud. 'He genuinely was innocent of that charge, honestly. We may have difficulty getting him made landlord, but there are ways and means, you know.'

Chris pretended to be horrified. 'Not a big brown envelope? I'll be delighted to deliver it to the council offices.' They both laughed.

Johnny recovered first. 'Does Deborah like the idea of you starting up a chain of Templeton pubs here in England?'

Chris nodded. 'She does indeed. She hasn't approved of me having nothing in particular to do every day. Great believer in hard work, is Deborah, even if you don't need to struggle to find the money for your daily bread. Bit puritanical, she is. She *loves* the idea.'

'Has she told you why she goes away for three or four days every month yet? Or is the time not ripe for the truth. Alice—'

'I know what Alice thinks. But I do believe that if we decide on this Templeton pub empire and I'm in charge and show promise, she will tell me. Something to do with my reliability. Needs to be sure of me.'

Johnny raised a questioning eyebrow. 'Who'd have imagined that Chris Templeton, of all people, would at last begin working for his money instead of just being good at spending it?'

Chris had to smile. 'Being married to Deborah has made me grow up, I suppose.'

'Right then. We'll go ahead with the pub! Welcome to the working world!'

Chris got to his feet and leaned across Johnny's impressive desk. 'We'll shake hands on it. Now I'm going to find Deborah and tell her what we've decided.'

'I don't want the pub's ambience changed in any way at all. Better organisation, strict accounts – things have slipped, I'm sure, since Dicky got thumped on the head, although Georgie's excellent, her attitude to the customers just right. Introduce new lines slowly and carefully and don't let anyone interfere in the recipe for the home-brewed ale. Keep a tight hold on the money and the rest will take care of itself. And remember, the village will already be bursting with gossip; I've learned they know before you do what's going to happen, so, be careful who you talk to until the sale is definitely signed and sealed. Not even a hint to anyone! Otherwise they will make us look not only silly but incompetent and that won't do. Right! Must press on.'

Chris found Deborah working in a part of the garden she had appropriated for herself. It was barely large enough to call a garden but she loved it. She'd bought an old stone garden ornament in a garden shop that specialised in them, a lady with a child clinging to her skirts, early nineteenth century and beautiful even if you weren't an artistic person yourself. The mother was about five and a half feet high and the child, aged about three, had long hair and a beautiful smile on her face, while the mother wore a charming brimmed hat to shade her from the sun. This was the centrepiece of her garden and Deborah hoped that one day it might look to be an image of her and a possible child of hers. This morning she was improving the quality of the soil. It was too late and too cold, to be planting – that would have to wait until the spring. Deborah heard footsteps on the gravel and knew

Chris had come to find her. Mentally she crossed her fingers. Had he or had he not chosen to run the new public house chain idea Johnny had come up with?

'Hello! Thought I'd find you here.'

'Where else? Do you like her?' She pointed to the statue.

Chris wandered right the way round the statue, studying every angle, and then finally replied. 'She looks like you, so yes, I like her very much indeed. And I like the child. I know all children wore dresses back then, but it is a girl, isn't it?'

Deborah nodded. 'I'm certain it is. Aren't they both lovely?'

Chris touched the hand of the child and casually remarked, 'Ever fancied one of these ... of your own I mean?'

Equally casually Deborah replied, 'In time, but not just one. I'm just one and I don't feel happy about it.'

'I see. Lots of people have to be because no more arrive.'

'I know. Of course I know, but for *me* ... do you think this garden is going to work out?'

'With you in charge, of course it will.' Chris grinned at her and the awkward moment passed. He was so much less determined to have his own way about every little thing, so much more relaxed. That mother of his had done him no good turn allowing him to have his own way so much when he was young. Nicholas and Jonathan must have hated him sometimes when they were boys.

'Have you decided, Chris?'

'About the pub idea? Yes. It's yes, if that's all right with you? Is it?'

Deborah got up off her knees and, looking straight at him, answered firmly, 'Yes. I know it means you won't be home every single day, because you'll undoubtedly be travelling about, seeking out new pubs for sale, but I'd rather that than have you bored to tears which is just beginning to happen. Isn't it?'

Rather surprised she was so close to him she even sensed his restlessness, Chris grinned.

'I'm right, aren't I?'

'You are. I shall enjoy building something new and I like achieving things. But don't tell anyone yet. Wait, as Johnny would say till, "it's signed and sealed".'

'Of course. Doesn't do to let the cat out of the bag too soon.'

'One day perhaps ...' Chris paused for a moment.

'Perhaps? What?'

'You might – might be able to tell me where you go every month. There should be no secrets, as Alice would say, between married couples.'

'We're getting there. Believe me. But don't mention it again. OK? It's my decision.'

'As you wish, Deb.'

She knew what a great deal that statement cost him. When they first realised how much each of them meant to the other he couldn't have said that even to save his life for he was convinced that his opinion was far and away more important than anyone else's. She replied, 'Love you more than anyone else in the whole world, Chris. Believe me I do.'

'Same here for me.' He waved a hand over the garden she was constructing and said, 'And this part of the garden will be the jewel in your crown, you know.' He patted the head of the child in the statue and smiled at Deborah as he left her to her garden.

What a change there was in his outlook. Once arrogant, confident and unbearable, now as she had said, he was the love of her life. One day very soon she would be able to trust him completely and then and then only would she reveal who and where she visited so frequently. But how would he react? Perhaps in his present mood he would laugh it off – or maybe not. Maybe the old Chris, who was still there, she supposed, would surface; and that would be the end of it for her and for him.

Chapter 22

The Christmas season came and went in a blur for Peter. He did as he always did: provided a church Christmas that excelled any that had gone before and they all, sinner and saint, rejoiced in his presence in their village. There couldn't have been a church anywhere in the country that had celebrated this Christian festival as thoroughly and as magnificently as they had in Turnham Malpas. Gilbert Johns, still choirmaster, had persuaded a youth choir that had excelled in a music festival in the county town to come and give an evening performance of Christmas music that involved not only singing carols but solo performances involving violins and wind instruments and even old English musical instruments from a collection owned by someone with a deep interest in youth and music. Everyone who attended loved each joyous moment.

The centre of the village had been turned into a fairy light paradise because every house in the immediate vicinity had gone to excessive effort to smother their homes in swathes of lights. The church even had fairy lights on the spire right from the top, reaching down to the entrance. On Christmas eve all the cottages in the village put the lights on in every room and opened the curtains so that their decorations were on view to everyone who walked by. So delighted were they by the response to this idea that most of them did the same after dark every day until Twelfth Night.

After reading about the idea in the local paper, dozens of people came from far and wide to walk round the village just to see the lights. It certainly put Turnham Malpas on the map. Georgie, for a whole week, had the most splendid time serving more customers than ever before; some came for a meal, on a 'we might as well' basis while others thronged the bar for a sustaining drink before heading home.

Peter put on a pretence of enjoying Christmas but inside himself he was distraught. He counted the days off in his diary to remind himself that Caroline was, very shortly, leaving, and most likely never coming back. She hadn't taken up his idea of the two of them leaving Turnham Malpas and going to live somewhere else more pleasing to her. In fact, she never discussed the next twelve months while Peter could think of nothing else. They were a man and a woman who didn't belong to each other any more. Parishioners came and went, some to sleep, some to eat, some to discuss their problems and needing Peter to cast a new, refreshing light on them, but the two who lived in the Rectory scarcely communicated.

Caroline worked out her notice at the hospital and devoted herself to making Christmas as delightful as possible for Beth and Alex and then, during the following four weeks, to sorting the Rectory out and planning for Peter's solitary life. Her heart hammered whenever she spoke to Morgan, which was quite often as they had a lot to plan.

Beth and Alex spent a curious Christmas. In the past this holiday had been a joy; this year it was more like a wake. Solemn, avoiding subjects such as, 'where will you be living, Mum?' Or, 'give me your address' and 'we'll need to Skype you too'. Worst of all was trying to keep their father involved and helping him as much as they could. But as far as the village was concerned Christmas was a triumph.

Beth seriously broached the idea of taking time off university and coming home to be with her dad, but he told her, very positively, that he didn't need her. It being the first time in all her life that he had rejected her she thought her heart would break.

'It's no good, Alex,' she said to her brother, 'he is quite simply devastated. Totally heartbroken. I can't believe she can treat him like this. What is the matter with her?'

Alex, equally concerned but not willing to participate in the whys and wherefores of this astonishing situation the two of them found themselves in, said, 'It will sort itself out. I'm sure. One can't love someone to bits most of one's adult life and suddenly not.' Then he remembered that girl in his first year at Cambridge whom he'd been convinced was the one for him and the pain when she dropped him after six months of passion. Maybe you could. It had hurt him. He remembered the hurt and thought of the hurt his dad must be feeling. He looked up from the breakfast table and saw his dad, as so often these days, was lost in thought. The pain registering in his whole being shocked Alex and convinced him he should try to stop what his mother was intending to do. No good asking Beth to assist him, because she'd go overboard emotionally the first moment she opened her mouth.

His mother needed a calm, sensible, sensitive discussion, not tears and passion and he was the man for the job. Sunday evening, that's when he'd catch Mum, after their evening meal when they were in the kitchen loading the dishwasher, just the two of them.

Peter retired to his study with, he explained, work to do ready for Monday morning. Beth, furious at being excluded from the plan Alex had outlined to her, had rung a friend from her schooldays and gone out to visit her.

As they finished, Alex said, 'I need a cup of tea, join me?'

It sounded more of a command than a suggestion but Caroline fell in with his idea because there was little else for her to do.

As they settled at the kitchen table, with Alex waiting on her, she said, 'Yes?'

'I know it's none of my business, but can you explain to me why you are going to the States with Morgan Jefferson? Really explain, not just tell me fibs to put me off. I'm old enough to need to understand, especially when I see how upset Dad is. He is devastated and you've not even gone yet, so what he'll be like when you do go I can't begin to imagine and Beth and me ... well, we can't be here to help him because of university. He's trying so hard to be cooperative and kindly but ... Mother, just explain, please. It's more than just boredom, isn't it?'

When Alex used the word mother instead of mum, Caroline knew he meant what he said. Very definitely. He needed answers.

'It's not what your dad thinks; I'm not going because Morgan is looking for an affair. We're just old friends and he needs someone compatible he can trust to help with the research. That's all. Absolutely all,' Caroline said, willing herself to believe that what she was saying was true.

'Well, of course, I know you, of all people, aren't going to leap into bed at the—'

Caroline leapt to her feet, 'Alex! Of all the things to say to your mother. I'm really angry that you should even think such a thing.'

'Mum! If you could see your own face when you talk about him it would be the only conclusion you could come to. Because your attraction to him is written all over it. And that's the truth. That's what Dad sees when you speak of Morgan. How about that for breaking his heart, eh?' Alex stood up. 'I've said all I'm going to say because I've got my answer. And I can tell you now it's not only me who is concerned: Beth is horrified at what you're doing.' He turned to leave the kitchen, his mug of tea disregarded.

'Alex! Come back!' But Alex ignored her, roaring out of the kitchen as though pursued by wild animals. He reported to Beth later and the two of them agreed they'd leave first thing in the morning, then Beth was overcome by her love for her father and immediately changed her mind. 'I can't leave him, not till I have to. He needs someone to care about him, and I don't mean making cups of tea.' She went to stand at her bedroom window, looking out into the darkness towards Turnham House.

'I love this view, you know, really love it. It's the best view in the world. In the daytime, that is, of course. I've never known any other, apart from college. If they part I may not see it again.' She turned to look at Alex. 'Do you think they will?'

'It won't be Dad's fault if they do. But if that's what she wants ... well, he'll give in to please her.'

They heard footsteps on the stairs. It was their father. 'I've got to go.'

Startled by his statement, Alex jumped to the wrong conclusion. 'You've got to go? Where?' asked Alex.

'Unfortunately it's Craddock Fitch. He's dying, and his son Michael has asked me to see him. Can't go dressed in mufti. That's not what people expect. Just get changed. I'll say goodnight in case I'm not back for a while.' Peter turned away to go in to his own bedroom, 'Goodnight, the two of you. And remember, your mother is doing what she needs to, that's all, and I'm going to be well looked after with Dottie helping, so don't the two of you worry. Right! See you in the morning.'

That night Peter only got three hours sleep because it was half past two by the time he got home again from Nightingale Farm, then it took ages for him to get to sleep. If ever he got called out in the night in the past he'd known he could get to sleep with Caroline's arms around him, because she could always soothe his cares away. Now that they were sleeping alone, it took Peter a while to relax. His anxieties about his marriage, his sadness about the death of old Craddock Fitch – such a tempestuous figure in the history of the village – all made his mind refuse to be at peace. Peace! When would he ever feel peaceful again?

Chapter 23

Peter still followed the same pattern of running three miles each morning, the same paths, the same speed as always. He knew all the variations of the seasons: where and when to look out for the bluebells in Sykes Wood, the wild orchids that appeared every year around the footbridge over Turnham Beck, the buttercups that flooded the field with bright yellowness as one passed where the Beck suddenly appeared out of the ground. He knew when the Beck was most likely flooding, he knew when and where he might meet other runners getting their exercise.

What was most unlikely was meeting Sir Ron Bissett as he had done yesterday morning. Poor Ron. It was obvious to everyone who knew him that losing Sheila had been a terrible shock. Suicide. It couldn't have been worse. He still refused to have anything to do with his daughter Louise and her children: grand-children he'd been so proud of since the day they were born. As for Gilbert, Louise's husband, a son-in-law Ron had admired for years, he simply did not exist as far as Ron was concerned. Worst of all, for Peter, neither did he. Since Sheila died he'd tried his best to make sure he saw Ron at least once a week but he was not allowed to. The door of Ron's cottage was closed to Peter.

But now, two mornings in succession, he'd met Ron no more than five yards from his very own front door in Little Derehams. All Peter got was a hesitant nod of recognition and for an entire week this pantomime was repeated. Finally Peter decided something had to be done about it. There he was again now. Peter reached out and took hold of his arm and stopped him dashing inside the house without a word, and said loudly and abruptly. 'Good morning, Ron. How's things?'

Challenged like this, Ron stuttered, 'I-I need a word.'

'Right now?'

'Right now.'

'I'll come in then, shall I?'

'Yes, please.' Seen close up, Peter saw that Ron was under-nourished, seriously undernourished.

Peter kicked off his muddy trainers and followed him in. The house was terribly neglected. Peter remembered how fastidious Sheila had been with her housekeeping. She'd be so embarrassed if she could see the sitting room now. Newspapers left where Ron'd sat to read them, used cups and plates and knives and forks needing a trip to the dishwasher, the ironing board piled high with clothes awaiting his attention. 'A cup of tea would be welcome. Have you had breakfast yet?'

Ron shook his head.

'Let's get it together then, shall we. You and I? Long time no see.'

'That's right.' Ron pushed a heap of dishes in need of attention to one side and got out Sheila's very best set. Nothing too good for this man, the keeper of all their guilt and their good turns.

They ate their breakfast in the kitchen, a fact which Ron knew would have given his Sheila heart failure had she witnessed it. He often thought she did know what he was doing, for a regular phrase or a quizzical look of hers came into his mind all too often.

'Ron, I know losing Sheila must have been a shock for you as it was for all of us, but she, of all people, wouldn't have wanted you to retire from life so completely. There comes a time when you need to accept it and need to take up the cudgels again.' Peter remained silent while Ron took his advice on board.

'You don't know the half of it, Peter. I don't want Sheila's memory be-besmirched by scandal.' Ron looked deeply into

Peter's eyes. 'How can I look our Louise in the face and more so, Gilbert in the face, knowing what I know, what no one else knows?'

Cautiously Peter asked, 'What do you know that no one else knows?'

Ron stopped chewing his toast, swallowed hard, and when his gullet had dealt with it he said, 'I've never spoken to anyone about what I know. No one knows but me, what Sheila did, and why she did what she did to end it all.'

Peter felt relief. Now was the time for truth. So Ron'd known all the time, had he? 'At home, in my study, locked away, I have a letter from Sheila that she posted to me the day before she died, justifying her actions. Apologising.'

Ron took a long drink of his tea and the cup rattled loudly as he put it back in its saucer. He wiped his mouth on the serviette, no, sorry, 'napkin' as Sheila always insisted upon calling it. 'You know the truth, then?'

Peter agreed he did.

Ron almost looked happy. He bit off another piece of toast and chewed it slowly.

Peter remained silent. What does one say in such circumstances when a man confesses his wife committed murder? He struggled to remain calm.

Ron looked him in the face, drops of sweat beginning to appear on his forehead. 'I shouldn't have done it, Peter, it wasn't for me to do it, but I did. No real human being could have allowed that travesty of a baby to have lived.' His voice trembled and shook. His hands did too. 'It's all very well these medical people saying we could do this and do that and then the other to give him a reasonable life! Maybe even get him walking. Huh! They don't have to live that life, but the parents do and the brothers and sisters do, and the grandparents. *They* live that dreadful appalling life, and less than half a life he'd have had with all the things that were wrong with him. He was already dead when Sheila used the pillow. I'd done it minutes before she did. She was so upset she didn't realise he was already dead. I watched her, and to my eternal shame I allowed her to blame herself. Neither of us spoke one word about it to each other. Not a single word. Absolutely taboo, it was. As if it had never happened. But it wasn't her, it was *me*. The machinery should have gone to alarm mode so that the whole hospital knew there was an emergency with it, and I was prepared for that. I thought, "When the alarm goes off I shall walk out with the police full of righteous dignity." But it never did. There was a fault with it, a blinking fault, a simple technical fault, and it saved me from going to prison so I never said a word. Not a word. And the hospital – no one there's ever let on. I think they ... no, I *know* they knew, I'm sure they did, but they kept mum. But it saved Sheila and me from ...'

A long silence followed this critical statement.

Over the years Peter had faced some hard-edged moments in his career but this ... well, this ... Ron picked up the teapot. 'More tea?'

'Yes, please.' Peter pushed his cup across the kitchen table.

'More toast?'

Peter shook his head.

'We saved that child from a life of torture, of operation after operation. His brothers and sisters from years of caring. His parents from agonising lifelong responsibility for bringing him into the world damaged as he was. It's all right for the scientists to feel proud of their skills, to gain international respect for what they have done, but they are not living *his* life, day in, day out. If it could be called a life, that is. Roderick his name was going to be. Roderick.' Tears began to fall down Ron's cheeks. Long, slow tears that he endeavoured to control but couldn't.

Peter cleared his throat from the emotions he was feeling and made a suggestion.

'Can I ask Louise or Gilbert to come and sit with you a while?'

'I can't look them in the eye. So, no.'

There came a knock at the door. Ron didn't move so Peter went to open it. It was Alex on his bike. 'You were so long I came to look for you, Dad. Knew your route and then saw your trainers.' He pointed to them laid outside Ron's door. 'All right, are you?'

'Yes. Tell Mum I've had breakfast with Ron. Won't be long now.' Peter smiled reassuringly.

Alex took the hint. 'OK then, I'll be off home. Bye, Dad.' He hesitated for a moment, not wanting to leave him without some support in the circumstances.

'Off you go, everything's fine.'

Alex cycled off and Peter almost wished it was himself heading home. Who should he ring for help? The only person Ron would tolerate was Chris Templeton. Ah! Right. Of course. He'd ask Ron if that was all right. Though Chris Templeton didn't seem to be quite the right sort of person for this particular situation.

Everything's fine ... Fine? Who was he kidding? Life wasn't fine for him nor for Alex and Beth, and it certainly wasn't fine for Ron at the moment.

'Ron,' he said, 'would you like Chris Templeton to come and visit? He always cheers me up.'

'It's not Thursday so he won't come. It's always Thursday when he comes.'

'I'm sure he would come today. Nowadays he's that kind of a chap, even when it's not Thursday.'

'No. He comes on Thursday to bet on the horses.'

'Yes, I know, but we could always try him, couldn't we? On the off chance he's free.'

'No.' Ron stood up. 'I'll clear up. Off you go. I know you're busy. Sheila loved you, you know. Thought the sun shone out of you, she did.'

'And I was fond of her too. Always so loyal, was Sheila, so pleased to help in any capacity. Would you like to read the letter she sent me?'

Ron slapped the milk jug down on the tray. 'No! Thank you, Peter, but best leave her where she is, in my heart, not in a letter to someone else.'

'Fine. Before I leave shall I ring Chris?'

'No. Thanks. And you do what I forgot to do, tell that wife of yours you love her. They need reassuring about that and I never realised all the years we were married. Tell her, whenever you can. Immediately, right now. Tell her how much you love her. Sheila would like that. And thank you for coming for breakfast, I enjoyed your company.'

'Can I call in another day, perhaps, and have breakfast? If you want me to.'

'You caught me on a good day; sometimes I have nothing for breakfast, too much of a recluse some days to want to leave the house.' Ron smiled and waved at him to remind him to leave.

Just before he shut the front door Ron shouted, 'Don't forget to tell her how much you love her, tell her Ron said that you should actually *say* it.'

'OK!'

So when he got home Peter did tell Caroline how much he loved her and told her to come home whenever she wanted, because he needed her like he needed no one else. His arms would always be wide open for her, waiting for her to come into them if ever she was in need of him. 'Believe me, Caroline! I love you, every inch of me loves you, so do what you have to do and then come home where you belong. Right? You will for ever be welcome, and deep down you know that, don't you? Believe me, one year, two years, a decade, however many years you are away I shall welcome you home with every fibre of my being. I can't say any more than that, can I? You go with my blessing, when you go.' He gently stroked her cheek with his hand and smiled.

Caroline looked at him so gratefully that Peter had tears in his eyes with the emotion her honest gratitude brought about. She was so grateful for his acceptance of her decision that she couldn't speak. Why she needed his approval she couldn't analyse, but having got it she realised she most certainly did need it. She mouthed the words 'thank you' and walked away before she completely broke down in front of him. He was so much better a person than she would ever be.

Peter stopped twice at Ron's house, after that. Once he got breakfast, the other morning Ron apparently had been up all night, unable to relax into sleep. He looked ghastly, said he'd nothing in the way of food for breakfast, sorry. So Peter carried on with his run but Ron stayed at the front of his mind so, when he was showered and dressed and had his breakfast, he drove straight to Ron's house in Little Derehams. As he parked the car he sensed a strange loneliness surrounding the house. Ringing the bell brought no reply so he was instantly pleased at the idea that Ron must have gone out. Just to make certain he went round the back and, shading his eyes, he peeped in the kitchen window. What he saw shocked him to the core. Surely not! He changed his viewing angle but found he was still certain that Ron was laid on the floor, almost under the kitchen table. Signs of breakfast having been consumed littered the table but what made his nerves scream was the blood on the floor. He tried the back door and found it locked; so too was the front door and, being winter, there was not a single window open, neither upstairs nor down.

Luckily his mobile phone was fully charged and he rang the sergeant in the police house in Penny Fawcett.

Three rings and a voice said, 'Sergeant Lloyd speaking. How may I help?'

'It's the rector speaking, Nick. Peter Harris. I'm in Little Derehams at Honey Cottage, the one on the corner just before the restored prison house. Ron Bissett's house. I rang the bell and there was no answer, looked in the kitchen window, the doors are locked, and, well … come as quick as you can, and you'll need an ambulance, OK? There's a body.'

'Five minutes, Rector. That's all. I'll be there.'

Peter heard the phone click. As he was putting his phone back in his pocket he discovered he was shaking from head to foot. He'd never found a body before. Usually when he was called in they were neat and tidy, in bed, covered up. Respectable. Still. Waiting the final rites. But this time – this time the terrible, appalling sadness of a suicide was there for all to see. What had Ron done? All that blood? Cut his wrists?

A neighbour called over the back fence. 'Peter! What's up? Couldn't help hear your voice on the phone because I'm laying a new path along the foot of this dividing wall. Didn't intend eavesdropping. Is it Ron?'

Peter nodded.

'Well, it couldn't be anyone else could it?'

Peter shook his head.

'Shall I come round? I haven't got a key though.'

'Nick's coming asap.'

'If you need any help I'm working here.'

'There's an ambulance coming as well as Nick.'

'Well, I shall be here till lunchtime – complicated doing a crazy-paving path - if you need help. He's not been too good the last few days. Been friends for years but he's cut us off completely lately, says we can't help with his troubles at all. But a problem shared ... Still, there we are. Sorry and all that. They've been good neighbours. Good morning.'

'Good morning.'

Nick, the sergeant, must have broken all the traffic rules because he was already getting out of his van and with a police van parked outside everyone would know there was trouble at Honey Cottage.

Sergeant Nick had the kitchen door open with three swift thuds of his large shoulders.

Peter delayed going in until Nick had tentatively checked Ron's pulse. 'You're right, sir. Cut his wrists halfway through eating his toast. No need to come in if you're feeling squeamish.'

'Not squeamish, just very sad. I'll come in and say a prayer if I may.'

'Avoid the blood, please. I'll leave you to it then. I'll just be outside if you need me.'

Peter stood by the table where he'd eaten his breakfast barely two weeks ago and prayed for Ron, then he went outside.

Sergeant Nick was making notes. 'Thank you for the prayers, sir. Nice man. First his wife and now him. Whatever was wrong with them both?'

'Known only to God, Nick.'

'Ah! Right.'

A head bobbed up over the neighbouring wall. 'I can hear the ambulance. It's almost here. Suicide is it? Or a heart attack? Eh?'

Sergeant Nick answered quickly. 'We're not doctors either of us, sir, we'll have to wait for the Coroner's verdict.'

'The bowling club'll miss him, one of their star players he used to be till Sheila died.' The neighbour leaned on the dividing wall. 'Since she died he's been hopeless. I swear he hasn't been eating enough. Could be that. Malnutrition. Poor old chap.' He was clearly longing to hear any gory details to pass on to his wife.

Peter remembered the practical side of suicide. 'Nick. You have my telephone number, don't you? And my mobile, so let me know if you need a witness. You know where his daughter lives, don't you?'

'Mrs Gilbert Johns. I certainly do. I'll be in touch if you're needed, sir. Thank you for your help.'

Peter answered by saying he would stay till the ambulance took Ron away.

'Just as you wish, sir.'

'I say, is there a lot of blood, then?' asked the neighbour.

Sergeant Nick turned his back on the neighbour, not wishing to be drawn into any explanations of what they had found.

★

Peter went back to the Rectory to find Dottie waiting for him. 'There's been three phone calls, Reverend. I've made notes for you and I'll make sure to leave you some lunch on a tray before I go. But has something happened? You look very strained.'

'It's Ron Bissett, Dottie, he's ... well, I don't know for certain till the post mortem, but well, it looks as if he's committed suicide.'

'Oh no! You found him?'

Peter nodded.

'That was unfortunate. Still, better for a friend to find him than some nosey old neighbour, making a sensation out of it. Got the police in?'

Peter nodded.

'I'm sorry you had that to face. Poor old Ron, he's been useless since Sheila died. Poor chap, couldn't cope without her, I suppose. Well, anyway, there's post for you and one that's been delivered by hand. Shall I bring your lunch into the study when it's time, Reverend?'

'Yes, please, Dottie.'

'I shall find some fruit and some cake too to finish off with. Cheese and tomato sandwiches? Bit of a shock, isn't it? Suicide? Not like a natural death at all.'

Dottie aware Peter wasn't in a chatting mood disappeared into the kitchen and set about the ironing. The poor man! As if he hadn't enough on his plate. She'd noticed on the calendar in the kitchen that there was only one and a half weeks to go before Caroline went off with that slimy toad named Morgan. She'd no time for him, she didn't. Not a single second, and what Caroline saw in the man Dottie couldn't begin to imagine. Well, truth to tell, didn't *want* to imagine. He was no good. And leaving the reverend, such a wonderful, wonderful, man, so kind, so considerate, so sympathetic – and so good looking. Really, she couldn't find any more words to describe him. Poor Ron Bissett, though; that family seem fated to face tragedy.

There, she thought, as she enjoyed making a good job of ironing one of Peter's shirts, that looks good; nothing but the best for the reverend she thought. Only her Maurice excelled him, though she didn't expect that anyone else would think that but herself.

He still looked upset when she carried the tray into the study.

'It was what he wanted, you know, otherwise he would still be alive. I expect he found that life without Sheila was too cold and bare to tolerate, even if she was a nag. Which she was. But now at least they are together in heaven ... aren't they?' she asked for reassurance.

At this moment in time Peter was not entirely sure that Dottie was right about that.

'Lunch, and you've to eat every single bit of it. Right? See you tomorrow.'

'Right! Thank you. This looks very tempting. The cake looks especially good.'

She smiled indulgently at him. 'My word! You've a sweet tooth, and not half. See you tomorrow. Bye!'

Despite his sadness, Peter enjoyed his lunch, checked his clock on the study mantelpiece, and reflected on how long that clock had belonged to him. It had been his mother's, then when she died it came to him, being the only child she had. It must have been at least a hundred years old. Gold, and a travel clock really, but it sat beautifully above the fireplace that rarely had a fire in the grate because of the central heating. The doorbell rang and there on his doorstep was Louise. He should have gone straight to her house. Blast!

'Busy are you, Peter, or do you have time to see me?'

'Of course I have. Come in, come right in. I was intending coming to see you, but I got delayed. So sorry about your dad, Louise, so sorry. But he was lost without your mother.'

She looked round the study, recollecting earlier times doing his letters for him when ... 'Still the same old study. It hasn't changed a bit, not one bit.'

'I don't suppose it has, Louise, you're right. I'm so sorry about your dad, my dear, it must be a terrible shock.'

'It was inevitable. It was the bitterness that killed him, you see.'

'Bitterness about what exactly?'

'About losing mother, though she'd been going downhill for a long while.'

'Can I ask you a question?'

Louise nodded in reply.

'She said she hadn't been seeing much of you the last time I spoke to her – was there any particular reason?'

'Something to do with Roderick dying, I think, but I never got to ask her because she wouldn't talk to me about anything serious, wouldn't let me near her. Do you know what it was? Exactly?' Louise looked him straight in the face, expecting the truth. Her mother, who'd doted on her all her life, suddenly breaking off communication and she honestly didn't know why.

But Peter failed to reply. It was something he couldn't – wouldn't – reveal. It could ruin the rest of her life and he wasn't prepared to do that.

And then he lied. 'I have no idea at all.'

'I have always expected the truth from you, always,' she frowned. 'It's a huge part of your make-up, being truthful. That's why I'm here today, right now. Wanting the truth.'

Louise waited a few minutes, expecting that eventually he would tell her but he didn't. She shrugged and then asked, 'How did his death come about? Sergeant Nick said he had to wait for the post-mortem.'

'That's correct, though it seemed to me he'd cut his wrists. But that's not official, of course. The post mortem will tell us.'

Louise looked around for a chair and plumped down on the nearest one. 'Oh my God. Neither of them have been the same since ... the same since, you know, the b-baby we lost. Little Roderick. Mother was heartbroken, just like Gilbert and I were. So was Dad. Genuine heartbreak. They've never been the same since then and neither have we. But both of them? I mean, *both*. It takes some absorbing, does that. I'm an orphan now. No mum. No dad. All I have is a brother who is a waste of space. He probably won't come to the funeral even, seeing as he didn't come to Mother's. Will it mean I'll do the same? Do you think so? Commit suicide?'

'No!' said Peter. 'You are as different as chalk and cheese to your parents. You're strong, you share the truth with Gilbert where in fact your parents didn't.'

'You discussed it with them? When?'

More lies. 'Your dad told me they didn't discuss things, not anything that was deep and hurtful. Told me one morning when I had breakfast with him.'

Louise was astounded. 'Had breakfast with him? When he wouldn't even see me nor eat the food I took round to him? Brought it all back, leaving it on the doorstep, didn't even hand it to me. That was cruel.'

'I'm so sorry, Louise, but he asked me to have breakfast so I did, felt I mustn't refuse for his sake. He seemed to need company that morning.'

'We'll have a funeral service for him but it's to be hushed up. I don't want a trail of trade unionists coming to it. They used him, and when he was no longer important to them, because attitudes had changed and they were trying to give the impression of being bang up to date, they shut off all communication and hung him out to dry, they did. That was cruel too. It hurt him badly. They didn't care if he lived or died, when he'd supported and worked for the union all his adult life and was so proud of its achievements and his contribution to it.'

'That must have hurt. I'm so sorry, Louise, about both of them, such a sad way to lose your parents.'

Louise stood up, obviously preparing to leave. 'I don't understand what triggered it all. One day I shall have to come again to ask you for the truth. Not yet, I know I can't cope with it yet, but I *know* you know the truth, and that's what I shall want from you when I'm ready to hear it. Thanks, Peter, for your time. Always had great respect for you. Always. Bye!'

Peter went to his study window and watched Louise begin crossing the green. She paused for a moment by the pond and appeared to be watching the geese strutting in and out of the water, paddling back and forth. He saw her hand emerge from her jacket pocket, saw the quick glance round to see if she was being watched and the surreptitious wiping of her eyes with a crumpled tissue. Poor Louise. Yes, she'd have to come to him and ask for the truth herself, because only she would know when she was ready. If indeed she ever was ready for such pain. He recalled his lies. Sometimes, just sometimes, lies were the best in certain circumstances. But he still felt ashamed of himself.

Peter remained at the window looking out over the village for a while longer, contemplating all the unhappy incidents that had occurred whilst he was there. The longer he stood there the longer the list became. He did wonder at one point if maybe Caroline was right in wanting to move where interesting, amusing things were happening. Frequently. They hadn't all been unhappy times, though. What about the race afternoon when so many of them bet on that horse that won the Arc de Triomphe race, Major Malpas was it called? Or the midnight skinny-dipping in Jimbo's pool when the police turned up. Or the Morris dancing at the Village Show when two different teams were booked by mistake to do a display and it almost turned into a fight between the two teams. It was one incident after another that sprang into his mind and made him laugh. Nothing happens in this village? He loved this village like no other; they'd have to carry him from it in his coffin, because whilst ever he had breath he couldn't leave it. Well, he wouldn't leave in the end in any case, because he'd bought a grave right here in the churchyard. So he wouldn't leave it, for ever. Good! That sounded like Caroline's car. He looked at his little gold clock on the mantelpiece. She was early, very early for her. How unusual.

He heard the back door being energetically opened and suddenly, standing in his study doorway, was the love of his life. Caroline. They stood looking at each other. Not speaking. Then she broke the spell and walked in smiling. 'I've left early.'

'Yes, you have, I wasn't expecting you for at least another couple of hours.'

'I got this sudden feeling halfway through the afternoon that you were needing me. Were you?'

'I found Ron Bissett. He'd killed himself. Had to call the police etc., etc.'

Caroline frowned. 'No! Surely not. Oh, that family. I could never stand Louise after that time when she fancied you, but this? Her mother. Her father. And also the baby. It's too much to cope with, isn't it? Does she know the truth? About the baby? Have you told her?'

'She wants to know but not right now, she's too upset she said. But despite my lies she knows I know the truth and will come to ask me when she's ready, she says.'

'She's brave. Very brave. I admire her for that. It must be awful. Just straightforward dying is bad enough, but two suicides *and* the baby. So terribly sad.'

Briefly Peter could hear the Caroline of yore and he longed for a permanent return of the old Caro, but it wasn't to be.

'I've had an email from Morgan. The flight and the accommodation are all confirmed. He's paid for first class and refuses to allow me to contribute my share so . . .'

'You're off then . . . definitely. First class! My word. He must have pots of money.'

'Yes, except it's all been brought forward.'

'Brought forward?'

'Yes, we're leaving on Monday instead of a week on Friday.'

'This coming Monday? I see. Only four more days then.'

'Yes. Four days is nothing, now is it? I'm going, so there you are. I rang Dottie as soon as I knew, then she knows where she is. You'll be fine, Peter. Absolutely fine.'

'Of course, I shall.' He turned to look out of the window again as she left his study and thought about his two children still at university. Well, no longer children of course, but still in need of support and not just financial. They were braver than he, for they'd taken on the idea of their mother being so far away more easily than he had once they'd got used to the idea.

But he felt tumultuous inside. Torn to shreds ... The phone rang. 'Turnham Malpas Rectory. Peter Harris speaking.'

'Morgan Jefferson. Hi, Peter. Can I speak to Caro, please?'

He loathed the delighted expression on his wife's face as she came in to speak to Morgan and immediately left his study before he snatched the phone from her hand and smashed it to pieces.

Chapter 24

The four days disappeared in a flash. Alex came home to see his mother before she left, but Beth – partly because she couldn't face the thought that Caroline was definitely going and hadn't changed her mind as she had confidently expected she would – Beth knew her goodbyes would be grim and made an excuse that she had work to do that had to be handed in the morning of Caroline's departure and she couldn't afford for it to be late, she said.

Alex, who had known his mother wouldn't change her mind, had made up his mind not to make a fuss about her departure so was at home to see her off. 'You'll have a marvellous time, I'm sure of that, Mum. Make the most of it. Dad will be fine, what with Dottie coming four mornings a week and everyone in the village bringing him food and stuff to keep him going.'

Caroline smiled. 'Thanks, darling. I think you must be the only one who is cheerful about it. Grandmama Charter-Plackett has promised to keep an eye on him too – though I'm not sure if that's a good idea!'

They both laughed and Alex said, 'She will, you know. She's really very kind underneath all that bossiness. Though she doesn't approve of what you're doing, she said so.'

Surprised Caroline asked 'She did? When?'

'Last time I was home. Very anxious she was. I told her nothing untoward would happen but she wasn't too sure about that.' He grinned at her.

'Well, honestly, what does she think I am? That woman!'

Bravely Alex admitted the truth to her, thinking it was best if she knew how others felt about the situation. 'She only said what everyone else is thinking.'

'But to you! I shall tell her off next time I see her.'

'You won't, you're going in the morning.'

'Yes, of course, yes, I am. Is it tomorrow? It is.' An unexpected anxiety came over her. 'Ah! But I *shall* see her. There's a special coffee doodah after morning service to say au revoir to me, so I'll speak to her then.'

But the special coffee doodah never actually took place. It was one of those occasions when that strange, unspoken, unmention- able thing happened. When the village took up arms together without a word being spoken and moved as one. It had happened before, but this time there was a sinister feeling about it.

No one put the teapots out. Got the cups out. Unlocked the cupboard where the jars of coffee and sugar were kept. Brought the milk. Put the nice white cloths out that Craddock Fitch had bought specially for such occasions. Turned on the water heater. Not even the heating had been switched on. And not a single member of the congregation set foot inside the hall.

When Peter stood at the church door to say good morning to everyone they shook his hand, but Caroline, who was outside too, standing some distance from Peter was given only the oc- casional handshake and other people, very positively, marched home immediately. Peter was horrified, but there was nothing he could do about it. It had happened.

Alex, who had purposely stayed on for the service, felt the mood of the congregation, that strange mystical pull of anger, disapproval, dislike. And this time it was his mother who had brought it down on their heads. His own mother. He felt ashamed for his mother, pity for his father, and despair for himself.

Beth rang his mobile. 'It's me. Everything OK?'

Alex disappeared into the downstairs loo to answer her.

Beth was as concerned as he was when he told her what had happened.

'My God! Surely not? That strange moving-as-one-without-a-word-spoken thing? How dreadful of them. Mum has a right to go, if that's what she wants. Surely?'

'Well, apparently Beth, that's what they don't think. As far as most of them are concerned she shouldn't be going. Poor Dad. It was appalling, believe me. Zack went into the hall, thinking he'd have all the stuff for a coffee morning to put away, and he didn't. All he had to do was lock up because everyone, to a man, had gone straight home.'

'I'm glad I didn't come home, then, because I would have told them what I thought about them.'

'That would have been difficult. There was no warning it would happen, they simply all melted away. Dad's gone into his study and shut the door with a bang so we know what that means, don't we? I'm going straight back to college after lunch. Want a word with Mum?'

'Not right now. I'm working. I'll ring her tonight as I intended. OK? Sorry about it all. It won't have been *arranged* by everyone, you know, it just happens at moments of extreme disapproval. Bye, Alex. Safe journey back.'

The three of them had an almost silent lunch. Until, just as Peter had spooned the last of his Victoria sponge into his mouth, Caroline burst forth with, 'How dare they? How dare they? Have I no rights at all? Just because I am the rector's wife it doesn't mean every waking minute is dictated by them. How dare they? It was so shaming. Even Jimbo. He marched off too, and Harriet. I could expect nothing less than for Grandmama to follow suit, but Harriet! I would have thought she had more sense, more understanding.'

'They have a right to their own opinion, darling.'

'Oh! So you wish to have me tied hand and foot to the Rectory too, do you?'

'Whatever you say, whatever we do, they still have a right to their own opinion.'

'It's none of their business what I do! They didn't even discuss it. They just did it. They didn't even put the heating on. Zack told me. So they *knew*. Scorned me in front of everyone. It's a good thing I'm going. Oh, I'm so right to go. Wait till I tell Morgan. It's downright sinister what they do, it is.'

'I don't expect Morgan will care,' replied Peter.

He hadn't imagined for one moment that the comment he'd just made would bring down such a torrent of abuse on his head. Alex left the table, put his pudding dish and spoon in the dishwasher, and said in a loud voice to make himself heard, 'I'm leaving. This I will not tolerate!' He went upstairs to pack his overnight bag and then, standing in the kitchen door, said, 'I'm going now. Bye, Dad. Bye, Mum, have a good time in the States.' Whether his parents heard what he said he'd no idea, but then he left them to it. Life was intolerable. Thank goodness Beth hadn't heard them shouting – she would have been so distressed. But then, so was he and trying hard not to show it.

When Monday morning came, Peter and Caroline were still not speaking to each other. But that scarcely mattered as Caroline was waiting for Morgan to pick her up and Peter knew if he saw him he would have that terrible temptation to thump him right between the eyes, which common sense told him was ridiculous but he felt like that nevertheless. He was deeply unhappy. Deeply, deeply, unhappy. Never in all their years married had he and Caroline had such a tremendous row. In front of Alex too, that made it worse still. He shut himself in his study and resisted answering the phone. Whoever it was they could ring as often as they wished because he was unable to speak rationally to anyone at all. He'd answer after – yes, after – Caroline had left. The things they had said to one another were absolutely appalling, using words they'd never used before about each other. All the years of contentment fell apart during their row. It had all been a sham, apparently. He hid his face in his hands. How could he have said all those dreadful things? It was as if they were saying things about each other that had been stored up, repressed, all their married lives. So their marriage hadn't been the glorious experience he'd thought it was, it had been a massive pretence all these years, she'd said. And he blamed himself. It was all his fault.

The doorbell rang. Again and again. He'd better go. Being Monday, Dottie wasn't here and Caroline was upstairs doing her final packing. He stood looking at the group of people standing on the doorstep, his mind so confused he couldn't understand what they were doing there.

'Hi,' said the good-looking young woman who stood there, accompanied by four beautifully dressed children. The woman had an American accent. American accent? Who on earth were they?

'Hello! Can I help you in any way at all? I'm the rector, my name is Peter Harris and you are … ?

'I've come to see Morgy. He is here, isn't he, though I don't see his car?' She looked up and down the village green. 'Isn't he here then?'

'Morgy? Morgy? Oh! You mean Morgan Jefferson.'

'That's right. Yes. Larger than life and the biggest liar under the sun. Unfortunately, I'm married to him. Well, I hope I am, although there is always a chance I might not be.'

Peter stood there, his mind leaping about seeking an explanation. Morgan Jefferson? A wife and four children and, by the looks of it, another on the way? He felt he should ask her in, well, ask all of them in.

'Please, do come in.'

'Is he here? Or not?'

'We are expecting him any moment.'

'Off to the States leaving us behind, he thinks, but no siree. He goes we go. Oh, the children need the toilet so can we use yours while you pull yourself together?'

'Of course, of course. This way.'

'Caroline!' He called upstairs, whilst opening the door to the downstairs cloakroom. He switched on the light and called upstairs again, 'Caroline, we have company. Can you come down a moment?'

She stood for a moment at the top of the staircase looking down at what seemed to be a horde of visitors gathered in the hall. Somehow they looked familiar but yet they weren't, not at all. Slowly she came downstairs and smiled in turn at those still standing in the hall. The boys were ... but she couldn't think straight. Suddenly the woman reached out to shake her hand.

'My name's Marianne Jefferson. I understand my husband intends to work with you.' She broke off to reorganise the children needing the loo. 'Sorry we're such a crowd! He's not arrived yet, then? I have to be honest with you, I've found out he's off to the States for a year doing some research and he thinks he's going without us, but he darned well isn't! I know he's going with someone called Caroline Harris ...' Marianne looked hard at Caroline and then added, 'And I assume that must be you if *he's* Peter Harris?' She nodded towards Peter as she said this and then left a silence. The children picked up on the tension and remained completely silent, looking at their mother and Caroline in turn.

Caroline simply couldn't speak. Her tired mind, tired because she had lain awake for most of the night, was not functioning properly. Peter tried to explain but didn't know what he was explaining nor to whom he was giving the explanation. Surely to goodness they couldn't be Morgan's children and his *wife*? He had told them he had never married. Never.

Marianne continued staring at Caroline. Finally Peter spoke.

'My wife is going to America to work on a research project Morgan's in charge of to find a drug to replace penicillin. That's it in a nutshell. I'm right, am I not, darling?'

Caroline nodded.

'I see. Right. Oh, Morgan's the biggest liar this world has ever known!' Marianne folded her arms belligerently.

'You mean there is no research project?' Peter asked.

'Oh, yes, there is, but he's not in charge and he can't just pick someone from his past and drag them along, because he isn't the boss. He's saying he is because he wants to impress everyone, you two especially I imagine.' A sarcastic smile spread across her face. 'I've been married – how old are you, Chuck?'

Son Chuck sighed. 'Fourteen, as you well know.'

'Fifteen years to Morgan and I thought I knew every trick in the book about husbands but now I find there are even more tricks up his sleeve than I ever imagined. Damn him. Damn and blast him!'

'Mom, I'm hungry.' This was a plea from the youngest of the children and Peter immediately offered to take the children into the kitchen and give them something to eat. 'Give the two of you the chance to sort things out.' Before anyone had a chance to say no he was herding the children from the hall into the kitchen.

'Everyone sit down on a chair while I get sandwiches ready.' When they were all seated Peter began reciting the choices for sandwiches and they listened until he asked for answers and then a torrent of replies poured out from them. Chuck offered to butter the bread, a girl called Ellie offered to get the plates out and, before they knew where they were, they were all seated at the kitchen table with cups of tea, glasses of fruit juice and a pile of sandwiches to attack. Which they did. Peter then brought out two cake tins, took off the lids, and they all chose which cake they wanted and silence rained again. More drinks were poured and, as the last of the cake disappeared down Chuck's throat, the doorbell rang.

Chuck sprang into life again. 'Quiet, everybody, Mom's parked the car well down the road, so if that's Dad, he won't know we're all here. Not a word. Mind. Remember.' He pressed his forefinger against his mouth and even the youngest one knew exactly what was expected of him.

Peter was surprised at how silent and still the younger children sat. It was obvious to him they'd done this kind of thing before and he whispered to Chuck that he was leaving them and going into the sitting room.

When Peter entered the sitting room the look of dismay on Morgan's face was very evident. This was not what he'd planned! Caroline looked to have been struck by lightning, but Marianne, accustomed to Morgan and the surprises he sprang on her from time to time, looked entirely self-possessed. 'I've come, darling. You look surprised,' she said, smiling brightly. She checked her watch. 'We'll have to keep an eye on the time. We don't want to miss our flight, do we?'

Morgan couldn't or wouldn't speak.

'I booked our seats when I saw where you were going. Luckily first class was only three-quarters full. I hope the apartment you've booked is big enough for us all. Is it?'

Morgan still couldn't reply. He nervously flicked a glance at Caroline and was appalled by her expression. It was taut, disbelieving, horrified, all those things, and she looked as though she would collapse at any moment with the shock of it all. Blast it! Just when he thought he had worked out every little detail and thought Marianne was totally unaware of his escape plans. Who the blazes would want a bossy wife and four, soon to be five children, with them on a trip the like of which he had considered was the best idea he'd ever had. It had been so carefully planned. And such a wonderfully interesting woman to be going with. He tried a second look at Caroline and saw all his well-laid plans lay shattered by Marianne and her uncanny ability to read his mind. He could see that Caroline was devastated. Completely devastated. Her shocked expression was the one thing he couldn't bear to look at.

'Who's looking after the children, Marianne? Right now?'

'Who do you think?'

He saw the answer in Marianne's eyes.

'They're here? Oh! God! You've got seats for them too?' That was finally the end. 'How did you pay for them?'

'With my credit card, of course, what else?'

'Your credit card?' Not wishing to give the game away about the limited size of their bank balance – after all, he'd paid for his and Caroline's tickets too – Morgan laughed, saying, 'I have to give you credit, I really do.' He stepped round the coffee table which was all that prevented him from touching Caroline, and, intending to embrace her to soften the blow she'd received, he put a tender, sympathetic hand on her upper arm saying, 'I'm so sorry, Caro, so sorry it's turned out like this. I meant for it to be all wonderful, a terrific time together, just you and I and now ... Please, I'm so sorry ... But I imagined you'd realised ... You *must* have known a man like me would have a wife ... I mean, a man like me still unmarried ... it isn't likely I'd be a bachelor, now is it? Thought you'd be astute enough to—'

Caroline spoke for the first time, her voice harsh and unreal. 'Peter, take this man and his wife and his children out of this house immediately.' She paused, swallowed hard and added, 'Please.'

'Surely you don't ...' Morgan began.

Caroline finally found her normal voice. 'Right away, right now. Marianne, I'm sorry, so very sorry. I had no idea. None. He never said. I thought it was just the two of us. Being married to a monster must be an appalling situation to be in. You're so brave. So very brave.' She hugged Marianne with real feeling.

'Don't you worry about me. I know every move he makes. Trouble is, I love the brute, can't help myself.' She shouted in the direction of the kitchen. 'Chuck! Bring them out, we're leaving. USA, here we come! The entire,' she patted her bump, 'Jefferson family in one fell swoop. Is the USA tough enough to cope?' She roared with laughter. 'Watch out, America! I ain't done yet. Come on, kids!' She glanced at Caroline and, for a very short moment, Caroline saw the pain that lay behind Marianne's eyes and almost wept for her.

214

She avoided looking at Morgan because she knew if she did she would definitely be weeping in front of the children and that would not be right, for surely life for them had never been worse than at this moment. Their father abandoning them! So cheerfully, too. She could have killed him this very second with her own bare hands. Slow strangulation, very slow, was what he deserved for his hideous, selfish deception.

Just before Morgan slammed the Rectory door behind them all he turned to look at Caroline and flashed a pleading look at her, as though begging her sympathy, as though he was blameless and deserved her forgiveness.

Peter said nothing. He, of all people, knew how blatantly Morgan had scooped her up into his plans. How could he imagine he deserved her *sympathy*?

Caroline went into the kitchen to get away from any comfort Peter might offer, and surprisingly there was Dottie calmly clearing up. 'I'm sorry, I came to say goodbye to you and found all this.' She waved her hands over the crash site that was the kitchen table. 'Don't begin to explain. I won't say a word. Not a word. You do what you want to do and I'll have the kitchen tidied up in no time at all and when I go I shall go out through the back door. Right? The reverend won't even know I've been.'

With her back to Caroline, Dottie began stacking the dishwasher, emptying the leftovers into the waste disposal and wiping up the mess the littlest one had left on the table.

'Dottie! Many, many thanks. You've saved my life for me doing this.'

'Not me, doctor, it's the reverend who'll do that for you, save your life. Just go and talk to him; the man is beaten to a pulp, believe me he must be.'

'It was me that did that, to my shame. Bye, Dottie, see you tomorrow ... will I? Do you think?'

'If it's Tuesday tomorrow then you will, of course, that's one of my days, isn't it?'

They both heard the two cars drive off and felt relief at the sound.

Caroline went into Peter's study and found him sitting at his desk, staring into space. All he did when he felt her footfall was to hold out a hand to her. He was speechless.

They stayed silent, both of them speechless.

Finally, when Caroline heard the soft closing of the back door and therefore knew for certain they had the house to themselves she spoke.

'Peter! I need time to myself. I'm going to pack a case, just enough for three or four days, and I'll stay at that little country hotel we loved so much that time. Do you mind if I do that? I need time to think. First and foremost I am saying to you that I am not running away, I'm simply taking time off, to adjust. To see where I stand. Where I am. Indeed, *who* I am. And to examine how and why I let myself get taken in like that. I never suspected his sincerity at all, not for one second, that's what I cannot understand about myself. I have caused you endless pain and, what's worse, I didn't care that you were hurt.' She caught his eye and looked directly into his heart, for it was there for her to see: in his eyes his heart and soul were there. Why! He still loved her! How could he, after the way she'd treated him? How could he? But he did, she knew he did, just by looking at his face.

Dear God! She didn't deserve him. Could she, should she, take that huge gift of his love that he was offering her, still as pure and honest as the day they married? Did she want it? Did she deserve it? 'Peter! Oh! *Peter!*' She left his study without saying another word.

He could hear her speaking on her mobile to the hotel, businesslike, grateful, relieved. Sounded as though they had space for her.

She needed time to think.

He needed time to breathe.

★

Caroline left the house, her handbag and one small weekend case with her. The only person who saw her leave was Zack the verger, pruning a shrub that had grown so much it left very little space for anyone trying to squeeze through the lychgate. He paused, pruning shears in hand, gave a vague wave and wondered. Going on a wonderful adventure? I think not.

Chapter 25

'She's left. I saw her go.'

'With *him*?' Marie asked.

'By herself.'

'By herself? In her own car?'

Zack nodded. 'In her own car.'

'So, where was she going?'

'I don't know. She was off before I could ask. It was none of my business anyway, I couldn't have asked, now could I?'

Marie laid his plate loaded with food in front of him. 'Apple sauce?'

'Oh! Yes, please, pork needs apple sauce I always think.' He delved into his food, eager for it after a whole winter's day spent outdoors. 'Aren't you having some?'

'I think you never listen to a word I say. Not one word do you hear. I told you, it's Sylvia's birthday so we're having a girls' night out. We're eating in the pub and if I don't hurry I shall be late.'

Marie raced off upstairs to put on her newest dress and refresh her make up.

She clattered downstairs, put on her faux fur coat, struggled with her fur boots – she never remembered to put them on *before* her coat.

'Marie! You got enough money? I went to the bank yesterday.'

Marie kissed the top of his head and thanked him. 'Oh, lovely, glad you remembered. I'll be off then. Thanks!' She stuffed the notes into her purse. 'See you when I get back. I shan't be late, I don't suppose. Possibly I might find out what the situation is at the Rectory. At least, apparently, she hasn't gone with *him*.'

'Remember you're driving and don't drink too much.'

'I never do, driving or not.'

'Bye, then. Have a good time.' He stuffed his mouth with another of Marie's roast potatoes and thought how good life was to him. As soon as she'd gone he'd get the football on. Roast dinner accompanied by brilliant football, what more could a man ask?

When Marie arrived at the Royal Oak, Sylvia was there, organising their favourite table, counting the chairs and explaining to Georgie that she'd already ordered the food when she was in the other lunchtime. 'Dicky took the order.'

Rather than panic Sylvia and more so get Dicky into trouble, Georgie said casually, 'Of course you did, he said. I bet I can guess what you ordered. Your favourite?'

'Not this time. You know I always have chicken Kiev with all the trimmings, and it really is delicious but this time I decided to have a change.'

'My word, you're really pushing the boat out. The steak, was it?'

'Exactly, we all chose steak but Greta didn't want the chips, she wanted jacket potato instead. There we are, that looks lovely! Thanks for buying the flowers, Georgie, it's a lovely touch – Sylvia will be pleased.'

'They're for her to take home, of course, if she pleases.'

'I'm sure she will.'

At that moment the others all piled in, admired the flowers and chose their seats, Sylvia at the head of the table and the rest of them spread around the sides. Though they'd all been in the Royal Oak more times than they could remember it still felt special, and being all women they wouldn't feel obliged to talk football or cricket tonight; they could talk about anything at all.

'Well,' said Pat, 'here we are with no rector's wife for a whole flipping year. We shall miss her. Always so willing to offer to help.'

'And it doesn't matter what, even if it's the washing-up she helps. Nothing too lowly for her to get involved in. It's Peter I feel sorry for; he'll miss her and not half. So will we all.' This was Bel Tutt speaking, who on several occasions had consulted Caroline with her problems about should she, shouldn't she, marry her long-time lover, Trevor.

'Wish it was me floating off for a year with *my* lover,' said Maggie, rather too loudly.

Very acidly for her Evie answered. 'Lover? Have you met him? The only person he loves is himself.'

'Evie! What a thing to say about him. That's not like you!'

'It's true, nevertheless. I came in here with Tom one night and he, Morgan that is, gave the performance of his life, but it wasn't as a lover, it was because he was just so fond of himself. Good thing he'd come in with the rector and not Caroline – she'd have been mortified. Peter just laughed.'

It was so unusual for Evie to have opinions about anything at all, and certainly not critical ones, that they felt compelled to take note.

Marie began to tell them what Zack had witnessed that very afternoon.

Dottie, knowing she would be the next required to share any snippets of information she had seeing as she worked for Caroline, found a sudden impossible-to-ignore need for the Ladies.

'She's gone, but not where you think she's gone.' This confusing statement of Marie's brought them all to a standstill. 'Zack was working in the churchyard pruning – wrong time of year I know but he never got round to it in the autumn and some of them, specially the rose by the lychgate, well, he declared it had to be pruned immediately or else they wouldn't be able to use the lychgate at all, so—'

Marie got no further because Maggie rudely interrupted, 'To

be honest, I've not the slightest interest in what your Zack was doing trying to catch up with his autumn schedules. What did he *see*? That's what we want to know.'

By the time Dottie returned from the Ladies they'd reached the stage of open-mouthed horror. '... and pregnant *again*. That'ud be five!'

'And their mother, was she really American?' they asked.

Marie nodded. 'American born and bred. Soon as she opened her mouth he knew she was.'

Sylvia suggested that Dottie might be able to contribute something, seeing as she worked there.

'I know nothing, nothing at all. Being Monday it wasn't my day for working, was it? Zack saw it all you say, Marie?'

'That's right. He did. This American woman arrived with all the children, and then next *he* arrived in that flashy sports car he drove and went in. Then about fifteen minutes later him and her and the children came out and disappeared in their two cars. Then later he saw Caroline with handbag and weekend case leave in *her* car. *By herself*, looking extremely upset. That's all I know.' Marie took a long drink of her home brew.

Dottie wished the food would arrive, then perhaps they'd all stop talking about the matter that had occupied her mind and heart all afternoon. She wasn't letting on about anything. Not one word. Thank God for Mondays, thought Dottie.

Maggie sarcastically stated that she wondered that Zack got anything pruned at all considering how much time he'd spent studying the comings and goings at the Rectory.

Marie, in rapid defence of Zack, said he'd finished pruning in the churchyard, and that if Maggie ever went to church nowadays she would be able to see for herself how much he'd done.

'Since I live opposite I can see for myself without undertaking a royal visit, thank you very much.'

Before they knew where they were a loud argument broke out that dominated all other conversations throughout the bar.

Marie got to her feet with the obvious intention of leaving immediately but fortunately for the birthday party the food came, served by Dicky and the temporary barmaid, and as they had all paid in advance they decided the easiest option was to sit down and eat it before they left. So in the end they all stayed there almost until turning out time. Dottie never needed to make sure she didn't tell Rectory secrets when she shouldn't because everyone was so disappointed that they had almost ruined Sylvia's birthday they kept a strict curb on their tongues for the rest of the evening.

It was only when they got home that they realised that the one person who could have told them all they wanted to know had been sitting there with them and keeping her mouth tight shut. Then they remembered that those privileged to work at the Rectory were clever at keeping their mouths shut. Sylvia had been just the same when she cleaned for Caroline.

But Caroline was back home by Saturday evening and when Peter preached on the Sunday morning some of his compassionate love for the human race had apparently been restored; they could hear it in his voice and see it in his face. Something had been resolved then.

Peter had recognised the sound of Caroline's car engine as she parked in the garage at the rear of the Rectory. He was in the kitchen emptying the dishwasher as the sound of the automatic garage door beginning to rattle on its way up confirmed her arrival.

She was back. They hadn't communicated at all since she'd left that fatal Monday morning. Peter, if he'd rung her wouldn't have known what on earth to say so he thought, in that case, that silence really would be golden. He put the kettle on, hoping they might have a cup of tea together while they talked and began laying a tray with cups and saucers, milk ... and there she was at the back door. She didn't come to him for a kiss as she would have done if things had been as they once were, but gripped his hand as though in need of support.

'Darling! You're back!'

'And to prove it I'm here.'

They both laughed.

'Tea?'

'Please. I drove back without stopping. Is there any chance of a sandwich or have you eaten everything up?'

'Eaten everything up! No, the fridge is packed with food. You can help me eat it all. They've all been calling with food for me so I've dined like a king at every meal and I'm sure I've put weight on.' He paused for a moment; what if she was simply calling to collect her belongings? 'That's if you're stopping and haven't just called in to collect your belongings.' The look on his face as he waited for her answer crucified her.

Caroline took a deep breath. 'If you'll have me back. Will you? What I want more than anything is to get things straight between us. Like it's always been, all these years.' She stood silently begging, awaiting his approval.

His answer was to open his arms wide and say, 'I did say even if it was a decade before you returned I'd welcome you back. And I mean that, every word. This house has never felt so lonely and the children will be pleased. Shall we ring them and suggest they come home next weekend? Mmm?'

'Let's leave that for now and talk, just the two of us, about what has happened and why? Please.'

Peter thought over what she'd said as he made her a sandwich. Sandwiches seemed to be his thing this week, first for the American contingent and now for Caroline. With the knife poised to cut the cheese and mayonnaise into four delicate portions he looked up and saw love, just like it used to be, gazing at him with delight. 'Oh! Caroline! So good to have you back.' He could have consumed her as well as the sandwich, but honestly didn't know if she would welcome him just yet. Instead he asked what the weather had been like and was the hotel as good as they remembered it.

'Better! It's changed hands and the new owners have absolutely transformed it. It was marvellous before but now it is fantastic! Better than before. Honestly.' She almost snatched the sandwich from him and began devouring it immediately. 'Thanks for this. Tea? Tea? Will it be ready to pour?'

Peter slid her cup and saucer across the kitchen table. She paused in the massacre of the sandwich and wetted her mouth with the best cup of tea in a week. *Almost* a week anyway. She'd forgotten how good a cup of tea could feel and taste. Took another sip and asked, 'Does it make a difference to the taste of tea if it's made specially for you by someone who loves you?'

He gave this serious question deep consideration before he replied. 'I'm sure it does.'

'So am I.'

He watched her consuming the rest of the sandwich and then she asked if there was any cake.

'You could have a slice of Grandmama's date and walnut, if you wish or one of Dottie's Maurice's specialities, namely Eccles cakes, or if you are really daring and courageous, a slice of Evie's lemon sponge.'

'My word, I'm spoiled for choice.' She couldn't look at him. Mustn't look at him or her need might be there in her face and she mustn't let him see that, at least not until she'd sorted things out between them. There were things that had to be said *first*.

'Evie's lemon sponge, please. In truth, sack cloth and ashes ought to be on the menu.' She took a large sacrificial bite and was pleasantly surprised. 'Oh! I say, it's not bad at all considering it's Evie who made it; in fact it's rather good. Have you had a slice?'

'No.'

'Try it.'

So they sat, one at each end of the kitchen table, munching Evie's lemon sponge. Peter had a second slice, then so did

224

Caroline. What a fool she'd been, she thought. What a fool. This perfectly splendid man offering himself to her because he loved her whatever she had done. Physically, nothing had happened, much as she'd wanted it to, due to some old-fashioned scruples she still harboured deep down where Peter was concerned. She gloried in the fact that she had resisted Morgan. It would have been such a barrier to a reconciliation that they would probably never have got together again – and the prospect of that made Caroline shudder with fright.

Caroline poured herself another cup of tea and thought about Marianne. She was tough, very tough. You had to admire her holding the family together like she did, but *loving* him despite his wanderings and five children with a man who treated her like dirt? That was love above and beyond what Morgan deserved.

She looked up and saw Peter was admiring her as though every inch of her was perfect and honourable. *He* was perfect and honourable, but she still had to earn her stripes.

What a fool she'd been. Allowing herself to be taken in by that shallow man. She'd get a new job – not at the hospital, perhaps in general practice make a complete new start. They'd stay here in Turnham Malpas, where she was loved and respected. They'd all been on her side when she'd taken Peter's twins on, and they'd never said a word to a newspaper or anything when she almost had that affair with Hugo. As an actor he was stupendous but as a man he was a bit of a waste of space, but such good fun and he'd been excellent at boosting her ego. Hugo had gone on to great things in the theatre – such a pity he was killed in that terrible train crash in the States, how many years ago was that? Ten perhaps. Thirty-one people killed. What a loss he was to the theatrical world. But neither Hugo nor Morgan were ahead of Peter in the love stakes. Neither of them would have been so forgiving, so full of genuine love, so caring, so loyal.

She stood up, walked round the table, and, standing behind Peter with an arm around his shoulders, she buried her face in his hair and when he turned his head to look up at her she kissed his lips. A familiar gesture.

'We need to talk first, don't we?'

Peter nodded. 'We do. You first.'

Chapter 26

When all his plans were signed and sealed, Johnny decided to visit the Rectory. He checked on his mobile that Peter was at home before he left Turnham House.

'Have you time to talk?'

'Indeed I have, Johnny.'

'Just some plans I'd like to run past you.'

'Coffee?'

'Most welcome. Leaving straight away.'

They settled down to talk in Peter's study. 'Caroline OK now she's back home?'

Peter nodded. 'She is fine, thank you.'

'Working?'

'Temporarily in general practice in place of someone on maternity leave.'

'Liking it after hospital work?'

'Loves it. Sugar?' Peter pushed the sugar basin across his desk and watched while Johnny spooned three spoons of sugar into his mug. 'You like it sweet.'

'I do. Right. I've come to tell you that I, or rather *we*, that is, Chris and I, have bought the Royal Oak.'

'I heard.'

Johnny couldn't hide his surprise. 'You did? I thought no one knew.'

'Everyone does, it's the talk of the village. No one knows the intimate details such as who's going to manage it, though.'

'Well, it goes like this: Chris and I have bought it from Georgie and Dicky now he's too frail to cope with the long hours and all the hard work and administration a pub involves, and I must say Georgie is very pleased to be relieved of the burden too, so as soon as they get organised they are moving out and ... well ... do you know who's moving in as well?'

'No, that's the big question of the moment in the village.'

'Ford and Merc Barclay.'

There was a short silence while Peter absorbed this news. 'No! I would never have guessed it would be them. Have they experience of the licence trade?'

'Some, years ago, but ~~Johnny~~ Chris and I will be the licensees and Merc and Ford the managers. They've got the right personalities, haven't they?'

Peter studied the idea for a moment and agreed. 'You're right, they have. I'm sure they'll do excellently well. Yes, I'm sure they will. But it will feel strange not seeing Dicky and Georgie behind the bar. They've been there a lot of years. Well, well! What a surprise.'

'Chris is going to be in overall charge because the two of us are going to buy a chain of pubs. None of this Slug and Lettuce style, we'll only buy old quality places with a long history and an antique building. What do you think?'

'Sounds like an excellent project. Excellent. A lot of work, though. Is Chris looking forward to it?'

Johnny smiled. 'I know what you're thinking: is that lazy idle chap up to making a success of it? Yes, he is. He's a changed man, you know, a changed man. Deborah has done him a world of good and Alice and I are very fond of her.'

'Am I at liberty to mention about this chain of pubs business to people in general, or is it till taboo?'

Johnny stood up. 'You're the first person outside the family that I have mentioned it to, but yes, you are; the sooner everyone knows the better. And you can also say we are keeping the home-brew recipe too, so those who favour it needn't even begin to worry. We're not going all cocktails, glass tables and chairs as hard as rocks and twice as uncomfortable and the like, we're keeping it just like it is with a few, just a few, new ideas and a complete redecoration. But I don't mean modernisation. Got to retain the feel of an old pub. Hopefully, the Royal Oak will be the first of many.'

'Excellent!'

Johnny was about to leave and then changed his mind. 'Something else to tell you. Becky Braithwaite and her Ben? You know them of course.'

'I certainly do.'

'Well, now this *is* hot news as it was only arranged last night. They are both coming to live at Turnham House.'

'Really?'

'Yes. When our new baby arrives Becky is going to be our live-in nanny and Ben is coming too, of course. Becky is brilliant with young children and she and Ben are both looking forward to working for us. Ben's proved to be excellent in the glasshouses and is now working full-time looking after them. Got some kind of instinctive ability, despite his disability, where grapes are concerned, and he's improved in leaps and bounds in his behaviour since I gave him the responsibility. He works all hours, totally devoted to them, he is, and he has Greenwood's approval and that's something as no doubt you know from past experience, because Greenwood was against Ben at first.'

Peter was delighted. 'That's wonderful! Becky will be delighted, I'm sure. She'll make a lovely nanny. Well, well! I'm so pleased; she really deserves a boost, such a hard-working girl! So pleased to hear that bit of news because life hasn't been exactly kind to her in the past.'

The two of them shook hands and Johnny made to leave. 'I do notice that the royal oak tree itself is not looking quite as lively as it always has. I did wonder about getting a specialist to have a look at it. If it starts withering or dropping branches off they'll all have a lot to say about it, end of the village etc. What do you think? Have you noticed?'

'I shall have a good look at it when I go out, Johnny, and let you know. You can't have the old oak dying just when you take over the pub because as you know, we shall all be blighted and, as you say, it will be the end of the village, and heaven knows what else! What's more, you'll be to blame!' Peter had always laughed at this ridiculous theory about the village dying if the oak tree died and he did the same this time.

'It's not funny, Peter! It could be very serious. Have a look and ring me. Right?'

'You are serious, aren't you?'

'I most certainly am. Thanks for your time.'

And so, before setting off to Penny Fawcett to visit someone who had just moved in to the village, Peter walked across the green and examined the old oak. Being winter and deciduous it had lost its leaves, but when one examined the bare branches they did look particularly pathetic. Peter tried snapping a twig off to see what happened. There were tiny ant-type insects congregated on it and, as an amateur, Peter could only describe it being as though they were draining the moisture out of the branches. Were the twigs and branches of ancient oak trees drained dry of moisture throughout the winter? Was that how they should be?

All the village needed at the moment was the royal oak dying. Surely not. He wouldn't mention it to a soul, not a single one, because the news would fly round all three of the villages faster than the speed of light and be exaggerated out of all proportion.

Penny Fawcett inhabitants would openly laugh like drains with delight. Little Derehams people would, in public, bemoan the tragedy but in private also laugh but with a smug look on their faces, and as for Turnham Malpas residents ... no, it didn't bear thinking about. They'd be holding candlelit midnight vigils and praying as they'd never prayed before.

Peter rang Johnny immediately.

Chapter 27

By chance, Chris Templeton was visiting Penny Fawcett the same morning that Peter went there to see the new people now they'd had a few days to settle in. The two of them met right outside the Slug and Lettuce. Chris had been inside for a coffee and Peter was walking by on his way to find the newly occupied cottage.

'Good morning, Chris. What's the competition looking like this morning? How bad is it?'

Chris looked taken aback by Peter's question.

Peter reassured him. 'It's OK. Johnny called to tell me your news. Congratulations!' They shook hands vigorously.

'Not up to much, is it?' Peter nodded towards the dead hanging baskets still on display in front of each window. 'Always been the same. I've heard people in Turnham Malpas say they wouldn't be seen dead in it. What is the matter with Penny Fawcett? They are totally useless, aren't they?'

'Never got over the plague, I expect, even though it was here so many centuries ago – thirteen hundred and something, I understand?' He smiled as though he meant it. 'They got hit very seriously, you know, much, much worse than Turnham Malpas did but not as bad as Derehams Magna – everyone living there died. Have you ever been to see what's left of the original houses? Very interesting. Takes a lot of finding, but you can still see the remains of the foundations if you persist. Deborah and I did; you go right down to—'

Peter, surprised that Chris was being intensely serious about the plague, interrupted by saying, 'You're not kidding me, you mean it, don't you? You've been looking at the remains of the cottages?'

'Oh yes. It's very interesting. Haven't you? Eight centuries ago and, believe it or believe it not, still no one owns the land, you know. Amazing! According to the council, anyway. Strange state of affairs, isn't it? Everyone wiped out in a matter of a few weeks and no one left to bury them. Anyway, what are you doing here in Penny Fawcett?'

'Visiting some new people just moved in.'

'Part of your duty as the rector, I suppose.'

'I make it so, yes. Must press on. Be seeing you, Chris. Deborah OK?'

'Yes, thank you very much.'

Chris stood for a moment watching Peter making his way along the main village street, checking the names of the cottages as he went. Even Chris himself found it odd that he was so fascinated about the foundations of the houses where Derehams Magna used to be all those years ago. But he had to admit he found the whole situation fascinating, mostly because no one had claimed the land or offered to buy it in the intervening centuries. In a country so closely packed as England was nowadays you would have thought ... His attention was taken by the pub again and he decided to go inside again and ask if the man behind the bar knew why the land on which Derehams Magna had stood was still owned by no one at all.

The reply to his question came swiftly and abruptly. 'No idea.' And the chap rapidly disappeared down the cellar steps. He was back up again in one brief moment to continue what Chris had hoped would be a worthwhile conversation. 'Why? You wanting to buy it?' he said as his head appeared above the bar counter.

'Well, no. Not really. I was curious, that's all.'

'Don't bother if all it is is curiosity. No one even mentions that land and the houses. Ever.'

'Why not?'

The barman leaned on the counter and glanced round to make sure no one was listening to their exchange, though that was no problem as Chris was the only other person in the bar, and then he leaned on the top of the bar and whispered, 'No one dare mention it. Strange things happen to you if you do.'

'Strange things?'

The barman nodded. 'Strange things. One chap fancied buying the land about a hundred years ago, asked the council about it, willing to pay their price he said. Get back to us, they said, in a week or two. He never did get back to 'em and they found him three weeks later, strangled, amongst the foundations. Been dead a while. They say soon as you get close to where he was strangled you come over all shaking and even if you're old and can't run, you do run without any explanation of it.' The barman wagged a forefinger at him. 'It's all, every inch of it, evil. Death stalks the foundations and not just at night, neither. Believe me: don't get interested in it. Now off you go and don't come back or you'll be the next.' It was his sepulchral tones that finally persuaded Chris to leave.

He and Deborah lay in bed that night, laughing themselves to exhaustion.

'Why on earth did you bother to ask? I mean, honestly. You, of all people, Chris. You've become more like a genuine villager than those who've lived here all their lives. What a terrible thing to have happened, though. And them all being so afraid. Why do they live in Penny Fawcett? No wonder they're all odd and the pub is never a success.'

'I could always buy it and make a success of it. I wouldn't be afraid. Not likely.'

Deborah sat up in bed, switched on the light and said, 'Under no circumstances do you buy that pub, Chris. I mean that. Make a success of the Royal Oak and then have a stab at the Wise Man, say, but not the Slug and Lettuce. Definitely not. Do you hear me?'

'Yes, miss.' He sat up and saluted her obediently and then lay back, contemplating the possibility of buying the Slug and Lettuce. What an exciting and unnerving possibility. A haunted pub. Was it the pub and the village of Penny Fawcett that was haunted or was it the overgrown foundations of Derehams Magna that were the problem?

'Are you ready to go to sleep, Chris? Or shall I enlighten you about where I go every month? Do you feel ready for it? I feel ready to tell you, if you are ready to listen. Mmm?'

This moment was a very very important step in their relationship and all thoughts of evil and mysterious deaths and centuries old folklore disappeared in a second. He put his bedside light on again and sat up, fully alert to this momentous statement.

'Ready?'

Chris nodded vigorously. 'Yes.'

Deborah sat up too, took hold of his hand and began her story. 'As you already know, I am an only child and have spent all my life in a family dominated by money. Money galore. Money no problem. Whatever we wanted – new house, biggest and most high tech television, latest washing machine, no prints on our walls, oh no, we had real oil paintings, genuine antique furniture. I was surrounded by people willing to get me, do for me, anything I might come up with, my every wish fulfilled. My parents never ever had to say to me "can't afford it". Best schools, best everything. Completely indulged. It should have turned me into the most dreadful person.'

'It didn't, though.'

'That was due to a scholarship girl who joined my school at thirteen, the same year as me, except I didn't have a scholarship: my father's secretary paid my fees.' Deborah paused for a moment. 'So that was my education taken care of: my father didn't even need to sign the cheque, didn't have to bother seeing me for most of the year except occasionally in the holidays if he couldn't avoid it. And I think I can remember my mother taking me to buy new clothes only twice because nanny always took me until I had my own bank account, then I went by myself or with a friend. Mother was too busy, you see. I thought she must work somewhere, like my father, but of course: she didn't, she just enjoyed herself. And just one child was too much for her, especially one who was plain and charmless like me.'

'Deb, don't talk like that! You're none of those things, not at all. You are very beautiful and utterly charming. *I* say so and what I say goes.' He placed a gently salutary kiss on her cheek, squeezed her hand and patiently waited.

'Love you,' she said 'you're so good for my ego.'

'Press on, darling.'

'Her name was Primrose Barraclough.'

'Oh, the poor girl! Primrose. Heavens above.'

'She was as tough as tough. She needed to be. Because she was a scholarship girl she got teased in the nastiest way possible. The others made her life hell, but I liked her and stood up for her and we became friends. Close, really close, friends. We sat together in class, we were in the same dorm, same swimming group, everything. We spent all our spare time together, and if they started plaguing her with snide jokes and things then I defended her. She'd never learned to ride a bike so I taught her. Hours up and down, up and down the school drive until she got the hang of it. Then I bought her a bike. It was delivered to school and she never knew who'd bought it but it was me. And despite all the cruel teasing she suffered, she was a wonderful friend to have, and believe me I needed a friend.'

'Where is she now, do you know?'

'Tell you one day.' Deborah's eyes filled with tears and Chris knew he mustn't pursue his questioning.

'Go on, then. You still haven't explained where you go.'

'I go to prison.'

Startled beyond belief Chris sat bolt upright, speechless.

'To visit my dad.'

'To visit your dad?'

'Yes. To see my dad.'

'Right. I see.'

'No, you don't Chris, not yet. What I hadn't realised for a long time was that the money we had was all, shall we say, *stolen*?'

'Stolen! My God! All of it?'

'Every penny. If he got an accumulation of money then he invested and invested so the money mounted up. But initially it was stolen. Bank robberies, mostly, but also anywhere where money was stored and that he calculated was comparatively easy to get at. He was educated you see, not some loud-mouthed rough with a Cockney accent, but a man with an educated accent and good taste so he wasn't suspected at all. It went on for years, I understand. He moved in the circles rich, well-educated men move in and none of them suspected what he was up to. He was a very, very clever man. Somehow – I don't know who – paid for him to go to a very good school as a boarder, so he had good connections right from being a boy.'

'Are you pulling my leg?'

His question made her feel indignant and she replied emphatically, 'No, I am not! You wanted to know where I went and I'm telling you, to prison to see my dad.'

'Your mother, did she know?'

'We never discussed it and she died just before I went to finishing school, where I met you for the first time. You were heaven sent.' She kissed his cheek.

'I'm so sorry.'

'I tried to be sorry and couldn't because I really didn't know her. Anyway, he made sure I had plenty of money stored away when he realised the police were closing in.'

'I suppose your luck can last only so long and then gives out. Did you ever guess how he got his money? Before he got caught I mean.'

'Never. Never suspected. When the police turned up to arrest him I was as surprised as it's possible to be. So that's where I am when I'm away. Now you know and it's up to you who you tell. I knew if I told you before we were married that if your mother learned the whole story she wouldn't allow you to marry me – and when she does know she'll more than likely never speak to me again.'

'He's been a mixture of very good and very bad, has your dad. Do you have a conscience about using money which has dubious ancestry.'

'Chris! I've never thought about it like that before. I honestly haven't. It's normal to me, always has been, you see. The food I ate, the schools I attended, the holidays I had, all paid for with stolen money.'

'If you think at any stage that you shouldn't be using money to live on that's originally stolen money, you could always give it up and I will give you money. I hasten to add that Templeton money is OK. None of it was stolen, not even years ago. My grandad and my dad earned their money by hard labour.' He smiled at his error. 'Hard labour! I meant working hard *legitimately*. Can I ask another question? Why do you put yourself through the pain of going to see him when he never really bothered about you?'

'Strange that, very strange. I don't know why. He begged me to go see him. Begged me. It was embarrassing.'

'He's your only living relative, I assume.'

'That's right. Chris, I need to know how you feel about it.'

'I think that one day the police may be after you for the money. How long has he been in prison?'

'Eleven years, almost. Nineteen more to do, if he lives that long.'

'Where is he? You know, where do you go to see him?'

'America'.

'America! My God! All that way to see a dad who doesn't care a jot for you and never has. Such devotion.'

'Apart from you he's all I've got who belongs to me, the only flesh and blood that's mine and, somehow, that matters to me. Do you still want to be married to me, after I've told you about my unhealthy beginnings?'

'You just try getting away from me! I want you for ever. For ever, do you hear me? For ever. There's no escape. I love you deeply and for always.' He kissed her very sweetly. 'There was no need to keep the truth about your family from me; it's you I married, not your family.'

Chris lay down again and stayed silent for a while, then he said, 'When or *should* I say, *if* you feel you can no longer use your dad's illegal money, you could always give it to charity and like I said I could provide for you. I would gladly do that if you prefer.'

Deborah felt it was time she said something positive. 'I admit, I'm beginning to feel distinctly uncomfortable when I think about it. You and Johnny are so honest and upright that I think I might have to do that. It's so embarrassing. My father will have a fit if I tell him what I've done. He's been rotten to the core for such a long time it doesn't bother him in the slightest. In fact, he's proud of his achievements. I'm not.'

'I've had a thought: if your father is clever, and obviously he must be if he was thieving for years and no one suspected, thirty years seems a long time for straightforward thieving, excessive almost. Why is that?'

Chris didn't get his answer immediately. After a while, he looked at Deborah and knew something far worse was about to come out. 'Did he ...? I mean was there something else?'

Deborah answered eventually. 'This is why I didn't want to talk about it, but I must, Alice agreed I must.'

Scandalised that Alice had known before himself, he said disbelievingly, '*Alice knows?*'

Deborah shook her head. 'No, of course not! We were talking about being honest to one's spouse, nothing else. She doesn't know a thing. And if I tell you, you mustn't tell anyone else because I can't bear the thought of the whole village knowing what he did, and once the whole village knows it won't be long before the whole world will recollect reading about him in the newspapers. You maybe know already from the papers, except of course you'd have been in Brazil or climbing some unclimbable mountain or other and wouldn't have seen the headlines. He did a desperate thing. Desperate. I'm so ashamed.'

Chris was afraid for her sanity when he saw how distressed she was.

'See here, tell me another day when you're feeling stronger. Not now.'

'I've got to right now, while I'm in the middle of it, while I can; another day I might not be able to mention it. Someone who worked for him in the office found out what he was up to. So Dad told three of his henchmen to rough up this chap and put the fear of God in him, and they did, but they hid him afterwards and the men who beat him up refused to tell Dad where he was and Dad never found him. The only thing in Dad's favour is that he deeply regrets what happened to that man. If he could have saved him he would have, but he couldn't find him. It was the end of Dad's lifelong career as a bank robber. Everything went messy, very messy and it finished him. He went to the police to ask them for help and that was when it all came out. He's never forgiven himself ...'

'His only redeeming feature, then.'

'He'd been so clever, but they finished him. And the poor man who died ...' Her next sentence came out in a great rush. 'I should have told you before I said yes to us getting married. I definitely should and I didn't! I'm as bad as my dad for deceiving people and I'm so sorry. So sorry, Chris.'

'Maybe the man isn't dead; perhaps they said he was left some-where to die on purpose, to get your dad in a state. Perhaps they just said it knowing full well they'd been paid to give him a kicking when in fact they never laid a finger on him. Could be, you know.'

Deborah shook her head convinced she was right in her assumption.

Chris realised Deborah didn't agree with his idea. 'See here, I love you and you love me, and that's what counts, Deb. Loving and being loved.' Chris wrapped his arms around Deborah and hugged her close, determined to make her feel worthwhile; if she hadn't been loved as a child then he would love her now and do his best to make up for her bleak childhood. How terrible for a child, to be aware they weren't loved by their parents; his own mother had smothered him with love as a child and still did.

He thought of Charles and Ralph and how terrible it would be for them if Alice and Johnny didn't love them. When he thought about how astute they were, how quick to pick up on insincerity and deceit, he was convinced they would know they were well loved. What dear boys they were, still untouched by the enormous inheritance that awaited them.

He turned to Deborah to tell her how lucky they were to be living in the loveliest place on earth. Nothing would make him move to anywhere else. Deborah and him in Turnham Malpas for ever felt like living in paradise. He'd enjoy the villagers' respect, possibly even their love before long, just as Johnny had done. But he'd need to earn it, and with Deborah alongside him that was just what he would do.